GW00701695

BARRY MERCHANT

A QUEST
FOR SELF-DISCOVERY

An East End lad battles poverty and depression
in his search for God and redemption

BARRY MERCHANT

A QUEST
FOR SELF-DISCOVERY

An East End lad battles poverty and depression
in his search for God and redemption

MEREO
Cirencester

Mereo Books

1A The Wool Market Dyer Street Cirencester Gloucestershire GL7 2PR
An imprint of Memoirs Publishing www.mereobooks.com

A Quest for Self-Discovery: 978-1-86151-590-2

First published in Great Britain in 2016
by Mereo Books, an imprint of Memoirs Publishing

Copyright ©2016

The address for Memoirs Publishing Group Limited can be found at
www.memoirspublishing.com

The Memoirs Publishing Group Ltd Reg. No. 7834348

The Memoirs Publishing Group supports both The Forest Stewardship Council®
(FSC®) and the PEFC® leading international forest-certification organisations. Our
books carrying both the FSC label and the PEFC® and are printed on FSC®-certified
paper. FSC® is the only forest-certification scheme supported by the leading
environmental organisations including Greenpeace. Our paper procurement policy
can be found at www.memoirspublishing.com/environment

Typeset in 10/16pt Century Schoolbook
by Wiltshire Associates Publisher Services Ltd. Printed and bound in Great Britain
by Marston Book Services Ltd, Oxfordshire

CONTENTS

Preface

Although this book is a work of fiction, there are some elements that are autobiographical which need brief explanation. Between the ages of 12-37 years, I went through some rather debilitating experiences that isolated me from the society in which I lived. Briefly they were sexual abuse, imprisonment, a neurological illness called dystonia, 17 years of addiction to prescribed medication, mental illness and chronic insecurity. I am not a victim, but I am a survivor!

Acknowledgements

First and foremost, I am indebted to Lis Bird for her unstinting commitment in correcting my manuscripts over a period of several months. Even during her holiday in Spain, she worked every day, without complaint, to support my work. Thank you so much!

I would like to thank Tony Green for his helpful support in correcting punctuation when my work was taking shape in its early phase. I would also like to thank him for various suggestions he made towards helping me with my work.

Finally, many thanks to Chris Newton, editor, and his colleagues at Memoirs Publishing, whose professionalism made this book possible.

To Lis Bird and Tony Green, my dear friends and co-walkers.

Chapter One

Raised in the East End

I had always thought I was one of the lower classes. You know what I mean, always at the
beck and call of my masters, whoever they might be. Those above me always appeared to have power and money in abundance.

Inferiority pervaded my everyday feelings. Even at home down in the East End of London, where I lived in a right old run-down gaff for several years with my supportive family, I was always told to do this and do that. Anyone could boss me about like a worthless, mangy old dog. My trouble was that I, Leslie Tatter, couldn't look after myself, although I toughened as I got older and began to spread my wings of autonomy just as a colourful peacock butterfly does in flight.

Unlike a lot of the Stepney boys, even some girls, I was frightened of fighting, rowing and bickering with others. I shared this with my kindly old mum, Ethel, who was quiet but had a heart of gold. Yes, I was the one who usually found himself at the back of the queue when it came to receiving anything worth having.

Not that I was angry - far from it. Others had far less than me and my family. Mind you my maternal grandmother, Bessie Smith, was a great old lady. She used to stick up for me and my sister Susan if anyone got a bit out of order. You know those jack-the-lads who were always prepared to clump me, and many others, round the head or kick me up my backside for a bit of fun. One word from Bessie was deterrent enough.

During the last year or so of World War One Bessie had run a large canteen, just like a sergeant major, in Trafalgar Square. She provided countless gallons of tea and mountains of cheese sandwiches for overworked fire fighters, police and ambulance personnel trying to cope with the effects of the bombing of her beloved London. Bessie, fat with rosy cheeks, a female version of John Bull, always put on a brave face against adversity. Any time of day she could be heard singing old London tunes from behind her counter, as she served those brave men and women who tried to extinguish flames in buildings ravaged by fire. Those tireless workers pulled out the dead, dying and mutilated living bodies from under fallen rubble as our anti-aircraft guns fired at the German airships and planes flying above. Yet the adversity of the war had a tendency to unite people.

Nearly every London family lost someone they loved at this time when the world was full of madness. Bessie Smith and many other people like her were the unspoken heroes and heroines who kept morale going. Afterwards, things for most people were never quite the same again. My grandmother died of breast cancer in 1940, aged 72, months after World War Two had started. She had herself lost her young son, Benny Kennedy, who died on the Somme in 1916, aged 29, in the deep mud and blood of one of the longest battle of the war, which lasted nearly five months. When Benny died, it was said, she was never quite the same person for one who had once loved being the centre of attention. Later I read that 30,000 soldiers had died in one day alone during the carnage of the Somme.

Bessie's young sister Jane, aged 48, was also tragically killed, in March 1917, as she sheltered from a German air raid. As a result of London buildings being bombed, Bessie lost her supervisor job working in a department store. She also lost the new friends and colleagues she had made working twelve hours a day making clothes ('schmutter', they were called in those days) in Sammy Bernstein's Mile End Warehouse, nicknamed the 'laughing house'. She left very little to show for 72 years of hard work. She didn't give a damn about money. Years later one of her old friends, Mabel Turner, said of Bessie, 'One of the fucking best. Food in yer belly and a good old singsong. That was Bessie. I lost one of my best friends to those fucking Germans,' as tears gushed down her soft old lined face.

One of the very few valuable things that my maternal grandmother did leave amongst her rags was a boxing medal, which belonged to her cousin Sergeant Henry Roberts. He was single, came from Hoxton and worked as a barrow boy. Another treasure she had inherited, but gave to me when I was young, was a military medal. It was awarded to Henry posthumously for bravery during the Boer War. I cried my eyes out when Bessie gave it to me instead of anyone else in the family. 'Don't fucking lose it boy!' she shouted in my ear. I carried that most wonderful gift around with me for the rest of my life, even during my sometimes troubled travels, to remind me of my East End hero.

Various groups and individuals played a significant role in helping to bring about radical changes to the East End of London. Sylvia Pankhurst based many of her campaigns around the poverty-stricken working-class areas of East London, and received much support there. It was the energy and commitment of East End people that organised the first Communist Party in England. In 1865, William Booth founded the Christian Mission. Later in 1878 Booth named his mission the Salvation Army; it was based in Whitechapel. Booth, along with many others, campaigned tirelessly for social improvement so that those less fortunate should have a better quality of life. Local people joined his growing army of Salvationists, who marched round the streets evangelising and performing social work among their own poor people. Many viewed the Salvation Army as a force for good, but it was largely ignored by the wealthy, those who had the political and financial power to change things. Many years later the Army still performs its Christian religious duties, and has built on the social and educational needs that William Booth first recognised as essential for the growth of impoverished human beings.

Another social reform charity, Toynbee Hall, founded in 1884 by Canon Samuel Barnett, did much to help local people by focusing on working towards a future without poverty. And let us not forget those working-class female heroines, like Bessie Smith, nicknamed the 'match girls'. They went on strike in 1888 for better working conditions at the Bryant and May factory in Bow. This brave action helped to found the modern socialist and local trade union organisations, as well as supporting the first suffragette movement. In time it was realised that the phosphorus from the matches the girls were producing rotted their teeth and gums, and in 1908 phosphorus matches were banned. These were some of the radical types of East Enders that helped change existing views, conditions and institutions.

The following lines from the poem *'The Human Abstract'* by William Blake, for me, sum up the above:

Pity would be no more
If we did not make somebody Poor;
And Mercy no more could be
If all were as happy as we.

Bessie Smith was born in a comfortable two-bedroom early Victorian terraced house in Lavender Gardens, Barking, in 1867. Her sister Jane was born two years later. Both girls thrived under the love and guidance of their parents, Tom and Florence Smith, both of whom were born down the East End of London somewhere or other, but no one seemed to know exactly where. All I know is that my great-grandmother's parents had met through someone on her mother's side of the family, probably the result of having a knees-up and too much beer, although Florence's parents, being devout Christians, would have hated such behaviour. Bessie informed me her parents moved to Barking in 1866, having been given the offer to rent their first own home together. Besides, Tom, who was just 20, had recently found employment working not that far from home, as a porter, at Fenchurch Street Station which opened in 1841. British-built trains would eventually transform the country into a commercial powerhouse.

Although mainly based at Fenchurch Street, Tom also worked at several other local stations when staff was short. Flexibility was the name of the game. During his working years, he made several good, lifelong friends at work. Like most working-class men in those days, no doubt on Saturdays he enjoyed a few beers in the local Victorian pub the Railway Arms, not a hundred yards from Fenchurch Street Station. For a few pennies they guzzled their way through several pints of ale in a convivial atmosphere full of men having an end of week get-together, before their wives found them something useful at home to repair. Like generations before them, Tom Smith and his colleagues would fantasize about getting a better job *(The working class can kiss my ass, I've got the foreman's job at last)*.

After drinking too much beer, they occasionally discussed ways of starting a revolution in the local railway stations. Of course, they realised the State and employers had them all over a barrel. Working-class men were powerless, and they knew it. Interestingly, when Tom was a young boy, he had read about politics and related subjects in various East End Libraries which local authorities, in 1850, were empowered to open. However, many libraries did not open until years later, as the powers that be at the time thought the working classes didn't need books because many couldn't read.

Unless he was working on a late shift, Tom always tried to get home on time for the Sunday dinner with his family. I remember Bessie telling me several times with a broad smile, 'When I were young, we 'ad a 'appy home. My parents always did what they could for us'.

From at least 1800, London was full of the roaming and ubiquitous costermongers, all selling their wares, fish, meat, books, clothes, ginger beer and ices, and numerous other items could be bought at any time of the day or night. A lot of the costermongers would have slept rough, which meant they could bed down for the night anywhere, and continue working immediately next day. That early start gave them the opportunity to sell their goods to East Enders who were off to work. Dockers, construction workers, street market vendors, cabinet makers, warehouse workers and furniture makers, among others, bought cheap food for the hard day's work ahead. Most of these workers would travel to work on cheap electric trams. The first underground line, which opened in 1864, would certainly have helped local working-class people to travel quicker to various parts of London. Further London underground trains followed when the Circle Line was opened in 1884.

Mind you there were a significant number of East Enders, mostly women, whose early lives as prostitutes were absolutely wretched. It was estimated that between 1840-1900, and well before in reality, entire streets in the slums of London were inhabited by prostitutes. Bethnal Green was one such area. The prettier you were, the more chance you had of making money so that you could open a small business of your own. But in reality many ended up in one of the 'foul wards' that were available in a few of the larger teaching hospitals. In Victorian London sexually-transmitted diseases were a major health problem. There was no known cure for syphilis. However, there were philanthropic societies, notably the Salvation Army, and various individuals, who did attempt to save desperate and outcast prostitutes from being left in the gutter. *'Time to put off the world and go somewhere, and find health again in the sea air,'* as W. B. Yeats said.

Overcrowding, poor wages, unemployment and prostitution caused appalling squalor, crime and short life expectancy. The Factory Act 1844 limited female workers to a 12-hour working day, and 8-13-year-old children to six and a half hours a day. Only three years later the Factory Act 1847 brought in a 10-hour working day for children aged 13 to 18, and this also applied to women. Although the two Factory Acts improved the lives of some people, a lot of working-class women remained in the same horrid, difficult situations living in overcrowded houses. Factory Acts were totally irrelevant to a huge unseen army of exploited mothers, who grafted for long hours at home making matchboxes and other goods, for which they received absolute pittances to try to feed their children. 'Twelve dozen boxes for 2.25d, and in addition, finding her own paste and thread! She never knew a day off, either for sickness, rest, or recreation... she toiled fourteen hours a day' - from *People of the Abyss* by Jack London.

A combination of coal-fired stoves and poor sanitation made the air heavy and foul smelling as raw sewage was dumped straight into the Thames. A new Public Health Act in 1848 was meant to improve sanitation, but it did not appear to improve things for those entrenched at the bottom of the social order. Thanks to that great Victorian engineer Joseph Bazalgette, who built over 2100 kilometres of tunnels and pipes, sewage was diverted away from the city. In 1854 a cholera epidemic killed 52,000 people. Several friends and family relating to our great grandparents' generation had died in the epidemic. Mercifully outbreaks of cholera dropped dramatically after Bazalgette's work was completed.

Amongst this maelstrom, it seemed, Florence Smith (née Donald) was born in 1842, apparently in the Bethnal Green area. She was the only child of Percy and Edna Donald. According to my mother, Florence was a skilled and experienced seamstress. For many years, she worked as senior seamstress to Harry Stern, a third generation Russian Jew, at his small factory in Whitechapel. The business did a thriving trade for years, covering the bodies of the rich, famous and infamous with their splendidly-sewn and crafted cloth imported from around the world. Several of Mr Stern's customers even visited the filthy factory to meet the workers, who included my great-grandmother. She informed my mother that they were dressed in some of the suits and dresses that she herself had made. One of the men, who had what appeared to be diamond rings on all his fingers, said to my great-grandmother, 'that suit you made for me is just exquisite work, darling. Thank you'. He was a dark-skinned, overweight man, aged about 70. *'God guard me from those thoughts men think'* - *A Prayer For Old Age*, W. B. Yeats again.

It must be remembered, of course, that working conditions in some factories in those days were at best bearable. Stern and a few others in the district were above average, and treated their staff with some concern. Others didn't give a damn about workers, as long as they worked long hours and continued to make the owners handsome profits. They were considered sub-human. My great-grandmother's Dickensian working conditions, thankfully, have long gone into the annals of social history.

The long hard hours at work, and three hours of travelling six days a week, took its toll on Florence's thin and overworked young body. During the long hours away from her children, who were being looked after by unofficial child minders, Florence was constantly concerned for their well-being. In agreement with her husband, even though they would desperately miss the money, Florence took a local part-time cleaning job in Barking Town Hall. She could now make sure that her children had a breakfast, take her growing daughters to the local school and have the time to walk to her depressing and poorly-paid job. Civic pride was crammed down the throats of the cleaners by those higher clerks who were in charge of maintaining the grandeur of Barking Town Hall. 'Everything seen by the public,' one bumptious old fart kept reminding the cleaning women, including my great-grandmother, 'must be spick and span and shining like in a mirror'. He loved shouting this every morning, like some workhouse manager addressing resident imbeciles.

Florence continued working there for years so that she could look after her children, her home and husband. She didn't complain in any way. Who would listen if you did? What she did earn she spent on decorating the home, and buying good-quality fabrics to make first-class clothes for her husband and children. She had many offers to make various clothes from some of the working-class mothers who cleaned with her. She turned down all the offers to earn some extra cash until her girls were old enough to take care of themselves.

Bessie, aged 10, and Jane, aged eight, had grown and developed in every way during these years, principally thanks to their supportive parents, who wanted to give them the best possible start in life. The two girls had been attending the local Protestant school, called 'God the Redeemer'. Other than in religion, education in those days was basic indeed. Many working-class kids didn't even bother to attend school. Many had to earn money in order to survive. Many parents did not even bother to register their children for a basic rudimentary education, which could at least have helped some of them find regular work, even if it was pitiful and demeaning. Many unscrupulous employers used working-class children as cheap labour: thin, malnourished kids took home a few shillings to help out their poverty-stricken families, as waif-like young figures roamed the dangerous and dirty streets. Everyone in authority knew about the child exploitation, but they did nothing about it. Those days when London children suffered so badly it reminded me later of a sentence I read in Maxim Gorky's book, *Childhood: 'Here and now of bestial, animal-like existence in industrial towns, where people go begging in the streets, taking their pickings from refuse heaps'*.

Although Britain was one of the wealthiest nations on earth, grabbing riches from nearly all the four corners of the globe, its subjects were, at best, treated like third-rate humans. Not just in London, but around the country, people lived, especially children, like feral animals. The Poor Law Amendment Act of 1834 established workhouses, which replaced, and exacerbated, the existing Poor Houses Law. In essence it was to save money by deterring poor people from using workhouses, which were considerably more austere than previously. Due to the great compassionate work of the Irish doctor James Barnardo who, in 1867, set up the first 'ragged school' to provide basic education for kids sleeping rough. His first home for rootless boys was established in 1870 at 18 Stepney Causeway. It was the philanthropy of Dr Barnardo and many other noble people which gave the opportunity to many boys and girls the chance of receiving a decent education, which led many to have productive lives. It was also due to the ceaseless campaigning of Barnardo, and many other like-minded people, that in 1880 education up to the age of 12 became compulsory. In 1890 elementary education was made free.

Mind you, things didn't change overnight for poor street children and many others. Another hero of the downtrodden was Albert Mansbridge (1876-1952). He founded the Workers' Educational Association (WEA) in 1903, and was its first secretary until 1915. He became the pioneer of adult education and many working-class people went on to be educated at the WEA. Due to the work of people like Barnardo, Mansbridge, Booth, productive opportunities were provided to countless East Enders at a time when it appeared that the powerful weren't even interested in wasting money on educating the 'dirty street brutes'.

Let us not forget what successive British Governments did to those men, women and children, many of them from London, who were unfortunate enough to be caught stealing, or something similar, by one of Robert Peel's police officers. Transportation banished or exiled them to the USA and Australia. In 1834 the Tolpuddle Martyrs were sentenced to seven years' transportation for holding an illegal strike. *Out of this tragic case eventually came the right to form permanent organisations of workers' unions.*

Fortunately I am not aware that any of my forebears were unlucky enough to have been transported. The Smith children made it through school to the age of 14 to become relatively educated. This was largely because of the extra learning support the girls received in the evenings from their parents, who wanted their children to find some kind of decent job. In 1881, at 14 years of age, Bessie, who was immature but attractive, found a job in Barking, working as a receptionist for a manufacturer of small engines for the commercial oil market. Tate's had owned the old manufacturing factory in Maybury Street, just off the High Street, for several generations. According to my grandmother, the factory had appeared to be falling down during most of that time. It was dirty, full of an acrid smell and plagued by well-fed rodents the size of cats. It was also in desperate need of a few gallons of paint. The only gallons consumed were of beer, by the owner, Alfie Tate, who drank like an army of alcoholics. He was tall, thin as a toilet brush, rarely ate, and was invariably drunk, even during working hours. Most of his clients did business with him over a few beers in the saloon bar of the local pub. My great-grandparents met him a few times at the various employee parties he held, but because they were shy and almost invisible, they never got the chance to have a conversation about their daughter, except on one occasion when Mr Tate was standing at the bar (where else?) when my great-grandfather introduced himself by saying, 'Allo Mr Tate, I'm Miss Smith's father. Nice to meet you.'

'Oh yes, of course, Mr Smith. Fucking good mechanic with a body like a brick shit house,' came the response from the refined Mr Tate.

Many years later I remember asking Bessie about

her childhood. 'Could you tell me what it was like when you were a young girl in Barking, grandmother?' I quietly asked Bessie as I sat on her warm, solid lap.

'I was born in Lavender Gardens, a terraced 'ouse, just orf Barking High Street. My sister Jane was two years younger than me. Both me parents worked very hard for us. We 'ad a 'appy home together, until I met that bastard Arthur Kennedy, your mother's, and uncle Benny's, father,' explained Bessie. She became upset and started crying.

It transpired that Bessie was only 16 when she met Arthur Kennedy, aged 25, at Tates. Young, slim and unworldly, Bessie's secure world at the time was work, family and the church. When handsome, smart-talking salesman Arthur Kennedy one day visited her boss trying to sell him machinery parts, he soon set his eyes on the attractive young receptionist.

'Hallo sweetheart, what's your name then?' he quickly enquired, having assured himself that no one was looking or listening. (In those days you could get the sack for something even less promiscuous!)

After various communications, Bessie eventually decided to meet the tall, slim, travelling salesman at a café a few miles from where she lived. No doubt he was well versed in chatting up women; poor Bessie must have been besotted after just one glance from Sir Galahad Kennedy. Having been thoroughly reassured by Kennedy of his good intentions, but anxious about her age, Bessie's parents eventually, and reluctantly, agreed for their vulnerable daughter to live with him. He had rented two small rooms, well decorated and furnished, in a lower middle class Regency area of Ealing. It gave residents like Kennedy some air of respectability, although his paltry wages barely kept their heads above water. Besides, living in Ealing meant he was far enough away from the prying eyes and ears of Bessie's family. Furthermore he worked for a small engineering company to the west of Ealing, which made contact with Bessie's family less frequent and kept big Tom Smith out of the way.

Bessie's first child, Ethel, was born in Ealing Hospital on 6th May, 1885. (Incidentally Ethel was the first name of Arthur Kennedy's mother.) Being a womaniser and a romantic, Kennedy spent less time at home with his young, lonely attractive wife. Once he realised that Bessie was pregnant, Kennedy arranged a quick lunchtime marriage ceremony at Ealing Town Hall register office witnessed by two of his male colleagues. He promised Bessie that at some stage they would get married in a church, but they never did.

Travelling around London and the South of England, trying to sell engine parts during the day to keep his family, and visiting many pubs and clubs at night, he had numerous sexual affairs with women. There were periods of time, from a few days to three weeks, when Kennedy was absent, away from his young family. During those periods of 'working away,' one must assume he was staying with other women. In common with sailors, he probably had a woman lined up in most towns. When he was at home he rarely took his wife and young daughter out for picnics or walks or visits to the theatre. In those days, communication was very difficult, even to contact her parents, who lived not more than ten miles away. Bessie did write to her mother a great deal explaining that she felt lonely, being on her own a lot of the time. She felt her husband didn't really love her or Ethel, but she felt sympathy for her overworked husband, as she saw him.

In June 1887, Bessie gave birth to a son, Benny, in Ealing Hospital. After a few post-birth problems, Bessie and her handsome boy were allowed to go home. During her stay in hospital, Ethel was looked after by an old family friend. Her husband had only visited her twice during the four weeks she remained in hospital with her son. One can imagine the packed and understaffed wards with pregnant women and screaming babies all craving attention. Staff did their best in overpopulated and under-financed public wards.

With her husband failing to visit her, Bessie must have felt miserable on her own, and with small resources to fall back on, she would have gone hungry most days unless some sympathetic mother or nurse helped her to eat. She was too proud to write to her mother to ask for help. Although her husband gave his wife inadequate money to feed her and their two children, he was at the same time spending longer periods away from his family. It was becoming obvious that it was just a matter of time before he would leave and never return. It was obvious he didn't want the added responsibility that came with bringing up vulnerable children.

One day in early September 1888, after shopping for cheap items locally, Bessie arrived back home with her children to find a large brown envelope addressed to her on the mantelpiece. It read:

I am so sorry that I have had to leave you and my beautiful children. I was unable to cope any more. I have left my job in Ealing and found a new one in another part of the country. I have also found a new girlfriend whom I shall live with. I realise that I am a irresponsible father and husband. I have paid three months rent up front to the Landlord and the £20 cash is all I have. I wish you and the children all the best wishes in the world.

May God be with you.
Arthur Kennedy

After that shell shock had subsided, Bessie, feeling guilty, visited her parents in Barking to explain what had had happened. They were a great support to her and the children. Not surprisingly, if they had known at the time about Kennedy's mistreatment of their daughter and grandchildren, they would have sought legal advice, even if that meant spending all their meagre savings.

Bessie and the children continued to live for another year or so at their Ealing address. Money was very tight, but her supportive family helped out whenever they could. She had to borrow money from the tallyman, or the 'never-never,' as it was called in those days, so that she had food for the children. There were a few times during her stay in Ealing when she had to hide when the tallyman came round for his money. Usually realising the day, but not the time, he called, she would push the children in a pram for miles around the streets, hoping that when she returned he had been and gone.

It was very tough in those days to get any kind of welfare or assistance, in London or anywhere else. The staff humiliated and stigmatised you, and you felt degraded because you felt you had failed yourself and your children. So it was no surprise that after her terrible experience with Arthur Kennedy, Bessie subsequently became a tough survivor. You didn't mess with Bessie Smith. If you were her friend, she treated you like a diamond, but if you crossed her, then beware! Thankfully, so she said many times, neither she nor her children ever cast their eyes on Kennedy again.

Months later Bessie received some great news that changed her life. The Peabody Trust, one of the few Housing Associations around to house poor, destitute people, had allocated her a two-bed flat, with indoor bathroom and toilet. With only a few second-hand items of furniture to her name, Bessie and the kids, supported by her family, moved into 37 Bradstock Road, Stepney in August 1890, as dirty, scruffy, shouting kids played hopscotch in the road outside. It was a very hot day, a scorcher even, as Bessie and her father sweated gallons from walking pieces of furniture from Bob Blacker's horse-drawn cart to her flat some sixty feet away.

'We've made it, kids,' she said to her little bemused children, Ethel and Benny, as they all tucked into saveloy and chips wrapped up in a old London penny newspaper.

It wasn't long after finishing their food that Bessie's children joined in with the gang of children outside. By then some of the kids had collected freshly-dropped manure from Bob Blacker's horse and were throwing it at each other. Welcome home!

Eventually in 1890, as a result of overwhelming pressure from many sources on inept governments to act, the Housing for the Working Classes Act set out to address the worst areas of housing unfit for human habitation. It was way overdue. But in reality it wasn't until 1919 that Government policy really made a fundamental change to the way working-class people were decently housed nationally. This was soon followed by the London County Council becoming the world's first council housing provider. Decent housing was desperately needed as successive waves of foreign immigrants were already adding to the overwhelming problems highlighted above. Yet in turn, those immigrants have been a positive source for change. For example, three large immigrant groups, the Huguenots, Ashkenazi Jews and the Irish, left legacies of success for London and Britain. It is noteworthy that 50,000 Jews fought for the UK in World War One. Also it is important to remember that in 1816 poverty was so bad in England that it caused many to emigrate to USA and Canada.

From this time on, Bessie never thought about looking back on her sordid marriage to Arthur Kennedy. All she knew was that there were two beautiful children she loved dearly from those times. In that respect, she thought, all the suffering was worthwhile, as the three of them had a new home together. They had each other, and of course the three of them also had the love and support of Bessie's family in Barking. They were going forward, and enjoying the security that had been missing during the past years with their absent father.

With the unstinting support of a welfare worker, one Janice Beech, at Stepney Green, Bessie was fortunate enough to be allocated two places for her growing children at nearby Charles Darwin School. On a lovely warm March day in 1891, with masses of snowdrops popping up in the council gardens, Bessie walked along the main road holding the hands of her children. They were going to school for the first time dressed in nice colourful clothes which their grandparents had bought them. They arrived at the wrought iron school gates and saw the Latin inscription on it. Bessie didn't know what it meant, and nor did she care. Children mingled around talking, laughing and eventually waving goodbye to their mothers as they walked through the gates and into the school. With tears in her eyes, Bessie kissed her young children before they too walked into Charles Darwin School to begin their education. Ethel was six years old and Benny four.

That afternoon, and many afternoons to come, Bessie was waiting to take her children back home for tea. As the three of them walked along the busy Stepney Green Road holding hands, Benny was excited to tell his mother about what he had done during his first day at school.

'Mum, we painted on paper with brushes, and the teacher, her name is Miss Holland, I fink, said I was very good' he explained.

'Well done luv,' Bessie remarked to her handsome, brown-haired son. 'What about you sweetheart, did you enjoy yourself on your first day at school?' Bessie asked Ethel, who was slim, with green eyes and blond hair.

'Yeah, it wasn't that bad. I was told off by Miss Holland for talking too much. But I did enjoy reading some of the books,' was her daughter's softly-spoken reply. As had been the case at home, Ethel's early reading development continued to grow. Bessie couldn't help noticing that Benny was taller and more confident than Ethel, even though he was two years younger, but for Bessie they were both her treasures and for whom she would do her utmost.

Charles Darwin School, named after the great Victorian scientist, had been built in 1888, to commemorate his original work on evolution. A few years later, I read that the Church Elders had scorned not only the building of the school, but more importantly, his blasphemous work against the name of God. Well done Charlie Darwin - he was one of the first scientists to put the Church in its place. Furthermore, his incredible ground-breaking scientific discovery of natural selection well and truly sealed the fate of theism, but the children were taught otherwise.

Of course there was a compromise, as there nearly always is, in that the school had to be constructed by the church surveyors. As there was a limited amount of money available, Darwin School could only be a single-storey building, which meant cramming in as many children as possible, to the detriment of their learning. Limited toilet facilities were available, but no washing basin was provided. Furthermore, no pictures, statues or any other article resembling Darwin must be exhibited on school premises. How about that for church hypocrisy? The same institution that ruled over the working classes for centuries was determined, it seemed, to keep them under the yoke for eternity. But as I have already stated, many Christians fought bravely for the rights of the downtrodden East Enders, and, of course, in other places in Britain too. As Bessie said, 'thank God for that bloke called Charlie Darwin'!

With the children apparently getting on well with their education, the time had come for Bessie to find a job so that she could look after her family. Ever since she had been deserted in Ealing, she had been given handouts by various institutions and individuals so that her children could be fed. With the children at school for eight hours a day, it gave her the opportunity to find a job in a local greengrocer's not ten minutes' walk from Darwin School. Her only job had been as a receptionist in Barking when she was a teenager. In those days she wasn't a particularly confident person. There in the bustling and busy environment of Stepney she was rather apprehensive, understandably so, about working with tough, mature men who had years of experience of selling fruit and vegetables to the public. Rough and ready people, make no mistake. Most customers were mainly working-class mothers whose days largely consisted of trying to get the best bargains they could for as little money as possible to feed their hungry families from starving. Bessie was still wet behind the ears, but she had enough experience of human life to know that local women, if uncompromising, were decent and friendly.

Besides, Bessie thought, I've got to learn somewhere, quickly, about growing up, feeding my family and earning a regular wage.

So in September 1891, Bessie started work at Harry Barnard's greengrocer's shop. The small brick shop, with a rented flat above, was in Turnball Lane, one hundred yards from Stepney Green Road. Harry was the third generation to own the shop his paternal grandfather, Alfie, a small-time villain, had bought by taking out a small bank loan. After a few years in 'stir' (prison), Alfie thought it easier to borrow rather than steal. Since then the business had flourished, and was patronised by local people.

By the time Bessie arrived at the shop it was nearly 8 am. There was already a long line of customers (punters, Harry called them), resembling people lining up in a soup kitchen or buying a ticket for a music hall performance, waiting to buy fruit and vegetables.

'Allo luv, put your coat in the kitchen out the back and put this white coat on,' said Harry Barnard, a tall, gangly chap, nearly bald and wearing glasses.

Bessie served her first customer. 'Allo sweetheart, are you new 'ere?' said the woman.

'Yes that's right. Me name's Bessie,' she explained rather nervously.

'Well give me five pounds of spuds, no eyes [over-ripe] luv. And three pounds of carrots and one of those hearty cabbages the size of 'Arry's 'ead over near the shelf.'

Bessie fumbled her way through, but she did her best, and customers realised that.

'Allo darling. You ain't 'arry's new bird are yer?' asked Ivy, a regular customer, ribbing Bessie.

'At my age Ivy, I'm nearly 60, I need nourishment, not punishment,' remarked Harry, as poor old Ivy, aged 70 and widowed, hobbled away with her fruit on severely arthritic feet.

'Five pounds of spuds luv, gotta be clean mind, and a hand of ripe bananas. No green ones luv, cos it gives me husband constipation. Ain't you new luv?' That was Rosie, another ageing local customer full of jokes and laughter but always ready to give you her lip (tell you off).

'That's right luv. Just started working today,' said Bessie, as she slowly began to relax and gain confidence.

'Well luv, don't you allow 'arry boy to overwork yer,' warned Rosie, as she slowly walked up the road with her goods, stopping and chatting to those who had time. Most local people had nothing, and some lived in dire poverty with no choice but to thieve, beg, take pickings from dustbins or prostitute themselves in any way they could. This scene was typical not just in the East End, although it was probably worse than most places, but over most of the country at a time when Britain's Empire was making fortunes from around the world.

Bessie's first working day, of about eight hours, was coming to a close. Other than two cups of quickly-drunk tea, she had been on her feet all day serving customers.

'Ow d'yer feel Bessie? Tired, I bet?' Harry Benstead said, holding a cigarette in one hand and a mug of tea in the other.

'Gawd Harry, I'm fucking knackered, but pleased to be working for the first time in years,' Bessie remarked.

Harry handed her a few pounds of assorted fruit and vegetables for the family. 'Thank you 'arry,' said smiling Bessie, who had realised her children must be collected from school within the next half hour or they would start worrying.

'You've done well luv on yer first day. Take care and see yer tomorrow at eight,' said Harry.

Bessie walked the few hundred yards to meet her children at the gates of Darwin School. Darwin, unlike most schools around then, allowed mothers to come in and look after other children whose mothers were working and couldn't get there on time. Bessie glowed with pride and happiness about her Peabody Trust flat, her growing, healthy children, who had apparently adapted well to school, and the pleasure of having completed her first day at work.

'Allo Mum!' shouted Benny and Ethel as they ran out of the front gate to their waiting mother. Bessie bent down and gave them both a big kiss and hug.

'Would yer like a banana and an apple each?' Bessie asked her smiling children. In those days Darwin school, like most schools, did not provide any food whatsoever for the young children. Teachers were allowed to give then jugs of water, but that was all. Bessie used to make sandwiches for her own children, as did many mothers, but a lot of children went without food all day, and sometimes all through the night as their parents couldn't afford it. Many young children, like those mentioned, just dropped out of school so that they could earn, steal or beg some food. Many youngsters used to travel to the hotels in the West End of London, where they were usually successful in finding good food thrown away by staff. If there was enough of it, most young people would take some food home for their poverty-stricken families. Families in those days, sometimes with six or more children lived, slept and ate in one room. They paid exorbitant rents to private landlords who could throw them out onto the streets without any prior notice. Some families were so poor that they took in male lodgers who slept in the same room as their children. And these were families living in the most powerful and wealthiest country on earth at the time.

LONDON

I wander thro' each chartered street,
Near where the chartered Thames does flow,
And mark in every face I meet
Marks of weakness, marks of woe

- William Blake

Chapter Two

Bessie battles to the top

Things had been going well for Bessie and her two children. They thrived generally, and what they failed to learn at school, even though the education was adequate, Bessie taught her children, just as her mother had taught her and her sister Jane. Ethel, although still thin, and Benny soon enjoyed playing with friends at school. Like some of those friends who lived in the same flats at Bradstock Street, they continued to flourish. Familiar games such as kicking footballs, playing hopscotch, drawing chalk figures and even kissing each other down in the courtyard below. Benny was a confident young boy full of healthy mischief. He was popular with the girls, but preferred to fight, run, shout and generally assert himself amongst the boys. Apparently he feared no one.

Like most healthy carefree boys, they would meet most evenings and weekends down at the bottom of flats to discuss anything from sex to smashing shop windows, and, if they had time or the weather was fine, off to the local park they ran at top speed, knocking over anything in their way. St Georges Park was only a few hundred yards from Bradstock Flats. (Incidentally there were three new blocks of Guinness Trust owned flats in the same street. They were all built with deep red bricks and looked very attractive.) Once there, Benny and his mates could be joined by any number of scruffy boys all waiting for a punch-up, or a game of football or running matches or smoke cigarettes nicked from their parents. Besides, their mothers having kicked them out of the house for some respite, most had nowhere else to go. Occasionally a few of them went stealing round the local shops, but the patrolling policemen were never far from the action.

Sometimes a few of the older boys used to take the train to Central London, usually Soho, and seek out middle-class men who gave them money for sexual favours. A few extra pennies helped in those days of hardship. All the boys looked the same: pudding basin haircut, stolen or charity or hand-me-down clothes, hobnailed boots if you were lucky. No one really cared what you looked like. Parents did their best. And it went on for years.

Since she had been young, Ethel had been a bit of a loner, and would remain so for the rest of her life. She actually enjoyed her own company, but occasionally she went for walks with one or two girls from the same flats.

With one of the girls, Joyce Jackman, a short, dumpy girl with a freckly face, she used to enjoy walking to Broxbourne Park. Other than the friendly alcoholics who slept there, it was a small quiet park, full of various flower beds, nearly a mile from their home, where they could sit down, talk and read to each other without being accosted by aggressive boys. That was how Ethel viewed most males during her life. Whether that attitude was related to the loss of her father at an early age is unclear. It could have been due to the confident gregariousness of her mother that she felt unable or unwilling to speak her mind.

As she got older, she avoided the boisterous Bradstock Flats boys altogether. Instead she either stayed indoors reading, an invaluable skill she taught herself, or went out riding on the omnibus to visit the London railway stations (motor buses were introduced to London in 1899). Ethel had a great fascination for large railway stations, even more so when she could stand on a platform only feet away from a large, hissing steam engine. She occasionally told Bessie and Benny of her utter enjoyment of travelling to King's Cross to watch the trains pulling out of the station amidst huge plumes of smoke that threatened to engulf her. That smoke, I believe, may well have given her some much-needed psychological anonymity. But most of the time she was secretive about what she did and who she saw or knew. I think she felt safe from people when she kept quiet about her activities. Sometimes days would go by without Ethel uttering a single word. She was locked up into her secure world. However, she was very interested in reading the story, and other similar stories, of the gruesome murders carried out by Jack the Ripper in 1888.

Bessie thought her world was complete when all her family were with her, which was usually on a Sunday for dinner. In one respect it gave her control of those she most loved. That was particularly noticeable one Sunday, 6th May 1895, when Tom, Florence and Jane Smith arrived holding a large chicken they had bought to celebrate Ethel's 10th birthday. Tom, aged 49, still worked on the railway, and Florence, 53, had returned to working as a seamstress. Jane, now 26, was short and slim and wore an attractive green dress. As for having a boyfriend, she had nothing to say on the subject. Due to her sister's experience of men, Jane was wary about associating with the opposite sex. She was still single and worked as a typist for a shipping company in Aldgate.

Jane was holding a flat parcel covered in pink paper and tied with white ribbon. 'Happy birthday to you, happy birthday to you, happy birthday dear Ethel, happy birthday to you,' all five people in the room sang loudly and harmoniously to smiling Ethel. She was probably embarrassed by all the attention.

'Granny and I have bought yer a birthday chicken treat, sweetheart' said Tom to his delighted granddaughter. 'And we've also bought yer a new dress, jumper and shoes. Happy birthday, sweetheart'.

'And this is my birthday gift to you,' said Jane as she placed a pink object into Ethel's hands. With smiling anticipation, Ethel opened the parcel to reveal three books by one of her favourite authors, Vivien Drake. Drake wrote about secret gardens and woods where only children played in a world of fun and happiness. These were ideal books for children with a rich inner life full of fantasy. Bessie informed me that my mother read and re-read them many times.

After an enjoyable dinner, pudding and a singsong, Ethel showed everyone the six birthday cards she had received from various friends. It was her day to celebrate. Finally Bessie gave her a large box from her and Benny, covered in red paper. When she opened it, shrill cries of happiness came from her. 'Thank you mum and Benny! I've always wanted a tray of paints, brushes and painting book'.

It was a most wonderful day, and something my mother still rejoices in, though her enthusiasm for painting was short lived because of her overriding passion for reading.

During the years she had been living at Bradstock Flats, my grandmother had managed to repaint the flat from the usual standard brown to various colours of her own choice. From a light green in her bedroom to light blue in the children's bedroom and beige elsewhere, the flat looked truly impressive. She had also replaced the old second-hand, clapped-out furniture she had brought along with her when she first moved in. Two new beds, a three-piece suite, table and chairs, pots, pans and curtains had helped make her flat into a comfortable home fit for a queen. A home where the vagaries of the harsh and unpredictable world were held at bay, until she re-entered that world early next morning to earn much needed money to sustain three hungry mouths.

All that redecorating and refurnishing was made possible by the cash she had saved while working for a number of years for the likeable, trustworthy Harry Barnard. The weeks and months had flown by selling fruit and vegetables to local people. She got to know customers well, not just from the shop but in local cafés and pubs. As her kids' independence grew, they would walk to school with their friends; that gave Bessie the time to meet more people and exchange experiences and information. All of London life frequented the East End cafés.

As time went on, she became confident and competent enough to run Barnard's shop on her own, which gave her more income. Business grew, possibly due in part to Bessie's gregarious personality. She trained two young local girls who served in the shop part-time. Bessie became an integral part of the community, well liked and respected. Other greengrocers and other shop owners along the High Street all offered Bessie the opportunity to work for them, as her competence was well known.

For the time being she stayed with Barnard, until information passed her way, as it did like wildfire in a place like Stepney, that a new upmarket furniture store was opening up in Liverpool Street. The large new store, called Ferguson's, was looking for all levels of staff, and interviews would be conducted two weeks hence. After enquiring about the vacancies, wages and hours, she posted her application form for the store supervisor position. Failing that, she made a second application for the cashier position. If she was successful finding employment at Ferguson, she, like her father, could use the faster and more reliable underground train to get to work.

Bessie was desperate to go forward with her life. But like her sister, she appeared not to be interested in finding a partner. Life with her growing children was safe and secure. There was also good news for Ethel, as one of the local contacts had been able to help her find part-time evening employment packing clothes in a small warehouse in Mile End. Mind-numbing work, but it brought a few shillings at the end of the week for her to buy books or travel around London.

It was March 1900, and after working at Harry Barnard's shop for over nine years, Bessie Smith walked through the posh swivelling doors of Ferguson's like a film star attending an audition, determined she was going to move on with her life. Green-suited security men told her where to find personnel. Wearing new clothes, bought by her own saved cash, not from money lent from the tallyman, my attractive, brazen grandmother was shown into the interview room.

'I've been reading your application form with interest', commented the tall, slim, well-dressed, educated middle-class woman interviewing Bessie. 'Tell me, Mrs Kennedy [although divorced years before, Bessie retained her married name], do you think you could handle a large number of staff on the shop floor, as well as helping, supporting and informing our sometimes demanding, but valued customers?'

'Yes I'm sure I could Miss Birt. During my present employment I've been managing the shop for the last two years on my own, but I had to serve a constant number of customers. Also on Saturdays I had to train, and supervise, at least four young people to support me in the shop (another porky). When my current employer became part time, he left me to negotiate prices for fruit and vegetables with various buyers that visited the shop.' She spoke in a calm and measured way, careful to speak correctly. The smartly decorated environment didn't intimidate her.

'But you are aware that your shop and this establishment are very different in nature?' explained Miss Birt.

'I can see that to a certain extent, but wherever you are customers have their needs and requirements. One must be aware of that and act accordingly,' said Bessie, who felt she had given a good account of herself.

The interview continued for another 40 minutes. Afterwards, Miss Birt thanked Bessie for attending and promised to write within four weeks to let her know whether she had been successful or not. As she said goodbye to my dolled-up, attractive 33-year-old grandmother, Miss Birt must have wondered where she had come from, dressed as she was in all her finery. No doubt, one way or another, Bessie Smith must have impressed her!

Three weeks later she opened the letter she had impatiently been waiting for, and it was great news. She would have dearly loved to wave the letter in front of her former husband and say to him, 'We haven't missed you since you walked out on us over ten years ago'.

'Look kids, I've got the supervisor job at Ferguson's and I start in two weeks' time,' she told them. 'I've done it at last. I've fuckin' done it!' She started jumping for joy all around her flat, kissing and hugging her two children.

After preparing herself for work at Barnard's, and seeing the children off to school, Bessie quickly ran round some of the flats to inform her neighbours of her good news. 'We'll 'ave a drink later to celebrate your success, duchess,' said Nellie Taylor, who had moved into the flat next door, with her three older children, the same week as Bessie had, all those years ago.

Bessie arrived at Barnard's at 8 am on the appointed day with an added spring in her step. Over the years she had never missed a day's work, and she had always been on time. Never late for work, that was something she was proud of. Harry Barnard and his many customers always knew Bessie would be there to serve them with their usual fruit and vegetable orders. She became known as the 'rock of Barnard'.

At the end of another busy day, Bessie took Harry to one side to explain all about her new job. 'Well done sweetheart. You deserve it after working 'ere for nearly ten years. I shall miss yer terribly, yer know that' he said, putting his arms round Bessie and kissing her on the cheek.

'Thanks a lot 'arry. I've enjoyed working 'ere all those years. I've met some good people and made lots of friends. People who are decent, kind, friendly and once they know yer, they would do anything for yer. I shall miss this place 'arry,' said Bessie, as tears fell down her chubby pink cheeks.

With all the well wishes from the many customers still ringing in her ears, my grandmother, dressed in a dark blue suit, walked to Stepney Green station. No doubt she received lots of wolf whistles from men working on the nearby building sites. She was only 33, chubby yet attractive, and most of all, she wanted to leave her mark on life, no matter how small that would be.

Sitting anxiously on the newish underground train, she felt self-conscious as the men opposite, all dressed in smart city suits and carrying briefcases, stared at her, some even smiling at her. Did they know she was a working-class girl from Stepney? She hoped they wouldn't ask her a question, because her Cockney accent would undermine her. Bollocks, she thought, that would be just too bad, wouldn't it? You must have confidence gel, Bessie kept reminding herself, as she reached the top of Liverpool Street station escalators.

Once on the main street she was accosted by three young ragged boys all trying to shove the newly-founded, free *Daily Express* into her hand. She looked straight ahead, focused only on presenting herself professionally on the first day at her new employment, only minutes from the bustling noise of Bishopsgate. Ferguson's, a former insurance building, was based in a side street called Old Broad Street, among other stores, banks, insurance companies and pubs. All life appeared to be here.

Once inside the grand foyer, with a huge glittering blue chandelier above her head, the large, high-ceilinged and beautifully-decorated hall at first overwhelmed Bessie. 'Yes madam, can I help you?' enquired a friendly middle-aged man dressed in a green uniform. She was directed to the third floor, where the manager was waiting for her.

'Good morning Mrs Kennedy, welcome to the carpet department. I hope you enjoy your time here. We're a friendly bunch of colleagues and we do our best to help one another,' enthused the manager, Miss Patel, a first-generation Hindu Indian, who was very short and slim and looked very smart in her pale blue suit with matching shoes. Bessie hadn't seen many Indians like Miss Patel before. After spending an hour in her manager's office sorting out and signing her employment contract, she eventually got to meet her six other colleagues in an adjacent office. After various formalities, she took her first tentative steps out onto the expensive dark green carpet of her new department. I bet she thought, if only those old, arthritic, toothless, former Barnard customers could see me now.

For the first weeks Bessie was being trained most of the time by her manager, but she did get the opportunity to serve and talk with some of the older, well-heeled female customers. Looking around at the expensive woven silk carpets, she was reminded of the bare-threaded rags she had first laid on her floors at Bradstock Street. It must be wonderful, she thought, to be wealthy, and have the opportunity to buy any carpet you wanted for your home. No doubt her thoughts went back to Ealing, Barking, Stepney and many other places where she knew people who didn't have 'two half pennies to rub together,' as they used to say down the East End. During lunch breaks, she slowly got to know her six colleagues, five of whom were women, all sales assistants, and one man, who was the porter. All of them lived not far from Bessie in the East End.

'Hallo, Bessie, we're all glad to meet yer luv,' said one of them, a fat and jovial woman with deep pink cheeks that were not that dissimilar to Bessie's. 'My name is Barbara, and these other urchins are Kate, Minnie, Betty, Mary and Joe, who humps all our carpets from the warehouse to the shop floor, but if we don't like the colour, we send 'im back to fetch another, but mind you he occasionally likes to pinch yer arse,' she said in a friendly, humorous manner.

'We're a good honest bunch 'ere Bessie. Fancy a fag?' said Minnie, aged about 50, who lived with her husband and four children in a shared tenement in Poplar. She had worked in numerous places during her hard life. Given the chance at tea break, Minnie always made her colleagues laugh at Ferguson's when she told them, in some detail, what she had done for money when younger. It appeared she would take middle-class men, especially after they had consumed alcohol, down one of the many dark alleys in Mayfair, or occasionally in Hyde Park, take down their trousers and give their penis ('percy,' she called it) a good pull.

'Mind you' said Minnie with a mischievous smile on her face, 'I always demanded cash up front. Most of the men were lonely middle-aged professionals workin in the city.'

After first complaining by letter about the sordid state of the expensive silk rug she had bought, Lady Dorothy Pilgrim marched into Fergusons' carpet department as though she owned the place. 'I demand to see the manager immediately!' cried the good lady.

'I apologise madam,' said Bessie delicately, 'the department manager, Miss Patel, is not here today. I'm the supervisor, can I help you?'

'What is your name, good woman?' demanded Lady Pilgrim.

'My name is Mrs Bessie Kennedy. I am in charge during Miss Patel's absence, madam'.

This was her chance, thought Bessie, to demonstrate skilfully what life had taught her so far. At that stage, Joe carried the expensive and beautiful maroon rug from the lift, having previously taken it out of Lady Pilgrim's carriage, and put it before her.

'Look at that awful discolouration in the left hand corner' said Lady Pilgrim. 'Can you see it, Mrs Bessie? Sorry, Mrs Kennedy'.

'Yes I can, Lady Pilgrim. It is a serious discolouration and spoils the whole pattern of the carpet'.

After some skilful and delicate negotiation, Bessie was able to persuade Lady Pilgrim to accept a new rug in exchange and a verbal apology for all the stress she had unwontedly experienced. The good lady herself wrote a friendly letter to the store general manager, Mr Cedric Rouse, thanking him for the most graceful attention she had received from his staff. A feather in the cap for a working-class girl from Stepney!

It transpired a few months later that it was Lady Pilgrim, with the professional assistance of others, who had helped the Quaker George Cadbury to set up the

Bournville Village Trust in 1900. The trust went on to house, employ and educate many people.

After several months of stamping her authority on the carpet department, though she was popular and well-liked by most, Miss Patel thought Bessie needed to gain more store experience. Many colleagues called Bessie, rather jokingly, Miss Patel's bulldog.

My grandmother got things done, if sometimes rather undiplomatic. Like the time she asked a young male porter to water the rather large dry aspidistra that was the centrepiece of the department floor.

'Ow can I do that Miss?' asked David, a thin, pale teenager with spots all over his feminine face.

'Piss in it if you like!' roared Bessie, like a colour sergeant on parade.

She was transferred to the furniture department, with the understanding that she could return to her original place of work, if she so desired, at a later stage. Already, she was getting something of a name for being outspoken and would stand no nonsense from those beneath her. Always at the front of her mind were the days when she had been vulnerable, insecure and powerless. Now that she had some control over her life, no one was going to take it away from her. It would take a fool or a madman to try. Now that she had one foot in the door, she would, in time, get both feet firmly entrenched. She was determined to succeed. That was her hope, anyway.

Just two weeks before Bessie's transfer to the furniture

department, Ferguson's store, along with most of the nation, closed for the day in honour of Queen Victoria's death. Her long reign (1837-1901) was over. Her German husband, Prince Albert, had died years before. This could have been due to the huge number of children he had produced. What a way to go, I remember my father joking about it years later.

Most of the staff did their duty and stood in silence, along with thousands of other people, throughout Central London. Not Bessie though. According to my mother, she went home, put her feet up and saluted the pampered old Queen with a large whisky from the comfort of her own home.

It made many of us laugh to tears when it was known that Queen Victoria's teeth had all rotted over the years through excessive consumption of liquorice. One could not have imagined, with teeth the colour of piano keys, the Queen passionately kissing her charming Albert.

By this stage Ethel had been working for more than eighteen months. She was over 16 years old, but still thin, reserved and not appealing to the opposite sex, according to her mother. Her packing job, which she did with other women, consisted of sorting out tons of second-hand clothes which had been donated by organisations and wealthy individuals. It was the responsibility of the warehouse owner, a middle-aged Jew called Sammy Hyman, to collect most of the donations from the local railway station. Once sorted and graded, the clothes were sent to various places including charities, hospitals and schools. Like most warehouses during that time,

Hyman's was dirty, cold and poorly lit, with one foul-smelling, rodent-infected toilet which several women had to share. There were others much worse than his. Many years later, not surprisingly, most warehouses were found to have contained high levels of asbestos, which had affected the health of many workers.

Considering all the difficulties Ethel had to face at work, she was nonetheless pleased to have a regular job. Mind-numbing as the work was, she was grateful to be able to have at least a pound in her pocket every week, which gave her the opportunity to go out for a ride on an omnibus, or visit a train station, or buy a book. She loved reading cheap novels, which she acquired from the second-hand bookshops she regularly frequented.

'It was something about those old shops that kept drawing me back to them,' she would explain. 'All the shops were quiet, and mainly used by middle-class old men. I think it was a mix of the musty-smelling books and tobacco smoke that I enjoyed.'

Given that she was intelligent, it must have been frustrating packing clothes for hours on end in such a stultifying environment. When I was old enough to realise these things about my mother, I had deep feelings of sympathy for the way her life had developed. I often imagined her resembling a frightened little bird cowering beneath the heavy burden of her everyday life. One consolation, if you can call it that, came when by law people aged 13-18 could not be forced to work more than 10 hours a day. Only three years previously, it was 12 hours. One could safely assert that the exploitation of child labour had been somewhat reduced, at least legally, yet employers still continued to flout the law, knowing that workers needed the money just to survive.

Even at the tender age of 13, Benny was a complete contrast to his older sister. Tall, well-built, confident and popular, he hung around with the local tough boys of the day. They had their own small gang which went round drinking, smoking and getting involved in petty crime. But his mother wasn't concerned about his antics, and nor were his grandparents down in Barking. Unlike Ethel, Benny often travelled down to the East End to discuss various things with his grandfather Tom, now aged 56, and still working on the railways.

'How's it going, Granddad?' Benny would ask, sporting well-oiled hair, tight blue slacks and a newish gabardine jacket he had bought cheaply from a costermonger.

'I'm all right son. Still working me nuts orf on the railway, other than that can't complain,' said Tom.

'How's grandma, is she all right?' Benny asked.

'Yeah, she's fit as a fiddle. Still grafting herself. Good old bird she is, your grandmother.'

Tom was beginning to put on weight round his stomach. My great-grandmother, Florence, aged 60, had been back working for years as a seamstress for a local dress maker. Unlike before when she had travelled at least three hours a day to work in Whitechapel, she could now walk to her place of employment. Mind you, like her granddaughter, she grafted ten hours a day in foul conditions. Besides, employers frequently wanted you to work overtime on Saturdays as well. Legally you didn't have to, but if you refused, your boss could make life difficult for you.

Benny soon found himself a job working as a labourer on a local building site, just as most men did from his background. His time had come to earn a living and make a contribution to the household. Two of his old school friends were working at the same place. Laing's were the main contractors and were responsible for constructing a hundred flats, in Poplar, for the Guinness Trust. In time the flats would provide a decent and secure home for working-class families who had hitherto lived in dirty, overcrowded tenements. Aside from making some money, Benny was pleased that he was helping others, so they could live a better quality of life. It reminded him of when he and his family, owning very little, had moved into Bradstock Road.

Along with his workmates, Benny charged around the site like a man possessed, carrying timber, bricks, cement and anything else that was needed. From his background you had to show you were strong and willing to take on anything, otherwise there were always many men available to instantly take your place.

In the evenings, he and his friends would go for a beer and talk shop. Having over a pound in his pocket most weeks gave him the opportunity to buy some modern clothes in the local market. Just like most of his local friends, he wanted to be a jack-the-lad. Dressed in new clothes, he soon had the chance to take out some of the pretty local girls he had known from his school days. One particular place he enjoyed taking his girlfriends was the cinema. The first cinema had opened in central London in 1905, the year I was born. Benny and his friends would go 'up west,' as they called it, to walk around the shops, drink beer and chat up the girls. It gave him a great thrill, when he could afford it, to ride in one of the new motor taxis that were first introduced in London in 1899. No buses for Benny, when he was out to impress different girlfriends.

By 1903, my Great Aunt Jane had left the office job she had had for several years in a large shipping company in the City. Still in the City, she had got a similar job at an insurance company in Aldgate. Now aged 35, attractive and slim, with years of office experience behind her, Jane could command a better wage and conditions.

She had also, with great reluctance, and to her parents' disappointment, moved out of their small comfortable house in Barking. Jane had realised at her age that, although her parents' home was secure, she had to move nearer to her place of work. After weeks of looking around, she found an affordable, if small, newly-decorated bedsit not far from her place of work in Aldgate. As she was still single, she wanted to improve her opportunities of finding a boyfriend. She had dated several male colleagues over the years, but for many reasons, they had all faded away. This was possibly due to living a long way out in Barking, or her parents' refusal to allow Jane's boyfriends to sleep with her in their house. In some respects my great-grandparents were old fashioned. Besides, she wanted a more interesting social life with the girlfriends she had already met at work. Jane continued visiting her parents whenever she could, but her life was moving forward. She also visited her sister in Bradstock Road, or sometimes they met for lunch in one of the many clean cheap cafés near where they worked.

Bessie, after her successful year-long stint in the furniture department, had returned to the carpet department. As usual, she ruffled more than a few feathers, but Miss Patel and her seniors regarded Bessie as a good worker. Miss Patel, aged 35, was intelligent and had raven-black hair flowing down her back. She had always lived with her parents and two brothers in a rented three-bedroom terraced house in Paddington. Her parents had moved from Delhi to London with the promise of work when they were young. For many years they had both worked in Mr Patel's uncle's factory, in Euston, making carpets and rugs for the overseas market.

Bessie liked working with Miss Patel, who she found to be hard-working, supportive and friendly. Never once, during the years she worked with her, did she ever see her be unfriendly to anyone, staff or customer. But knowing Bessie as I did later on, she must have given her manager a hard time, although it appears she took it all in her stride. Miss Patel and my grandmother continued to develop a positive professional relationship.

My mother, Ethel Kennedy, aged 20, was slim and underweight when she gave birth to me in the early hours of the 6th June 1905 at St Saviour's Hospital, Stepney. I was christened Leslie Tatter. Her young boyfriend, my father, Billy Tatter, later her husband, was there to support her. That was something she had always cherished, especially as she had observed so many young girls, all alone, no one to love them, with illegitimate children.

Apparently the hospital wards were so full of babies and pregnant mothers that the beds had less than six inches separating them. So that the hospital could cater for nearly everyone, they also put beds out in the corridors. It was said that the hospital was so short of space that two beds found their way into a large cleaning cupboard amongst buckets, pans and toilet rolls. Not an auspicious start. But that was life then; you just got on with it and hoped for the best.

Those mothers who could afford it not only brought in clean napkins, food and clothes for their own kids, but for those mothers who had little or nothing to provide for their children. Mothers also helped the overworked nurses, who did their best in difficult conditions.

After two weeks the young doctor informed my mother that as I had put on weight and was growing, I was now healthy enough to be taken home. With financial help from my grandmother, my mother had managed to put down four weeks' rent on a small shabby ground floor bedsit at 10 Davis Street, Stepney. In those days they were called tenements, and were typically found in the poorer parts of cities like London. They met minimum standards for health and hygiene. As most of them were privately owned, tenants had no real legal rights, which meant that houses were rarely repaired and eventually became slums. The Public Health Act of

1875 laid down rules for sanitation for all houses, but most owners did not adhere to them. Most owners didn't give a damn about their tenants' health or hygiene. I can't forget how we had to share a bathroom, toilet and kitchen, which were all on the second floor. Imagine the smell! Cramped conditions indeed, but the families who lived there did their best to keep the surroundings clean. The hallway, stair carpets and walls were all rather dark, dull and somewhat depressing, but it was our home and I soon found myself running up and down the stairs enjoying myself.

The constant childish noise I made delighted the father of the Turkish family who had the room above us. He and his wife were kind, friendly people. They had two children, called Hassan and Idris, I believe. Mother told me later that they were asylum seekers, but I did not really understand what that meant. Mr Ecevit, the Turkish chap, was always giving me sweets or sometimes fruit, whenever he saw me playing around the house or in the garden.

The one consolation that came with our dog kennel of a home was that we could use the large garden. As time went by, all the children, Hassan, Idris, Ted, Shaun, Paddy and I, used to play games together in the garden. With my confidence growing, I used to encourage all the children to play together. We all rushed round at a million miles an hour screaming and trying to catch each other, or playing football, cricket and rugby. We regularly kicked footballs, nearly always on purpose, over our African neighbour's fence. As they usually landed on Mr Mbewe's well-tended prize-winning roses, he was reluctant to return them without first receiving an apology.

I got to like Mr Mbewe. He was from Africa, wherever that was, and spoke with a funny deep accent. As he had a massive stomach, we always thought he was pregnant, until mother explained that men couldn't have babies. That was our first and only sex lesson in a Victorian world that preferred Christian values and hypocrisy to honest sexual education for the illiterate mas

Poor Idris didn't have the energy to play with five rough and ready boys prepared to try anything available. With our encouragement, Mr Ecevit climbed to the very top of the highest oak tree in the garden, but he was unable to climb down until the fire brigade arrived to help him down safely. These were great times. We fought each other with bare fists. I punched Shaun, Paddy's brother, on the nose. Paddy punched me on the chin, which knocked me to the ground. Ted beat up Hassan twice in one day, until the latter's father found them boxing gloves to wear. Some time later, with gloves at the ready, Hassan, encouraged by his father, started throwing punches at Ted. We shouted for Ted as he swung wildly at the shorter, lighter Hassan, who eventually fell, out of breath, onto the multicoloured bedding plants belonging to Cedric Blom-Copper, the owner of the early 19th century tenement. All the parents received a written warning from the aforementioned about our future conduct. That did not deter our boisterous behaviour. 'Stop pissing on those flowers, Paddy,' I heard his father shout on more than one occasion.

It was time for Ted and me to go to the local Protestant school, St Benedict's. With such an inspiring name, we both felt at the time that we had been chosen to follow Jesus into heaven. Well that's what the religious instruction teacher told us one morning after she saw us help an old lady across the road. Mind you she didn't see that the lady had given us a penny and boiled sweets.

As they had Catholic parents born in Dublin, Paddy and Shaun went off to attend St Patrick's school, somewhere near Limehouse. They told us that they were going to a different heaven to us. Their heaven was to be found somewhere near Highbury Football Stadium, because their father used to watch Arsenal play football, and he used to shout at the centre forward 'Jesus bloody Christ!' as he had been sent to them by the Almighty. This was all great banter, and kids believed it in those days when the Church dominated everyday life, especially working-class urchins like us.

Hassan and Idris went to an altogether different school from the rest of us, a Muslim school in West Ham. In those days we thought Mr Ecevit, a religious teacher, had sent his kids to that part of London because West Ham United players were Muslims. We often asked Hassan when he was going to play for the Hammers, the nickname given to United. He said Muslims didn't play football, they preferred to pray instead.

Although Mr Ecevit was a friendly and likeable man to us as we grew up, Paddy, Shaun, Ted and I often felt there were odd things about him and some of his friends. For example, we were rather confused as to why Mr Ecevit was nearly always wearing his pyjamas out in the garden during the day and on the public paths. Most of his friends also wore pyjamas when they visited the house. The men wore funny-coloured hats similar to a fez. Paddy surmised that they were all circus clowns and were going to Hassan's father's room to tell each other jokes.

At other times when we played in the garden, without Hassan and his sister, we used to hear funny sounds and noises coming from their room overlooking the garden. We used to hide underneath their open window giggling at the various sounds, which were completely alien to us. At the time we just thought they had unusual taste in music. My mother couldn't explain it either. She thought they might be holding a séance and having conversations with the dead. But Paddy thought only God could do that. 'No he can't Paddy, only Jesus can,' wailed Ted, who with a pudding basin haircut, and wearing dirty charity clothes, looked just liked a young costermonger.

It was only some time later, when our teacher explained, that we really understood why the Hassans and their friends, wore different clothes and played different music from us. In those early days, before the Great War, other religions and cultures were barely known or understood within working-class communities. For example, one of my local friends, Harry Drake, himself a former Romany, thought Sikhs wore head bandages because they were prone to injury or accident.

At St Benedict's School, Ted and I made many friends among the local young children living in Stepney and surrounding areas (or manors, as Father called them). White kids played all day long with other kids from around the world. We didn't care where they came from as long as the boys could run, play football and fight. There were children from Africa, India, Australia, Jamaica, Italy and many other countries. Most of us dressed in hand-me-down clothes previously worn by our older siblings or other family siblings. Many times my mother had bought adult trousers at the local charity shop, and after shortening the legs by two feet or more, I would wear them to school held up by one of my father's ties. We didn't care much about appearance – besides, who was going to look at us except the school doctor looking for lice and malnutrition?

I vividly remember two Indian boys first attending our school in bare feet. Their parents explained to the welfare worker that in their country it was so hot they didn't have shoes or many clothes to wear. 'Besides,' said Mr Savananda, 'we don't have enough money to buy them any shoes'. He explained that they had just arrived very poor from Bombay.

Mrs Webster, the welfare officer, a decent middle-class woman who really helped the dispossessed, arranged for the Savanandas and many other children to collect various items from the local Salvation Army. Most families went there at various times of near-poverty to dress their children, especially around winter time, when most households had little heat to keep them warm. In fact a lot of the local men used to steal coal at night from the trucks held in the large sidings near Stepney Green Gas Works. My father, though he worked in the Ritz Hotel as a porter, didn't earn much money and was nearly always skint. Along with other men he knew, he would leave home around midnight armed with shovels and small coal bags. Three or more hours later they returned with many bags of coal that kept us warm, as well as others down the road, during cold times. It was something special to get out of bed, around 5am, already dressed and walk into a warm room to eat our breakfast of bread and dripping and washed down with hot tea.

Another friend of Father's, a labourer in one of the Royal Docks, provided us with the stolen tea. Other times he gave us nicked bacon, potatoes and fruit, although I didn't have a clue, most of the time, about the name of the various funny-shaped and funny-coloured fruit we ate. So although times were always hard, we invariably got by one way or another.

When I came running home from school one day, when I was about six years old, my mother was sitting down on the old charity-provided armchair holding a small bundle in her arms. My father sat next to her on a small rickety chair. I remember him kissing my mother softly on her lips. 'For my beautiful princess,' he said to my tired mother. That was the endearing name he called her throughout the years. Mother smiled at me. 'I'm holding your new sister, sweetheart, do yer wanna see her and give her a kiss?' said Mother in her usual soft voice. 'We've named her Susan.'

Susan was born on 1st March, 1910. When mother unwrapped some of the clothes Susan was wearing, there appeared the most beautiful, yet small and fragile, sleeping human being I had ever seen. Her face was white as snow. She only had a few white wisps of hair spread over her small head. I bent down to kiss her cheek and smelt milk on her clothes.

'So what do yer think of her, Les?' asked father, who picked me up and sat me on his lap.

'She's great, dad. Is she going to live with us?' I asked my father.

'Of course she is, boy. She is our little girl and I hope you look after 'er when I'm not around. We've just brought her 'ome from the same hospital where you were born son.'

'Where did you get her from, Dad? I asked him, confused on seeing her for the first time.

'We'll tell yer one day, son,' father reassured me.

In those far-off days children were expected to be told very little about the facts of life. Our teachers said nothing about sex, nor did our parents. We had to guess, and in time things sort of fell into place. But we were all naïve and embarrassed when the taboo subject of sex reared its ugly head.

Susan grew bigger and stronger, and joined the children, nearly always minus her knickers, playing in the large garden at Davis Street, Stepney. Father had made a swing for us, tied to two of the large ash trees at the bottom of the garden. We all had to take our turn at being swung from one side of the garden to the other, but it was Susan who commandeered it most of the time. Being the youngest, it was not surprising that she was spoilt by all the children, and their parents, during the seven years we lived at Davis Street. I was compelled to look after my darling little sister during those times when my parents were busy elsewhere.

Occasionally all the four families in the house used to have a party together in the garden. Those were great times when we had the opportunity to eat different things, such as the exotic Turkish food made by the attractive, slim Mrs Ecevit. We all loved her food. It contained various delicious herbs and spices. Certainly different from the stew and steak, dumplings and offal Mother cooked, though that was also very good to eat after eight hours of fighting, shouting and reading at school. Besides, in those days school didn't provide food. Lunch for Susan and me, and most of our mates, used to be several large chunks of bread covered in dripping and jelly, and occasionally a few meat bones to gnaw, like wild dogs, from the previous day's dinner.

The other two tenement families, the Philips and Maloneys, were kind, decent people. Patrick Maloney, aged about 30, was tall and well-built. He worked for a large building company carrying out various slum clearances in the most poverty-stricken areas of London. He himself was desperately hoping that one day his own family would be moved into better accommodation. Mrs Maloney, of similar age, plump with long red hair, had worked in Redwoods, a factory making lampshades, for about ten years. She loved a pint of ale, a cigarette and a good laugh, sometimes to the disapproval of her husband. After too many drinks, Mrs Maloney would get to her feet, if she didn't fall over first, to perform her version of an Irish jig. After ten minutes of jigging, she invariably had to be picked up off the ground by her patient husband. But the children thought she was a great laugh.

Ted Philip's father, Ian Philip, originated from Alloa, Scotland. He moved south seeking work on various building sites. Just three years into his marriage to a local girl, June White, she was tragically knocked down and killed by a London bus near Trafalgar Square. He and Ted appeared to live happily together in their small ill-decorated room, although later on the house was redecorated both internally and externally, which lifted the gloom somewhat. 'That fucking fat capitalist owner slapped a few coats of paint on the gaff,' father used to say angrily after a few beers.

The decorating of our tenement, and others in the area, was in no small part thanks to the political badgering of many different charities such as the Salvation Army. Mind you the quality of housing in most of London, especially in the East End, was still very poor, unacceptably so.

My father, William James Tatter, was born in Bow in 1884. Both his parents died young. Apparently, they both contracted consumptive diseases. Neither Susan nor I ever met them. My father had two older siblings, but I don't recall meeting his sister at the time. His brother Joe, on one occasion, invited my family to a party above a pub in Whitechapel.

My father's sister, Doreen, moved to a small village in Suffolk when she was young. My sister and I would live with her during World War One. At the party there was lots of singing, dancing and drinking, and some of the men gave me pennies to spend. Late in the evening, I remember, father and other men went outside to buy jellied eels from a fish stall owned by Lenny Fox. He came from a family of villains, most of whom had served many prison sentences for robbery, fraud and larceny. My father left school at about 12 years of age. He needed to earn money to look after his ill parents and unemployed brother. A friend of my great-grandfather's, Bobby Kemble, put in a good word as was usually the case in those days, and found my father a job working in the local market selling fruit and vegetables. He worked long hours, as everyone did, from 5 am, when he pushed all the market stalls out to be filled with the day's goods. After serving customers non-stop for twelve hours, with only a brief stop for tea and sarnies (sandwiches), he would eventually arrive home around 9 pm absolutely knackered.

There were perks of the trade (as father called them). After a few weeks, when his colleagues got to know him, they would provide him with plenty of vegetables, fruit and meat that had 'fallen off the back of a lorry'. He carried on with the market job for a number of years. My father was the only breadwinner for years, after Doreen moved out and Joe was in prison for robbery, while he lived at Cecil Street, Bow.

In 1910, after many years of hard demanding work, my father successfully applied for a porter vacancy at the Ritz Hotel in the posh West End of London. Apparently he was very proud walking in and around the hotel showing off his green and gold uniform to anyone interested. He must have fantasized that he was like some high-ranking military man. Several members of his family, including me, saw him standing on the expensive marble steps outside the Ritz, opening large car doors for the rich, famous and infamous. He once told me that Charlie Chaplin gave him half a crown for carrying his case into the hotel foyer. That story is plausible, but many were not. For example, when he opened the back door of a chauffeur-driven car, the occupant, the actor Charles Laughton, is supposed to have told my father that he would get him a job as a driver in his forthcoming film. On another occasion father informed us that an unknown film company was going to make a documentary film about Ritz Hotel employees. After being asked several times by his family, he eventually explained that the silent films company had changed their minds about the film due to cash shortages.

There were other stories which he also no doubt made up. His fantasy world was a way of impressing people that he was quite an important employee. In reality he did skivvy work and was poorly paid. But the job was regular and gave him more security, now that he had a family to keep, than working long hours down a street market. Besides, grafting long hours in a fruit and vegetable market is made for young, energetic men who soon tire after years of daily hard work - 12/15 hours a day, six days a week. Come rain or shine, you had to keep performing tip top in that tough male environment. Years of pulling, pushing, bending, carrying and so on leaves your body physically impaired. Many blokes ended up with severe arthritis, which affected most parts of their weakened bodies.

In 1912 strikes badly affected the East Enders of London, my family included. The docks were lying idle due to national coal strikes, and garment workers walked out in their thousands seeking better pay and conditions. Labour disputes became very bitter and acrimonious between employers, employees and the unions. In essence, the problem was that Britain's one-time industrial powerhouse was now on the decline. Industrial output had been taken over by the USA and Germany. Britain's industrial base would never recover to its once great might that a worldwide empire, with plenty of raw cheap materials, had once conferred.

Around the turn of the 20th century, St Benedict's, like a lot of London schools, used to provide very basic education for the working classes. It had been illegal since 1880 not to provide state education for children up to the age of twelve, which was a major step forward for working-class children. But rather than trying to better themselves in school, many had to work to bring home much-needed money to support their poverty-stricken families. So many people were destitute that it took all their efforts to fight off starvation. In one way or another, if you could not pay your dues, then there was the real threat of ending up in a workhouse. They were pernicious places that ruined the lives of thousands of London families. Either that, or you could be incarcerated in one of the many different inhumane institutions the Victorians had opened to control thieving by the mad, bad and unruly British working classes.

Nevertheless, Ted, Susan, I and most local kids enjoyed playing all manner of rumbustious games at St Benedict's School. Most of the teachers were kind middle-class people who, with very little support from the State to buy books, did their best for us. Kids weren't placed in different classes according to their educational ability, age or sex. It was really a lottery as to the class you attended. For example, young pupils of about four years old would have been in classes with children a lot older than themselves. When I was about five, I was in classes with pupils of 10 years or older. The main reason for this was that most school kids' attendances were irregular at best. That made planning difficult, if not impossible, for the teachers.

Teachers, of course, realised that most of the pupils in front of them were unable or unwilling, even incapable, of learning how to read and write. My favourite teacher, Mrs Molly Masters, certainly thought I could read and write well. She encouraged me to 'keep up a daily practice, not only of reading and writing, but also learn how to use numbers as well. Regular learning will become useful later on in your life, Leslie'. How right she was.

Before the advent of World War One, the so-called Great War, we had quite a few enjoyable family parties in our new home. In March 1912 we moved from Davis Road, our home for seven years or more and a home I had enjoyed living in, to 50 Sandhurst Street, Stepney, an early 19th century two-bedroom terraced house with a back garden, which was allocated to us by a small local charity. We were fortunate to be given the tenancy, as most houses in those days were privately owned until after 1919. I would miss all the friends I had made at my last home and at St Benedict's School. My father had also enjoyed living there, but mother was over the moon not to have to share her own front door with anyone else again. I was pleased for my mother as she was not a gregarious person and found being in a group of relative strangers, as in Davis Road, rather difficult at times. As a placid person, she preferred being with her own family, although she wasn't anti-social by any means. Ever since her birth in Ealing in 1885, Mother had found life difficult and painful, but at times bearable.

It was around this time that Mother started to have tics, or shakes, to her head. We assumed that they had been brought on by her life's problems, but no one used to say anything, we just got on with things. I remember, when as young children, Mother insisted we play in the garden and not in the harsh world outside. Sadly, fear preoccupied her life, but she was always a loving mother to Susan and me. I felt so impotent, being unable to help my mother. The violence of war made her nervous and introverted, and she hated humanity's obsession with destruction. As she aged, she withdrew from others at every opportunity. She would have loved the solitude and reassurance of living alone on a desert island.

My larger-than-life grandmother walked in through the front door accompanied by Benny. 'Ere you are Ethel and Billy boy, a big bottle of bubbly to celebrate moving into your new home,' boomed Bessie. No sooner was grandmother in the house than she was marching from room to room inspecting her daughter's new home. 'You've got a good un 'ere gel,' she remarked. ''Ow much they chargin' you for this lot luv?'

'Too bloody much Mum, but it's a new start and we ain't got to share the kitchen and things any more like we did in Davis Road. Come and see where the kids can play,' said Mother, as the six of us walked out into filthy fifty-foot long garden.

Just like the house, the garden had been somewhat neglected, but in time we would all play our part knocking it back into shape. We carried out some remedial work by dismantling the rotten old shed, which was full of dead rodents. Rubbish was strewn all over the place, as it hadn't been used for some time. Being at the end of a row of terraced houses, it was convenient for local kids or workers to use the shed as a toilet. Turds were stacked two feet high, just like an anthill. Mother had already bought several different coloured roses, daffodil bulbs and a small Cox's apple tree from Flanagan's shop, two minutes round the corner in Nelson Street. Father reckoned she had nicked them from the local Victoria Park. In time, we hoped, the garden would look colourful and creative just like Kew Gardens. But the house itself, we realised, would take a lot of hard work to clean and decorate before we could call it a comfortable home.

The Sandhurst Street house had been boarded up for two years following a murder, in which a man had killed his apparently promiscuous wife. According to Bessie, who was a walking newspaper, the husband, who had a few bob, was thirty years older than his attractive young wife. He worked in the City as a solicitor's clerk, a well-paid job in those days. During the day his wife earned a decent wage, if you include the many tips the older gentlemen gave her, working in a West End bar near Soho. It transpired that she had had various paid sexual liaisons with some of her upper-crust customers in the evenings. Eventually the husband, one Norman Clarke, found out, and one late evening he killed her with a knife in the heart, in the bedroom where I was later to sleep. The poor chap went to the gallows.

Although, we realised, our house was in desperate need of a few coats of paint, we managed a rough clean for the visit of Queen Bessie. We had only moved in a few days before, so the Ritz it certainly wasn't, but father and his mates had cleared out rusting old beds, one of them probably used by the loving Clarkes! The woodworm-riddled furniture wasn't fit for a doss house. Father had several pieces of second-hand 'bent' furniture delivered by another friend, Jimmy Golding, who had lots of 'form' (previous convictions) for theft. He had more form, so father informed me, than the previous three Derby winners put together. Anyway, in the back room, as mother always called it, we had six chairs, all wobbly like a drunken sailor, an old table, covered with a clean copy of the *Daily Mirror*. The table was full of stew, dumplings, potatoes and green vegetables. 'There's much more scran [food] in the kitchen. A meal fit for a king or in our case, Queen Bessie,' said father, as he disappeared, and quickly returned with six old chipped cups, Bessie's bubbly and six bottles of pale ale.

Father poured out the champagne. 'Cheers everyone. You 'ave a new home at last. Fuck 'em all!' shouted Bessie. No doubt the whole street overheard her sweet. gentle words penetrating their plaster lined walls. Look out, Bessie was about.

We all tucked into the mother's well-cooked food. She underestimated her cooking ability, and with a bit more confidence she could have worked in a decent eatery somewhere in central London. No, I wasn't thinking of one of the spikes either. The bubbly was quickly consumed, and followed not long after by the beer.

Father walked down to the packed local pub, the Queen Victoria, to buy more beer. An hour later, he informed us he had had a quick beer with an old friend who had just been discharged from Broadmoor. Back indoors, father had bought five more pint bottles of ale, one each for the adults and one between my sister and me. For the first time in my life, not surprisingly as I was only seven, I had this queer feeling of being drunk. I consumed nearly all the bottle of beer.

Ten minutes later I ran to the outside toilet, where just in time I was sick into the dirty, cracked ceramic bowl. 'You alwight son?' asked Father, who was standing outside the wooden toilet door holding a bucket.

Upon my return from the toilet, I was now about half sober as Bessie started singing a number of her favourite London tunes. In full flow, Bessie's voice sounded like a regiment of soldiers practising for a royal event. She must have had lungs the size of a horse's, as she didn't stop singing for an hour. 'Less 'ave a drink and a singsong Ethel. Fuck em, that's what I say,' said a drunken Bessie.

Mother was much too inhibited, but father stood up and sang several songs I had not heard before. Another toast was had by all, except Little Susan, who wasn't yet three years old.

'Come on Ethel, 'ave a drink or give us a song,' said an over-enthusiastic father.

'Oi, just leave her alone Bill, all right?' Bessie replied, quickly coming to the defence of her daughter. 'What about you Les, you up to it?'

'No he is not, Billy. Ethel and Les don't wanna do that, for fuck sake. Leave alone,' Bessie once again replied. Father took the hint.

After an enjoyable meal, Mother cleared away the crockery and cutlery and returned with a large pot of tea. Benny and Father started smoking.

'How's things going at Ferguson's, Mum?' enquired Ethel.

'I love it there, sweetheart. Do yer know I've been workin' there now for nearly 12 years? Doesn't time fly! I'm still supervisor of the carpet department, but I've worked in several others to help out, yer know what I mean. I get on well with my colleagues and Miss Patel, she is my manager. I get on famous with 'er. Yes, that was my best move, to go and work at Ferguson's,' said Bessie, her chubby face beaming at everyone.

'And what about my handsome brother?' asked Ethel, who felt secure among her own kind.

'I'm alright Ethel. I've got a job portering in Spitalfields fruit and veg market. Early hours but good pay. As I told you about a year ago, Brenda and I are living in two private rooms in an old 18th century house just orf the Bethnal Green Road. Bit of a dump where we are. I painted over the old dirty brown wallpaper with a light cream colour. Looks a lot better. We've washed the floors and basin. The rooms wouldn't 'ave looked out of place at the spike. We share toilet and kitchen with three other families. Sometimes people leave shit in the toilet and don't wash the kitchen sink or stove, but what can you do about it?' said Benny, trying to be upbeat.

'How's Jane doing, Bessie?' asked my father.

'She's all right. Doing just fine, so she told me the last time we met for coffee in Fenchurch Street. She doesn't 'ave a regular boyfriend, but lots of girlfriends at work and they go out to the cinema and dancing together. She is still workin' at Eagle Insurance. She likes it there. Gets good money, I can tell yer,' said Bessie enthusiastically to the assembled gathering.

'That's good to know about Aunt Jane, that is,' said Mother, with a rare smile on her usually anxious face. 'We're all fine 'ere Mum. Bill is still working at the Ritz. Thinks he owns it, he does. And the children are well. Les is at a new school called Danetree Road, and Susan being only three years old, I'm lookin' after 'er till I can get a place at the same school in about a year. Then I can find a part-time job.'

'And more importantly Ethel, said Bessie, 'your grandparents are both very well. I only saw them the other day.'

My new school, Danetree Road, was built in 1833, and was originally used as a workhouse. By the time I arrived, September 1912, it had been used as a school for 30 years. It was said that during the night you could hear the faint voices of former inmates walking along the dark corridors. Due to various political and other pressures, state education continued to improve, somewhat, for the masses.

I shall never forget the first day at my new school. All the boys and girls were ordered to line up in the playground, like rows of urchins ready to be sent down a coal mine, by an old, frosty-looking middle-class man. *'Cruelty had a human heart'* said William Blake. Mr Matthews was about 50, tall and thin, but with a fat belly. He dressed rather formally, as most people in authority did in those days, in a suit, shirt and tie. Apparently, he had fought in the Boer War.

'Pay attention you lot to what I'm about to say. I hope everyone can hear. When I call out your name, I want you to march into the school building where a teacher, Miss Abel, will show you your classroom,' shouted the regimental man in front of us. Thus we marched, like workhouse skivvies, to our allocated prison. There were about 40 girls and boys, all about the same age, in my class. Mind you, if you had asked them their ages, I assumed only half would have answered correctly.

I didn't recognise one person in the classroom. Most of them looked a terrible sight. Half of us boys were minus socks and nearly all the pupils had holes in their jumpers, shirts or trousers. Most needed haircuts, and very few of their faces had seen water recently. As for teeth and gum hygiene, most mouths were truly disgusting. I rarely brushed my teeth with the sort of power cleaner mother bought down the local Cable Street market. It tasted like cow shit and felt like your teeth and gums were being cleaned with a wire brush. Incidentally, as mother got older she enjoyed wandering about the market talking to various characters where she bought any old lotion, potion or polish they recommended. That was one probable reason why I had several black teeth in the front of my mouth. However, compared to most of the other ragamuffins, my Hampstead Heath (teeth) were quite presentable. Welcome to the academy of life.

We were told to sit down by the teacher, Mr Wright (who always thought he was right), as he drew our attention to three large pictures on the classroom walls. 'These three people you see before you are great British heroes. Can anyone name them?' asked the half-smiling, half-scowling Mr Wright.

'Yus, I can governor!' shouted Tommy Foreman, who was dressed in a terrible state, mind you who wasn't?

'You address me as sir, not governor. I hope you understand that, all of you. Who can you name, boy?' the teacher asked once again.

'The one wiv a patch over his mince pies [eyes], didn't he use to play for the 'ammers?' asked smiling Tommy, who had only one tooth left in the front of his mouth.

'You stupid boy! That man with a patch over his eye is none other than Lord Horatio Nelson, who won many great sea battles for Britain and the Empire. Stop laughing all of you, at once! At least the boy had a go,' said the red-faced Mr Wright. 'Does anyone know who the other two immortal figures are?'

At this stage he was becoming a little irritated by the

thick bunch in front of him. I put up my hand. 'Yes boy?'

'Is the one with the grey hair from the bible sir?' I asked rather nervously, hoping not to receive such anger from the teacher as Tommy Foreman did. 'No it isn't boy. But well done for trying,' said Mr Wright rather reassuringly. 'That great figure upon the wall is Charles Darwin. His great legacy to mankind is discovering that human beings are descended from ape-like ancestors. Darwin didn't believe in a God that ruled the universe. His research, which he carried out around the world, convinced him that human beings have evolved by natural selection. That means we became stronger each time our environment changed,' said the stern Mr Wright, but not many of us really understood what he was on about. 'The third picture is of another great Empire figure called the Duke of Wellington, who was a victorious figure in many battles. He also, boys and girls, became Prime Minister from 1828 to 1830,' he explained.

Mr Wright went on talking and reading from a textbook about further great qualities the noble British heroes had. 'Now we have been talking here for more than three hours, I think you should all go and have a dinner break,' he finished.

Incidentally, many poor kids, even before Victorian times, had all their teeth pulled out by dentists, even if they were healthy. It was common practice, and children had no say in the matter. The main dental problem was that the sugar Tate & Lyle had shipped from the West Indies into the London docks, was rotting working-class children's teeth. Most working-class mothers gave their children lashings of sugar on nearly everything they ate or drank to keep them quiet. So as a precaution, many kids, not all, had their teeth yanked out, sooner rather than later, to prevent infection and costs later on. Fortunately it didn't happen to anyone in my extended family.

Back we went to the afternoon class. After eating our bread and dripping sandwiches, the short, stout blue-suited Mr Wright continued explaining about various heroic (he loved that word) individuals who had left an indelible mark on the hallowed soil of Britain. If my memory serves me correctly, one of the two men he spoke about with great passion (another favourite word in Mr Wright's vocabulary) that afternoon was Charles Dickens.

'Who has heard of Charles Dickens here amongst you lot?' said the surly teacher. Up went the dirty hand of Lilly Grainger. 'Yes girl. What do know you about Dickens?'

'Sir, he was well known for helping poor people.'

'Yes, that is correct girl.'

'Charles Dickens was known for writing immensely popular novels, which highlighted his concerns about the problems of poor people. He also took an active part in schemes to help the poor. He also became the editor, in 1846, of the newly founded *Daily News',* said Mr Wright. I got the impression, even after the first day, that our teacher had already written us off as incapable of doing no more than unskilled work. After such an intense day, I was pleased to rush out of the school and run back home to the safety of my family.

For the next 20 months or so, until World War I started, we beavered away at Danetree Road School. I desperately wanted to learn, and to keep up with the good work I first started with my former teacher Mrs Masters at St Benedict's School. Understandably, most of my class came from homes where life was tough. It was tough for nearly all working-class people, but some kids were poverty stricken. People lived from hand to mouth to exist. Most parents didn't have the time or the inclination to encourage their kids to learn. They were out long hours trying to earn money to put food on the table. Many of my classmates frequently missed school so that they could earn money to help the family out. I was fortunate; my father was earning a living wage at the Ritz, and my mother was by now, March 1913, working part-time in a local factory making boots and shoes. My mother, just as Bessie had done, supported Susan and me with our learning.

I often use to share my food with others who had nothing to put into their empty stomachs. We lived in a city that was full of middle and upper class affluence and indulgence, yet young children who lived just a mile or two from where those pampered poltroons lived went to bed starving. And yet it was precisely those same men who would regularly make forays into working-class areas to have sex with the women, girls and boys they otherwise disdained. Ever since I had been a young boy, I had realised and felt the injustice of the inhuman burden carried by the working classes.

Occasionally I used to miss school and take the omnibus

into the heart of London to see how other people lived. Although still young, I nonetheless walked round Mayfair, Knightsbridge, Chelsea and other wealthy areas. I walked miles along clean pavements, looking into large, beautifully-decorated rooms with glittering chandeliers and highly-polished tables and chairs. Sometimes there were large paintings hanging on the walls, and various coloured bowls full of scrumptious fruit on the tables. Occasionally, I looked in dustbins to see what I could find to eat or take home with me.

Most of the luxurious three-storey Georgian houses had new cars parked outside. Once when I stopped to look at a new blue car, to admire its leather interior and mahogany dashboard, a man with a grey uniform and peaked cap told me to piss off. Young women wearing black and white uniforms, hair short and smart, could be seen frequently from the pavement, cleaning various pieces of furniture, mirrors and other expensive and beautiful ornaments. These wealthy people had their own private gardens, where I often saw mothers, or nannies, playing with the children on the well-maintained lawns that resembled miniature football pitches.

One place in particular where I enjoyed sitting down to watch middle-class people walk by was a public bench in Mayfair. The very few people who even bothered to look my way, dressed as I was in near rags, did so with disdain written all over their spotless, clean faces. I felt, of course, that I was intruding into another world where I definitely didn't belong. Men, women and children wore such fine, colourful attractive clothes and shoes. They must have cost a fortune, I said to myself, on many occasions. I surmised that the cost of one long dress would have kept me and my family well fed for three months. How unfair it all was. The place where you were born, it appeared, would dictate the future of your life.

One teacher at Danetree who was altogether different from those before her was Miss Cohen, who used to teach us geography. She was young, short, funny and friendly with a large dimple on her left cheek. Her poor maternal great-grandparents had migrated from Russia to the East London in the early 19th century. They had found menial work in various factories, but they encouraged their two children to learn, and they in turn did likewise, through the family to Miss Cohen, who lived with her parents in Whitechapel, a rough and ready place!

Miss Cohen glued a huge map of the world on the classroom wall. In her own calm manner, she would mention the name of a country and encourage pupils to walk up and point to where they thought it was on the map. At first we got things wrong, but it was good fun trying to find Rhodesia, Peru or France. Most of us couldn't even find Great Britain. In fact, it was the first time most of us had ever seen a detailed map of the whole world. Some of us had seen maps of Britain, even France and Italy, but the other countries were alien to us.

In time, most of us knew where various countries were by name. We developed some understanding of land and sea, and the distribution of plant and animal life. Over a period of eighteen months, Miss Cohen taught us about human life and the various industries we had developed. It was a truly interesting subject, one which I used to read about at every opportunity when I got home from school or in the park. I thought Miss Cohen actually liked teaching us, unlike her colleagues, who given the chance would have put us to work in a local factory.

When father wasn't working or we weren't all trying to redecorate our home, arduous as it was, my parents used to take Susan and me out to visit various interesting places around London. When we lived at Davis Road, we had the large back garden to play in along with several other children. But our new garden at Sandhurst Street wasn't yet clean enough to plant flowers or play in. Besides, we were growing, becoming more inquisitive about the world.

My parents took us, when they could afford it, to the local newly-opened cinema in Southwark. Most of the time the cinema was packed with working-class children watching mainly American silent films. Cinemas had only been around in London since 1905. I remember Benny telling me about the exciting action-packed films he watched, and during the interval how a lady walked round the cinema selling ice creams.

We went for long walks in Hyde Park and Green Park and usually had our sandwiches in Regents Park. Susan and I loved to chase the large flocks of pigeons that could be seen in all the London Parks at the time. We used to entice them to eat bread from our hands, but catching one was very difficult. Father, Susan and I enjoyed playing football together. We always tried to put father in as goalkeeper, which he didn't always enjoy as most of our shots went wide, and he had the strenuous job of retrieving the ball.

My mother appeared to enjoy the walks we had through numerous London parks. She didn't like being in crowds of people. Space for her was safety. Above all else, mother was fascinated by the size, shape and colour of the London plane trees. She adored the many well-maintained flower beds, especially those with red roses, to be found in most London parks.

On one occasion, she unofficially planted a few daffodil bulbs in a flower bed in St James Park. 'I'll come back next year when they're flowering,' said mother. Things like that gave her comfort. Many times of a Sunday, the whole family used to walk to our local Victoria Park to be entertained by one of the many street singers around in those days. Most of them would sing for about an hour. Sometimes the crowd joined in. They were great characters, who certainly knew how to survive. Afterwards appreciative onlookers threw pennies in the cap as the singer walked round trying to collect enough money for a few beers and a night's kip in the local spike.

You always saw a costermonger trying to sell his various goods. They too were a great sight on London streets. Many a time I bought fruit, vegetables, kippers and even on one occasion, a tin of paint. They sold virtually anything. An old coster called Jake was a regular face round our manor in Stepney. Nearly every morning at five, Jake could be seen in a local café, Solly's, drinking tea and telling jokes by the dozen. When he died, it was said, he was 96 years of age, although he looked years younger.

Finally, the place to see thousands of congregating pigeons was Trafalgar Square. Father used to buy small containers of peanuts for all the family to feed the birds. With food in your hands, you could have half the London pigeon population climbing all over you. Mind you, you had to be prepared for the crap they dropped indiscriminately to 'anoint' you. With many tourists from around the world flocking to Trafalgar Square, the pigeons were guaranteed to be fed.

The London music halls were also great entertainment for people from all walks of life from the 1850s to the 1930s. After that most theatres closed down, as people preferred to visit cinemas and listen to the radio. The Yiddish Theatre and the Russian Jewish Operatic Company, both originally in Prescott Street, Stepney, eventually found new homes in Princess Street, Spitalfields. I loved the music halls, the spontaneity of the many local singers, the audience participation and appreciation. Not to say the stand-up comics, who were a laugh a minute. It was for me and my family a great experience, which in London today in 1950 regrettably does not exist.

During the next year or so life carried on as normal for my family. With Mother and Father working and Susan and me at Danetree Road School, all our other waking hours were spent frantically scraping old materials from walls, doors, window frames and floors of our home. My father and I carried all the rubbish out to the front of the house, where it was taken by a local builder. Whenever anyone had any spare time, including little Susan, they were encouraged to paint one of the many walls which were now bare for the first time in many years.

We were all hopeful that the exposed walls would reveal hidden money or something similar. No chance! But we never did look under the floorboards. One day, I came home from school only to find my mother's head and shoulders covered in paint. Apparently she had upset a large bucket of white emulsion she had been painting the ceiling with. Even after washing her hair many times, small flecks of white paint could still be seen three months later.

Weekends were the time when most work was accomplished. 'We've got to work methodically,' father used to keep emphasizing to the three of us. That meant Father and I decorated the two bedrooms upstairs and the front room down stairs while Mother and Susan decorated the back dining room and small kitchen. Although it was used by other people, I also painted the communal outside toilet as well. We had hoped that a clean toilet might encourage others to aim in the right direction, and keep their written sexual fantasies to themselves.

We scrubbed, washed, rubbed, cleaned and did whatever else it took to make our little home not just habitable, but comfortable. Mother hung various coloured curtains around the windows. The inside of the house was nearly complete when father laid down dark blue floor lino and bought second-hand furniture he had acquired from the back of a lorry.

All that was left was to sort out was the back garden. It was apparent, when father and I started to dig the soil over, that the garden hadn't been touched for years. Everything was rock hard. At times our spades just bounced off the soil, it was that tough. Two feet underneath the soil, someone had dumped various pieces of rubbish consisting of hardcore, clothes, cement bags and even a potty. Father crowned me King Farouk with it. It took us many sessions to clear up all the rubbish and dump it on the cart, owned by Paddy O'Sullivan, which had previously taken our house rubbish away. Paddy, who lived nearby, had ten children to feed, no doubt preordained by God. We thought we had problems!

Undeterred, we all carried on until our second-hand shed had been reassembled, Mother's plants planted and a little concrete patio laid for people to sit outside. It had taken a true family effort to complete the Herculean task of redecorating our home and redesign the garden, but we were determined to have a home fit for the Tatters. Kings and Queens, the pearly sort, would have been pleased to have resided there.

Only a few days after this, the newspapers reported that someone important had been assassinated hundreds of miles from the shores of Britain. This event would have severe repercussions around the world, as we were soon to find.

Chapter Three
A city in wartime

On June 28 1914, a Serbian student, Gavrilo Princip, according to the Evening Newspaper, assassinated Archduke Franz Ferdinand, heir to the Austro-Hungarian throne. Austria-Hungary demanded an explanation, but none was forthcoming, so they declared war on Serbia. Russia, Serbia's ally, immediately mobilized its army. Germany, Austria's ally, demanded that Russia stop mobilization. Then Germany declared war on Russia. Next came France, Russia's ally. Germany bypassed the French frontier by going through Belgium. This move brought in Britain, which had guaranteed Belgium's safety. From Austria-Hungary's declaration of war, it took just ten days before Britain too declared war on Germany. It was August 4 1918. World War I had begun.

On a wet and thundery day, Father walked in through the front door soaked, holding aloft the *News of the World*, the so-called 'working man's newspaper' (incidentally first published in 1843) exclaiming that Britain was at war with Germany and her allies. My father's colleagues, family and friends were all naturally worried, as were most other people, for the safety of our country. Not surprisingly, wherever you walked people were talking about the war. It was on the lips of the local neighbours; shopkeepers, workers and even police officers were concerned about the future of their Great City.

Within weeks, local people were alerted, that government departments had started sending information to employers and employees explaining to them their responsibilities, and the necessary precautions they must take, if London was bombed. They were informed about reducing lighting, fire drills, first aid, where people should go in emergencies and many other things you were required to carry out. Local council workers started handing out information, in case of an emergency. Training was vital for all concerned.

Father had arranged a family meeting at our house in Sandhurst Road. We all congregated into our small newly-decorated back room. Father, Mother, Bessie, Benny, Jane, Susan and I sat round the second-hand wooden table laden with cooked food. 'Dig in to the food,' Ethel remarked, pointing to the steaming pot of stew and spuds.

For the next twenty minutes, or so, very little was said. Usually talkative, even Bessie for once was quiet. All the assembled continued to eat, until Father broke the ice.

'Well those German bastards will be coming over 'ere soon to bomb us. Is there anyfink we can do to help our family?' he asked, concerned.

In a split second Bessie boomed in, telling us what she thought. 'Fuck those Germans, who do they think they are? We can look after each other can't we?'

'No we can't mum' interrupted Ethel. 'We must get things sorted by asking the council about it.'

'What do you 'ave in mind Ethel?' an animated Bessie asked her worried daughter.

'Fuck knows!'

Bessie interrupted. 'That's no good, Ethel, is it, saying fuck knows,' she retorted.

'Let's take our time everyone,' said Father in a calm manner. 'It's no good being angry with each other.'

It was understandable that family members were worried and anxious of the unknown, but after a while things settled down. Naturally we were concerned for each other's well-being, including, of course, that of my great-grandparents down in Barking. What was uppermost in people's minds was that if there was an emergency within our family, we could make some contingency plans, sooner rather than later, to help each other cope, which sounded practical. These emergency plans were already in place where Bessie, Mother, Benny, Father and Jane worked. The teachers at our school had already told the pupils what they should do in case of an emergency.

According to the Evening Star newspaper, Britain was the only country without a huge reserve of trained men - there were no more than 100,000 in 1914 - troops began landing in France. Britain depended on volunteers until conscription came into force in 1916.

Many miles away from war, in relative peace and security, Aunt Jane took Susan and me out for an afternoon treat near Liverpool Street. It had been two years since we had last been taken out by our aunt. On that occasion she had taken us to the Jewish Music Hall in Prescott Street, and what a great time we had eating bagels with the cast. Afterwards she treated us all to sandwiches and tea in Freddy Cole's, greasy spoon café, near Stepney Green station. The latter was near our home, which made it easy for Aunt Jane to travel back into central London, where she lived with female colleagues. She was always smartly dressed, but didn't use lipstick, although she wore sexy high-heeled shoes that made her much taller than Susan and me. Jane reminded me of the sexy models I used to ogle on the front page of various newspapers. As she was so attractive, I assumed she must have many boyfriends, not that I ever saw her with more than two men. On both occasions she brought them round to visit our family in Sandhurst Street. Both times she had bought presents for all of us, including a large box of assorted chocolates, something we hadn't seen before. Susan and I devoured them within days. We loved being in the happy, warm company of our Great Aunt Jane.

One of Aunt Jane's boyfriends was called Sammy. He was tall and thin, like a beanpole, mother quipped. He wore a flashy blue suit, smoked incessantly and told us funny jokes. Even Mother, who was usually quiet when strangers visited, joined in the frivolity. That pleased me, because she then became more relaxed and less self-conscious of her head twitching.

Jane's other boyfriend was totally the opposite to Sammy. Pedro was a short, stocky, dark-skinned fellow from Barcelona. I fantasized that he must have been a matador or cowboy. As his English wasn't very fluent, he sat quietly in Mother's armchair all afternoon saying very little. But every 10 or 15 minutes he would stand up to stretch himself and smile at everyone. Mother thought he was from the local 'laughing house'.

As we arrived at the restaurant Aunt Jane frequented with friends, not far from the hustle and bustle of Liverpool Street Station, newspaper sellers shouted about the war intensifying in Europe. Outside the station the Salvation Army was singing Christmas carols in front of a spruce tree, about thirty feet high and decorated with many coloured lanterns. One of their army colleagues, a young boy, was standing in front of the singers rattling a charity collection box. The small eatery, called Masons, was dimly lit with red bulbs, which made the place look rather exotic. A young dark-haired, dapper-looking man, sporting a black suit and white shirt, escorted us to our reserved table. For the first time in my life I had been reserved my own table, and for once I felt rather special.

When I was seated, and less anxious, I began to take in my surroundings. I noticed men and women chatting, smiling, laughing, drinking and smoking. Most of the blokes looked like the jack-the-lads you see in East London. One end of the restaurant was difficult to see because of the cigarette smoke. I thought the dreaded London smog had descended upon us.

One old bald chap, who was sitting to my left, had a huge stomach that hung over his black, shiny trousers. In front of him was an enormous plate of meat and vegetables, enough, I thought, to feed four normal-sized people. Apparently, nearly all the well-dressed diners were enjoying eating and generally having a good time. From my background, I couldn't help but notice the gluttony in front of my eyes.

'Stop staring at people Leslie, it's embarrassing,' scolded Aunt Jane, who looked so posh dressed in a white shirt and long dark green skirt, which was not dissimilar in colour to the wallpaper.

The dark-haired young man brought over the menu. I was rather bewildered by all the different names of the various dishes available. Susan, who was now over five years old, looked at me as if to say, I'm confused too.

Aunt Jane asked both of us what we would like to eat. The choices were overwhelming. 'Tell you what. Shall we all have chicken, chips and peas? Would you like that, Leslie and Susan?' asked Jane. In unison, we replied, 'Yes please Aunt Jane and could we have apple pudding with custard?'

'Of course you can,' she replied.

The customers continued enjoying themselves, totally oblivious to our presence; I couldn't wait for my meal to arrive, because I hadn't eaten for hours and was starving.

Looking to my right, my eyes were met by a fellow

about 30 years old, wearing a dark suit and smoking a cigar the size of a cricket stump. A typical 'wide boy', as father called them. He winked at me. 'You alwight son?'

Embarrassed, I just smiled and immediately turned back to face Jane. While I was preoccupied elsewhere, Jane had ordered us all Coca Cola. Minutes later three steaming chicken dinners arrived at our small table, which was covered by a lemon cloth spread over it. No sooner was the food in front of me than I tucked into my chicken leg like a man possessed. Five or six times I raised my fork, full of food, into my open waiting mouth. Within minutes the plate was empty. It was delicious. The best meal, I reckon, that I had eaten in ages. She would be most upset if I ever mentioned that to my mother.

'Where have you put all that food so quickly?' Jane asked.

'I was starving Aunty. I ain't eaten for hours,' came my spontaneous reply.

Another Coca Cola found its way into my half-full stomach, soon followed by apple tart and custard, which was brought to our table by an older waiter with long grey hair and a moustache. Susan and I had soon gobbled down our pudding. I felt like asking Aunt Jane for another pudding, but all of a sudden, I remembered mother warning me to be a good boy.

'Are we full, Les and Susan, and did you enjoy the meal?' Jane inquired. Noticing that she had left a small tip on the table, I learnt later that one usually left a few coins in gratitude for good service.

We made our way home on the packed 67 bus to Kings Cross. Most people appeared to be hidden behind their newspapers, reading, no doubt, about the war. From there we took the underground to Hyde Park Corner. On our way out, as we stood on the noisy escalators, we noticed that on either side of the white tiled walls were war propaganda posters encouraging people to think of their country and to help out whenever or wherever possible. There were posters of smiling young men dressed in a variety of military uniforms, all lining up to take the King's shilling. Other posters encouraged young men to volunteer to fight for their country.

Outside the station, Aunt Jane explained to Susan and me what it all meant to young innocent children like us. 'Our country needs young men to fight in France against the Germans,' she explained. We crossed the road and stood outside huge metal gates that depicted powerful-looking warriors from antiquity. The three of us walked slowly along a road holding each other's hands until we arrived at a large lake full of various birds, including mighty swans protecting their young cygnets. Many families sat on the seats around the lake talking as their children threw bread to the ever-growing crowd of wildlife that congregated waiting to be fed. Two or three dogs ran up and down the water's edge barking incessantly at the birds, which were more concerned with eating the abundant food being thrown to them.

To our delight, Jane took out a small parcel containing bread from her red bag so that Susan and I could make our contribution to feeding the hungry multitude of ducks. By this time dirty pigeons, many with deformed feet, had outnumbered both humans and ducks in their determination to eat whatever rubbish was available.

After two hours, with the warmish autumn sun beaming down on us, we walked slowly through the park. All the trees had shed their leaves. Everything was in hibernation, except for the tall elegant Norwegian conifers that had been sparingly planted around the large park. Life shone from its dark green foliage. One old gentleman, wearing a large thick coat and bowler hat, was sitting on a park bench reading the *News of the World*. As we passed him, I read the headlines on the front page 'Five months into war, and Christmas approaching, Britain continues to hold her ground in Ypres'. I didn't have a clue where Ypres was, but I guessed that it was many miles from London.

We carried on walking until we reached what Aunt Jane called 'Speakers' Corner'. 'Look children, fancy a hot dog and cup of tea?' Jane asked us as she joined the long queue of men wearing flat caps and winter jackets.

Susan and I sat down on a bench watching a number of men, standing on boxes, talking about many different subjects I didn't understand. There was a tall, thin, shabbily-dressed middle-aged man ranting on about the evils of war. Two similar-looking men stood either side of him holding placards that said, 'God punishes the Devil,' and 'Seek the Lord while he can still be found'. Susan and I looked at each other and started laughing. 'Where can you find God?' asked my sister.

'According to Miss Cohen, God is in Heaven,' I replied.

Another man, much younger, standing on his so-called soapbox, was speaking about the bravery of British soldiers fighting in the war against Germany, and how we must all be patriotic and support them. 'We must save Britain from the German tyranny!' he shouted at the assembled people, who were listening intensely to his rhetoric. Some of the crowd cheered and clapped him. 'Up with the British soldiers!' another speaker, wearing an old army uniform, shouted. There were a few dissenting voices.

About fifteen minutes later Aunt Jane, whom I had forgotten all about, arrived at our bench carrying three hot dogs and a large bottle of lemonade. 'Here you are kids. Sorry it took so long but there was a long queue,' she said apologetically. She sat down on the bench between my sister and me.

Once again, I was ravenously hungry. In three mouthfuls my hot dog had disappeared down into my stomach and was soon followed by the lemonade.

''Ave you got a tapeworm inside you, young Leslie?' asked a smiling Jane.

'Give me a bite of yours Sue, I'm starving,' I pleaded with my little sister.

'No sod off, you've ate yours already,' protested Susan.

Aunty Jane pulled a paper bag out of her pocket. ''Ere you are Leslie, a few buns for you'.

I couldn't believe my luck. Six Chelsea buns full of sugar, currants and sultanas! I kissed Jane on her rosy cheek, which smelt of perfume.

We sat looking at and listening to the speakers in front of us. They were all men, except for one placard-carrying woman, from all different walks of life and were doing their best to be heard above the din of voices vying for attention. I jumped up from the bench and walked along to the other end of the line of speakers. There was a Muslim, according to his placard. He was short, slim, about 50, who grabbed my attention because of what he was saying to the crowd that had gathered round him. His message was about peace for all living beings. 'Love yourself, your neighbour, your animals,' he went on.

As I drew closer to the man, who was two feet higher on his soapbox, I realised that it was Mr Ecevit, with whom we had lived at Davis Road. He was a kind, friendly gentleman, I remembered, who once used to give me sweets. Susan and I had played with his friendly children in the large garden we had. More people gathered round Mr Ecevit and his company to listen to his loud yet gentle voice advocating human harmony. He sounded very convincing. With Mr Ecevit was unaware that I had been a part of the crowd taking in his spiritual message, I rejoined Susan and Aunt Jane some fifty feet away.

After an enjoyable day, we took the underground from Green Park back to King's Cross. Outside the station, paper sellers, mostly scruffy young boys, were shouting of the battles being fought in various European countries. Thankfully war had not yet reached mainland Britain. At Stepney Green, Aunt Jane took us back home through the lonely dark streets, where our mother was waiting to greet us.

'Ad a good time kids?' asked mother, as she gave us both a warm hug.

'Yeah thanks Auntie Jane'.

After a quick cup of tea, Jane made her way back to her Liverpool Street home. Christmas was only days away, although because of the state of war, there were very few decorations on the outsides of buildings.

However, mother had made her own festive decorations and had bought a small tree down Cable Street. She always enjoyed dressing a Christmas tree. Besides it was the one time she always attended the local church, St Dunstan's, where she loved singing carols along with others she knew. Every Christmas, St Dunstan's Church Choir used to sing carols, and provide hot tea and mince pies, in Stepney Green to promote community spirit. For mother it was the time to celebrate with all her family and she enjoyed the close support she received from them. What Susan and I didn't know at this particular time was that it would be our last family Christmas until the war was over.

I vividly remember the first German Zeppelin airship raid on London was 30th May 1915. Many people hid down the local underground station for safety. There were to be more than fifty bombings raids mounted on the United Kingdom during the war, many of them targeted at London. During that first bombing raid of Stoke Newington, Stepney and Leytonstone many were killed and injured. Among the dead was a lifelong friend of my father's, Ted Newman. They had first met at school, worked together occasionally down the market, frequented the local pubs and made visits to various racetracks. My father was very upset over his death.

The realities of war were now on our doorstep. The local church, St Dunstan's, founded in 923, was bombed. Many other local buildings and houses were razed to the ground. As East Enders have always done, they rallied around helping each other by giving food, clothes and shelter. They would certainly not be deterred by a few

German bombs. 'Fuck em' - that's what local people thought of the Germans. My family, and no doubt thousands of other local families, sat quietly behind closed curtains, petrified by the horrific sound of bombs dropping not a hundred yards from our home. Poor Mother shook in fear for days.

After the 30th May raid, the public were informed by media that the British Government issued a (so-called) D notice, prohibiting the press from reporting anything about future attacks that was not mentioned in official statements. Previous press reports had contained detailed information about where bombs had fallen, but such information was viewed as detrimental to British security.

Chapter Four
Exiled to the countryside

Several weeks later, following on from the first family meeting, mother arranged another to be held at our home. The meeting had come out of discussions my parents had had concerning the security of Susan and me. They both thought it would be best if we were sent to stay with my father's sister, in Suffolk, in relative safety. My Aunt Doreen, whom my parents had already contacted, thought it a good idea and said we would be most welcome. All the family, my great-grandparents, Tom and Florence, grandmother Bessie, Aunt Jane and Uncle Benny were in agreement and supported my parents' idea that Susan and I would be better off in Suffolk.

I vividly remember that it was a very emotional family meeting. Susan and I didn't want to leave our home, where we felt safe and loved, to live with someone else many miles from London. Susan and I cried in our parents' arms for hours, refusing to physically let go of them. My parents also cried, as did everyone else in the family. We all hugged each other for what felt like eternity. At the end of that day, Susan and I were sufficiently reassured by all the family that they would write a letter to us, enclosing some money, every week.

My sister and I wouldn't set eyes on any of our supportive family for over three long years. Fortunately we had little concept of time.

On the 16th June 1915, as storm clouds formed ominously above, my parents took Susan and me by bus to Liverpool Street Station. Wearing our best clothes, as mother called them, and each carrying a small case, we cried and kissed and hugged our parents as we boarded the near-empty train for Stowmarket. We looked out of the window and kept waving to our parents, who became smaller and smaller as the huge green engine hissed and smoked slowly out of the station. Then all of a sudden they were gone. My sister and I were all on our own alone for the first time in our young lives.

We were expecting to be met at Stowmarket Station by our Aunt Doreen, aged 33, two years older than our father. According to my mother, I had met her years before. That was before Susan was born.

Torrential rain fell from the heavens. Susan, smiling broadly as usual, opened the large bag containing sandwiches mother had made for our journey. 'Bloody cheese sarnies again,' I said to Susan. She looked so young, only six, and so vulnerable to be living away from the security of our family. Father had told me, just before we left, that I should look after my little sister, whatever it took. If that meant thumping, kicking or shouting at someone, just do it.

Two hours later we arrived at Stowmarket. It was still raining. Holding our cases in one hand and train tickets in the other, we jumped down onto the wet platform. It felt as though we were in a different world from the one we knew so well in London.

'Hallo Leslie and Susan, I'm your Aunt Doreen,' shouted an attractive, blonde lady, only feet away, sheltering under a large red umbrella. She gave us each a large hug and kiss, and quickly took us to a waiting car outside the station.

'Well, how lovely to see you both at last,' she said. 'Your parents' letters told me a lot about you both. Anyway, let us drive home to the little village where I live with my partner, Robin. He's a nice bloke.'

I noticed she was wearing red lipstick and green ear rings. On first inspection my aunt reminded me of a sexy film star or model, similar to the Daily Mirror's Jane character, of the kind you see in the newspapers or on billboards.

We drove out of the station car park, which was full of hoardings encouraging people to become war volunteers, and down a main road for about three miles. Aunt Doreen drove her blue car, of which I forget the make, overtaking many other cars, until we turned left at a sign saying 'Compton 3 miles', our destination. 'Don't forget it's Compton where you'll be living,' Mother had explained many times.

We sped past detached houses with large front gardens and cars in the drive. I enjoyed being in a speeding car and looking out of the window at different things I had not seen before. The only time I had seen houses of a similar size was when I had walked round the posh areas of Chelsea and Knightsbridge to see how the other half lived. I wondered whether my aunt lived in a big house in Compton.

Another left turn and we were driving down narrow Compton High Street, with small terraced houses, former labourers' accommodation, on either side. Nearly at the end of the High Street, Aunt Doreen took a sharp right onto a bumpy road full of large puddles. Fifty yards down Jacobs Lane (another name mother had told us to remember), we pulled up outside a small detached cottage. It didn't look much of a home, I thought to myself, when compared to the houses we had just sped past.

'Here we are children. My home is called Rose Cottage. Let us all go inside, get warm and have some food to eat,' she said reassuringly. Food was the word I wanted to hear. With our old second-hand battered cases in our hands, we followed our aunt, like children being taken into a children's home, into her cottage.

We placed the cases to one side, took off our jackets and shoes, and were shown a posh brown leather settee to sit on. The front room we were sitting in was small, with a white ceiling and pink plastered walls. There was another similar-sized settee, one small wooden table and a writing desk with a lamp and I thought the wood fire, the first I had ever seen, was magnificent. The fireplace was surrounded by three large pieces of secured stained timber. I remember seeing something like it in one of mother's magazines at home. You didn't find these sorts of homes round Cable Street, Stepney, I can assure you. Compared to our home, or the noisy block of flats where we lived, it was so quiet that you could have heard a pin drop. There were no rough snotty-nosed kids like me here shouting at each other as we did in Stepney.

As we were on our own in the room, I got up to have a look at the framed wall pictures of horses, a cart carrying hay, a pond and a large field. The name 'John Constable' was written on all of them. Minutes later Aunt Doreen came in from the kitchen holding a tray of pies, bread and margarine and three steaming mugs of tea. I couldn't believe my luck as I had been dreaming about food ever since I finished eating mother's dry sandwiches in the train.

'Do tuck in children. A plate for you, Susan. Take a pie and bread and tea. And the same for you Leslie,' said Doreen, as we both got stuck into our first solid meal of the day. Mind you, Mother had given us porridge, scrambled egg, toast and tea early that morning, but I was a growing lad and needed plenty of grub to keep me going.

When Doreen disappeared once again into the kitchen, I said to Susan that I hoped country people liked eating big meals just like those that mother cooked. 'Course they do silly,' Susan said, grinning at me.

'As it is getting late, and you've both had a tiring day,

I will show you the bedroom you will be sharing ,' said a concerned Aunt Doreen. 'By the way children, Robin is away on business, but he will be home soon. Sleep tight'. After all the strained emotions that day, Susan and I soon fell asleep.

We emerged from our comfortable bedroom ten hours later after recovering from the anxieties of temporarily moving home and travelling down from London. Our small twin bedroom, not unlike the bathroom and toilet, had recently been painted all white, offset with dark blue curtains. We had put our few clothes away in a four-drawer tallboy standing in one corner. The furniture and decorating were all tastefully chosen, just like the rest of the cottage. On the window ledge were books on farming. Not many farms where we lived. The only meat to be found was dead and on sale in Jack's butchers shop in Cable Street! Aunt Doreen, I thought to myself, must have lots of money to be able to buy so many expensive items for her home.

'Good morning Susan and Leslie. I hope you have both slept well after yesterday's upheaval. If you walk through that door into the dining room and take a seat, I will bring you out some lunch,' said Doreen, pointing to a door behind, which led to another small, comfortable and pleasantly-decorated room. There was a wooden table draped with a white cloth, four chairs and a side cupboard for storing crockery and cutlery, so we were told. A pink glass chandelier hung from the low ceiling. They must have been short people in the days when this cottage was built. Those over 5' 8" would no doubt have banged their heads on the door surround, but I thought it fitted in well, as did most of Aunt Doreen's home, with the lime green walls and oak beamed ceilings.

Aunt Doreen must have had a fortune to be able to spend so much money on such an attractive home. I wondered many times during those first few days whether mother and father had ever visited Rose Cottage. My father earned so little money working at the Ritz Hotel, yet here was his sister living a very comfortable life. When I thought about it more, I realised that Father and Aunt Doreen didn't even speak the same language. And besides, come to think of it, why hadn't Doreen lived in London for many years?

Aunt Doreen entered holding the same attractive green tray as yesterday with two plates of liver, bacon and potatoes. In addition there was bread, real butter (not margarine as I thought it had been yesterday) and two large mugs of tea. 'There we go. I hope you are both hungry. Afterwards I'll show you round the gardens,' she said.

Well-fed, the table contents removed to the kitchen (another fine-looking room) and with our teeth brushed, we followed our aunt into the small front garden. It was a warm summer day and every tree, shrub and flower appeared wonderfully colourful. Our temporary landlady led us round from plant to plant, explaining its name, origin, growing life and so on. For some unknown reason I felt like one of the handicapped people that lived in a small hospital not far from where my grandparents lived in Barking. Some of them made funny noises, and others screamed and shouted.

Most of the front garden was full of multi-coloured

roses, petunias and gladioli. The latter, explained Aunty, was a genus, whatever that was, of African plants of the iris family. I was impressed by a large buddleia shrub, with drooping purple flowers, which was exposed to the sun. Several tortoiseshell butterflies flew round the shrub, constantly moving between heavy scented flowers.

The rear garden was magnificent, just like the rest of the property. They must have a gardener, I thought, to carry out all this hard work. Surely little Aunt Doreen and her partner Robin, who so far had been non-existent, could not have achieved this standard of gardening on their own.

The central feature was a dark green lawn about fifty feet long, not unlike a large billiard table. Dotted around the garden were several different flowering shrubs. The horseshoe-shaped borders were a mix of soft fruit bushes, roses, dahlias, carnations and pansies and climbing yellow clematis flowers were growing all over the small tool shed. Wow, I thought, what magnificent gardens to maintain.

We all moved out of the strong sun and into the shade to sit underneath a wide yellow parasol on the patio.

'Sit here, children, and I shall fetch orange squash for us all,' said Doreen, as she walked towards the back door dressed in another different-coloured dress with matching pale yellow shoes.

'Gawd, the old gel has got a few bob Sue, ain't she?' I asked my smiling little sister, who really didn't give a damn.

We survived the first seven days with Aunt Doreen, or

Doreen, or Aunt, the different names I gave her depending on how I felt about her at the time. Other names I called her to myself are unmentionable. I didn't know Susan's opinion of Aunt Doreen, but I found her a little snobbish, if on the whole well intentioned. Not a brilliant start for a tenancy that would last for over three years. Little did I realise that things were about to get worse.

As the three of us sat in the lounge talking, the front door opened and in walked the absent partner, Robin Knox. 'Hallo children. How are you? I'm so sorry I wasn't here to welcome you both to our lovely home,' he said, with a large grin on his scrawny face. He was 55 years old, medium height, excessively thin, bald and dressed like one of the tramps we see regularly around Stepney. 'I've been away working, children. I'm an architect, if you know what that is? Now that the Germans have started bombing the UK, it's becoming harder for me to do my job, what!' he said rather pompously. 'Glass of sherry, darling?' he asked Aunt Doreen.

'While you're there Robin, please make the children orange squash, won't you darling?' she asked.

From then on, a deep, dark despondency would occasionally permeate my inner life. Whether moving from home to Suffolk caused this reaction, I didn't know. Although this couple, our legal minders, if you like, had taken the time and responsibility to take us into their home, I felt very little gratitude towards them. I know that was ungenerous of me.

I was a little relieved of the weighty burden of depression, if that what is was, and keeping Susan safe, when Mother's first reassuring letter arrived three weeks later. She apologised for the delay in sending the letter, but the war made it difficult for trains to adhere to any kind of schedule. Nevertheless, Mother didn't forget to enclose a two-shilling postal order for Susan and me. She hoped we were being good and helping our Aunt Doreen and that we were also keeping ourselves clean and tidy. And helping Robin, which was important so that we could show our appreciation to him, as he was the owner of Rose Cottage. Well, I thought to myself, he might just make things difficult for me if I don't conform.

There was some bad news regarding Grandmother Bessie's job. Due to her department store and several adjoining buildings being bombed, she became unemployed. The good news was that she had found herself a job in a Mile End warehouse. Father was kept busy at the Ritz, as the American top brass had requisitioned a lot of the rooms, unofficially, for the war effort. He had also joined the local Stepney Home Guard, although mother felt he spent most of his official duty glugging beer with his colleagues, instead of keeping watch for the enemy! It didn't exactly inspire confidence in those deemed to keep our great London city secure!

My great-grandparents were both still working hard, even though my great-grandmother, now 70, was eligible for the state pension, which was introduced in 1908. Apparently she remarked that they could 'shove it up their arseholes'. She wasn't going to be means tested by some mean civil servant rummaging through her personal house contents. The rest of the family were all fine. Benny had found a new portering job in Caledonian

Market and Jane still worked in insurance. Mother was at pains to explain in her letter that the Prime Minister, Herbert Asquith, had formed a coalition government. Mother's letter lifted my spirit, if only for a few days, and made me feel hopeful of better days ahead.

According to a village booklet I found in our bedroom tallboy, Compton Village was first recorded in the Domesday Book in 1086. It hadn't grown a great deal since that time. In essence the village, in 1915, consisted of the following: St Paul's Anglican Church, the Jolly Farmer Pub, blacksmith, village school, general store, a doctor, who also covered many outlying villages, and one large mixed farm, called Little Ashburton. According to the 1910 census, about 100 people lived there. Five years later there were at least 40 more. The farmer, Jake Goodheart, owned a large detached house adjacent to the farm.

Most of the women were housewives with young children, yet made time to volunteer, as did Doreen, for one sort of activity or another. These were the kind of village people that held the place together. My aunt was a churchwarden; others painted the church, organised fetes, and on the whole supported each other.

One could say Brompton was like most small British villages at that time. Even though Compton was miles from the nearest town, it was still vulnerable, not from direct enemy attack, but from misdirected bombs or machine gun fire, I overheard Robin comment to the neighbour.

I had a positive impression when Doreen took Susan and me to the village school to attend our first lesson.

Rather anxiously, we entered a small corrugated building and were confronted by an old-looking chap of about 65. 'Hallo Mrs Knox. Hallo Susan and Leslie, how nice to see you both in our little school. There are two classrooms. One where I teach, I'm Mr Helling, and the other teacher next door is Mrs Lane. Now sit down both of you at those front desks,' Mr Helling explained quietly.

Doreen had no sooner left the building when the teacher told us to remove our jackets and collect paper and pencils from his desk immediately. It appeared that within a few minutes of Aunt Doreen leaving, he had changed from a kind, gentle old man into a cold disciplinarian. The more he spoke, the more I wanted to strangle him or smash his face with a shovel. I bit my tongue and said nothing.

Around 4 pm, lessons came to an end. Quickly I told Susan to put her coat on, and we rushed out of the school back to the refuge of Rose Cottage. Susan asked me what was wrong, but as I didn't want to upset her, I made up some story to pacify her. Fear had entered my heart. I didn't say anything about the schoolteacher's behaviour to Doreen. In Stepney you were taught to keep your mouth closed to outsiders- police, teachers, welfare or anyone that looked official- if you didn't know or trust them. Sod it, I wasn't going to push my luck by telling Doreen. She would probably tell Robin, who would, no doubt, go squealing to the whole village about those London troublemakers. Then I would be sent back to London. No Leslie boy, keep your mouth firmly shut tight.

During the night I had constant painful thoughts of harming Mr Helling. Because I had found it difficult to sleep, I overslept and had to rush around next morning to have my breakfast and prepare for school. School was something I wasn't looking forward to.

'Have an enjoyable day at school, children,' said Doreen. Susan and I walked down the narrow high street feeling outsiders in an alien world that didn't want us. I assumed Susan was unaware of my strong feelings of apprehension about being in Compton. Perhaps, I thought, I'm being irrational. We had only been there for a short time, and I felt just as I had first felt when I had started at my new school in Stepney. Be patient, I thought, it takes time for people to get to know you.

As we passed the local pub, the Jolly Farmers, the landlord was outside watering his plants. 'Good mornin' children. I'm Mr Peck. I runs this 'ere pub. I 'aven't seen ye before. What are your names?' asked the big, middle-aged man with a huge red beard and large tufts of hair growing out of his ears.

"Allo sir. My name is Leslie and this is my sister Susan,' I replied, thinking I should not have told him our real names. 'Don't forget what they say in Stepney' kept coming to my mind.

'Off to school then?'

'Yes sir,' I responded.

When we arrived at Compton Village School, Susan and I were placed into different classes due to our ages. My class was for children over eight, and Susan's was for all those under that age. The school, the teachers and the teaching were basic indeed, compared to my last school in London, but I had to try and make the best of it during the war. Give it time, I kept saying to myself.

We all abruptly stood to attention when Mr Helling walked into the classroom like some battle-wearied soldier. 'Sit down!' he shouted. 'Open your history books at the Battle of Hastings, and you, Tatter, start reading.'

After taking some time to find the relevant page, to the teacher's annoyance, I hesitantly began reading. After a few minutes he told me to stop.

'Were you taught to read in London, Tatter?' he demanded.

'Yes sir,' I nervously said.

'Well it doesn't sound as if you were taught properly does it boy?'

'No sir,' I said, more anxiously.

'Well carry on, for God's sake!' he bellowed across the classroom.

I continued reading for what felt like an eternity. I read words incorrectly, lost where I was reading twice, and after many minutes Mr Helling told me to stop. He beckoned me to stand in front of the class like some idiot from the handicapped school in Barking. I wanted to run out of the class, as I felt I was being humiliated. The other twenty class pupils, most of them boys, were laughing at me.

'Now here we have a smart London lad,' the teacher said sarcastically, 'yet he is even unable to read properly'. He told me to sit back down, and another boy continued reading. I felt like a trapped mouse in a cage, but without any cheese to eat. Yet to survive, I had to conform or else I was done for. My father could do that old bastard in - no problem. I could write to Benny to seek his help. He would be down in an instant to sort out this old git in front of me.

After dinner (the locals called it lunch), other pupils continued the aimless reading in the afternoon, until Mr Helling told us all to 'piss off home,' around 4 pm. By this stage I was angry and feeling frustrated.

Outside the school, some of the boys came up to me. 'Hard luck Les. Helling is a bastard sometimes. He loves undermining those he thinks are weak or vulnerable,' said David Cecil, whose father was the village doctor. I took some reassurance from what my fellow pupils told me. Apparently he had made many local people's lives a misery, including those individuals who were now parents.

It was common knowledge, the more I became aware of village tittle-tattle, that Toby Helling, now aged 69, was born in 1846 a few miles from Compton in a hamlet called Reepham, the only child of the local vicar, Charles Helling, of St Nicholas Church. His Victorian upbringing, socialisation, private school and Cambridge education were austere, as one can imagine. Even though he had lived in Compton for many years, no one I asked actually knew how long. Very little was known about his life. He lived on his own, hardly surprisingly, in a small cottage not a hundred yards from Aunt Doreen's home. He was known to frequent the local pub, especially at weekends, and was a keen gardener, an avid reader of novels and enjoyed walking the local woods. Occasionally he would take a taxi to the local Stowmarket station, and take the southbound train, but where to, no one knew. Being a chronic loner, he was always, therefore, on his guard to make sure he wasn't being watched or followed. That behaviour, I realise later, could have explained his anxious preoccupation with the actions of those around him.

He certainly didn't like me, from the very outset. At times his face carried utter hatred for me. If he had presented himself in or around Stepney in the way he dressed in Compton, most people, understandably, would have assumed him to be a homeless vagrant. There was nothing endearing about him. I hated him, most people I met hated him, and he probably hated himself the most.

The other teacher Mrs Lane, as others explained to me, was aged 63, was similar ilk to her male counterpart. Although she had been married, her husband had died five years previously of cancer. Some said he couldn't get away from his wife quick enough. Their one child, Simon, aged 40, had moved away when he was young to live and work as an engineer in Manchester. Those that remembered him said he frequently returned to visit his parents, although he hadn't been seen for some time. Mrs Lane was born in Lancashire, in 1852. As I hinted earlier, if you dig a little deeper, wherever you are, things will be decidedly different from what you expect. This place was no different.

From here on, I realised that my time at Compton would be difficult and a question of survival. From a young age I was aware that people, most people, didn't take kindly to living in close proximity to others. It was no different in Stepney, Catford or Barking. I suppose it had something to do with evolution, tribe, space and food. Besides in our case, it was one of class and snobbery. Susan and I just didn't fit in this middle-class area. It was only due to the war, and family ties, that we had landed up here. I was aware that some of these village morons had it in for me and Susan, but I wouldn't let on to her; I would use cunning, stealth and my young experience to keep us safe, as I was used to being undermined. It wouldn't surprise me if Helling, Mrs Lane, Robin Knox and even the vicar of St Paul's, Simon de Montford, were at this moment colluding to get rid of us. Incidentally the vicar's left arm had been blown off in the Boer War.

'Good morning children, how are we this bright Saturday morning?' asked Aunt Doreen, as she placed our breakfast of porridge and toast on the dining room table. We didn't say very much. 'In the last few weeks you have appeared increasingly quiet, Leslie. Very different to when you first came here,' she asked rather inquisitively, but understandably concerned as she was looking after us.

'I'm all right Aunty,' was my misleading response.

'School going well for both of you, I hope?' she asked.

'Yes,' I said.

'What about you, Susan? You don't say very much darling do you? I know you miss not being with your parents, don't you?'

'Yes Aunty,' was all Susan, not yet six years old, could say.

'Well, after breakfast I want you to meet our vicar, Simon, at St Paul's Church,' explained Aunt Doreen. Robin was not often around, I realised.

After breakfast, we cleared the table, one of our house jobs, and washed them in the spotless white kitchen sink, unlike our kitchen sink in Stepney, which was always brown with tea stains.

As we walked along the old bumpy road to the church, Doreen acknowledged good morning from several local people. One old couple, Mr and Mrs Ogden, residents for many years, now retired, enquired into who we were. 'Hallo Doreen, and who are these delightful young folk among us?' asked Mr Ogden. Aunt Doreen explained our story about being sent from London to live here away from the dangers of German bombing.

Fifty yards further on the vicar was standing outside the church waiting to greet us. 'Good morning Doreen, and hallo, children,' he said. 'Your aunt has told me all about you.' He invited us all into the 9th century church. The vicar went on to explain facts and figures to Susan and me which frankly went over our uninterested heads, although I do remember him mentioning that the Danes in 869 had occupied East Anglia and killed its last King, St Edmund. Apparently the King had hidden from the Danes in St Paul's until he was captured. The church had been re-modernized several times, the main benefactors being the local wealthy Stevens family.

As my aunt was a churchwarden and knew the vicar well, we were invited to the adjacent vicarage for tea and sandwiches. Susan and I found that experience excruciatingly painful. I went to the toilet three times just to get away from the pompous conversation between my aunt and the vicar. This also gave me the opportunity to see if there was anything worth stealing. There were large wall paintings, grand-looking furniture and colourful carpets, all of which would be out of place in

Stepney, but there was nothing I could slip into my pocket. I went looking round the vicarage like an excited cat burglar. Conditioning is very powerful!

These were the sort of people I didn't trust - not even most of my fellow pupils, whose parents had money and influence. But one pupil with whom I did manage to develop a friendship in time was David Cecil. His father was the village doctor and had moved to Compton from Ipswich when David was five years old. He too didn't like most of the local people. Unlike Ipswich, he found people, especially Mr Helling, at times unfriendly and old-fashioned. He told me that his young parents felt the same.

One cold frosty morning in November, 1915, David took me for a long walk round the area, explaining names and features of places along the way. We jumped over one of farmer Jake Goodheart's fences and made our way over several lush pasture fields, full of autumn speedwell and a few clumps of common ragwort, which eventually took us into Grange Woods. There we climbed the tall oak, beech and elm trees. Most of the trees appeared to be very old. All that remained on the bare trees high up in the canopy were the scant remains of crow and rook nests from the year before. A huge number of crows and rooks sounded their 'kraa-kraa' noises menacingly above us. It was a wonderful new experience for me to climb trees in woods away from the prying eyes of adults. Alas, poor Susan had to stay indoors with our aunt. The freedom, joy and unbounded excitement I had with David will stay with me forever. In London, where I lived, there weren't any woods as big as those in Compton. There were a few clumps of trees here and there in the parks, but the larger woods were further out near the suburbs. Most of the East End was concrete and tarmac; in Compton it was lush grass, fruit orchards and old walking tracks. Nevertheless, back in the smoke we were always out playing on the streets looking for mischief and adventure.

'Allo there boys,' came a voice from thirty feet below us. It was Jock, the local simpleton, who had worked for years as a farm labourer for Mr Goodheart. 'I've got somin' to show thee,' he shouted up at us. We decided to climb back down to the ground.

'What do you want Jock?' asked David, slightly irritated. Within seconds Jock had dropped his trousers to the ground and was holding his erect penis in his hand, laughing. 'What ders yer think about that boys?' remarked the scruffy-looking man in front of us.

'Put that fucking thing away Jock or otherwise we will tell the police,' threatened David. With that deterrent ringing in his ears, Jock pulled up his trousers and ran off over the nearest fields to safety.

David explained that he had been born illegitimate. Jock (that wasn't his real name) had been cared for in various children's homes until he was old enough to be admitted into St Bride's Hospital, Stowmarket. He thought that at about the age of 20, he had been placed by the local council with Farmer Goodheart. He had worked for him for at least 20 years. He was considered a nuisance, but not dangerous. I must say that I was frightened by all six feet of him, standing there holding his erect penis without any idea of the offence he was causing. Of course, I had seen that kind of thing among my friends at school, and in the local parks in London.

Jake Goodheart, aged 50, short, fat and married with two sons, had inherited Little Ashburton farm from his father, who in turn had taken over from his father. Both his sons were at agricultural college. His rather fat wife was one of the village army of volunteers, who loved helping out as long as there was gossip, rumour and scandal involved. Goodheart, it was said, loved his beer.

Goodheart had been born in the village. You could say that he was born with cow shit under his nails. His wife, however, had been socialised by her uncle and aunt in Colchester from the age of six, after her parents had both been killed in a railway accident. The endearing village joke insisted that Jake met his wife in a beauty contest, which probably explains the nature of the farmer's surname! Like most of the village people, Jake and Cynthia were outwardly decent enough, but deeper down they could make your life a misery. Anxious, and sometimes frightened, I realised that I had to grow up fast.

We were back at school in front of the pathetic self-ordained commander-in-chief Mr Helling once more. Standing there like a field scarecrow, his shaking arm pointed to a picture on the blackboard of Lord Nelson. I was familiar with the chap with one arm and patch over his eye, as one of our teachers in London had told us his story.

'Now, Tatter, who was Nelson?' asked the ugly teacher in front of me, no doubt determined to undermine me. Sod him, I thought, I will get him riled up this time.

'He was an officer born in 1066 sir,' I belligerently answered.

'You bloody cockney fool Tatter!' shouted Mr Helling, as the class roared with laughter. 'Shut up laughing at this buffoon's ignorance,' insisted the red-faced teacher, who had clenched his fists in anger. Given the chance, no doubt, he would have hit me round the head, or worse. 'Boys, please don't fall into the mire of ignorance where it appears Tatter has already gone,' fumed the old teacher in front of us.

That was the last straw. 'I've ad enough of you, you old bastard!' I shouted at the teacher. I stormed out of the classroom and ran as fast as my legs could carry me over to Grange Woods. I sat down under a bare oak tree not knowing what to do. The more I thought, the more I became confused as tears rolled down my cheeks thinking of my parents, grandmother Bessie and others in my family. If I wrote to Bessie, I thought, she would come down and permanently sort out that nasty Mr Helling.

I calmed down as I lay on the short, tough grass. All manner of thoughts and ideas went through my head. A large brown male fox was foraging for food nearby and saw me. It stared for more than a minute, wondering who was on his patch, then ran off in the opposite direction like a fired arrow.

After sitting around in the woods for about three hours, I was getting cold and worried again. Being February, it would soon be dark and I was becoming hungry, so I decided to walk back across the field to Rose Cottage. No sooner had I opened the front door than Aunt Doreen pounced on me, asking numerous questions regarding my awful behaviour in Mr Helling's class. I explained how the teacher had tried from the outset to undermine me and today's incident was about all I could take. Susan sat watching, too frightened to move. I reassured Doreen that pupils would confirm what happened to me in class.

'I most certainly will ask them, Leslie. I realise you are young and missing your family, but that is no way to behave,' she said looking anxiously at me.

Aunt Doreen made it her mission, above all other concerns, for the next few days to enquire into what had happened regarding my behaviour at school. She contacted most of the parents whose children were in class that day, and asked if she could discuss with them what they thought had happened. Being an assertive woman, she questioned all the children, with their parents in attendance, about their personal feelings of the incident. What did the teacher say? Was it directed at me? Did they think it led to my subsequent outburst and exit from the school?

Most of the class pupils supported me during the questioning. In particular David Cecil and several other pupils thought Mr Helling had provoked me into acting disrespectfully and leaving the classroom. When she later discussed the matter with me, Aunt Doreen was satisfied that I was the victim of Mr Helling's irrational behaviour. There the matter was concluded. Of course, most local people knew that the good Mr Helling was unfit to teach, especially children, but Britain was in a state of war. End of the matter.

It was letters from our parents, Bessie and other family members that sustained Susan and me during those difficult times. On 1 March, 1916, Susan's sixth birthday, she received many birthday cards from the family, as well as from friends at Sandhurst Road flats and her former school friends. We had an enjoyable party at Rose Cottage to celebrate her birthday, which was attended by Doreen, Robin and a few friends from Compton School. It was so kind of Doreen to bake a special cake with six candles burning brightly in the middle. Everyone there appeared to enjoy themselves, especially when Robin started acting the fool and telling us jokes. I felt I loved Susan so much. For one so young, she had adapted to a new way of life so well. Probably more so than I had. Remembering what my father had instilled in me, I was mindful that I would always try my best for my darling little sister. To ensure that no one would come between us was of paramount importance.

My Aunt Doreen's background had intrigued me, as I mentioned earlier on, for some time. She went to the same local schools as her two brothers. At the age of 14, she found a job working as a filing clerk for a property developer in Charing Cross. Not a bad job for a working-class girl. During the next four years she enjoyed working for the same company, and socialized with colleagues in the local pubs and dives, seedy places where young men were always ready and able to take liberties with a young, naive attractive teenager unused to such decadent environments. It appears, though, that she did meet one friendly working-class boyfriend during that time from Stepney. It was also around about this time that she and her colleagues began talking to Robin Knox and his friend, in a local bar used mainly by middle-class people in trendy Leicester Square.

To cut a long story short, Doreen and Robin Knox started dating on a regular basis, and after a year they started living together. For the first six years they lived in his posh Chelsea flat, then moved to a much larger house out near Richmond. Doreen had certainly 'gone up in the world', as they would say down the East End. By this time her wealthy boyfriend had found her a job working in the Home Office. No one actually knew what kind of work she did for a living, but she was always well turned out in new, pretty numbers that only money, Knox money, could afford to buy.

When they moved to Suffolk in 1908, it was Doreen who undertook most of the hard work restoring the cottage. To her credit, she had taught herself several of the skills that were needed to take on and finish the year-long project. It must be remembered that Robin was 21 years her senior. Most of his life was shrouded in mystery. Suffice to say that he came from a middle-upper class family. He was educated at a private school and Cambridge University, and from there on, little was known about him, at least by outsiders like us.

As most of the family have asked many times, what did she see in Robin that appealed to her? Doreen came from a hard working-class background where you fought for everything you ever owned. In Robin Knox she found security, a comfortable home in quiet surroundings, her own car, travel, fine clothes and dining out in good restaurants. For her, no more living in cold dirty rooms, no more eating pie and chips, or drinking beer down the local and ending up with a local, yet decent, unskilled fellow with no prospects. From Bow to Compton! All I can say on the matter is, bloody good luck to her.

As is usual with young boys, regardless of race, class or whatever, we loved fighting each other. Evolution has made sure that boys constantly play-fight to keep us fit, to keep us healthy for work, sex and war. During my time at Compton school, I had many battles with different boys. I won some and lost the rest. Even David Cecil and I fought each other at least six times, winning three each. Although pampered in my estimation, he was a tough well-built boy who didn't frighten easily. When it came down to fighting, David was a strong match for anyone.

One of those battles happened in the classroom, just after lunch break, when scruffy Mr Helling walked in and caught us fighting. 'Stop immediately, you thick shitheads!' roared the teacher. 'Yes, I thought you, Tatter, would be fighting, but you Cecil, I'm most surprised. Both of you will do extra reading in front of me this afternoon'. Helling's number one preoccupation, given the opportunity, was to intellectually beat up anyone he deemed vulnerable in front of him, and that certainly included me.

On the 6th June 1916, I celebrated my 11th birthday. Susan and I had been in Compton for one year. Several letters and cards and a parcel were delivered to Rose Cottage for me. Mother had bought me a pair of stout boots that I had asked for, in my last letter to her, so that I could take longer walks, over tougher terrain, with David. They were just what I needed, and must have taken all of her savings. Doreen had also made a delicious sponge birthday cake for me, just like Susan's, but this time with 11 blue candles all burning bright in the darkened room. We had lots of games, tasty food and, a new drink called cream soda that Robin had bought for me. Everyone had a good time, including pupils, of both sexes, from Compton School. It was good to see Robin jumping up and down in some of the games we played. Having been around Robin for some time, I got the impression he missed having children of his own. I was also so pleased that Susan had, in the last few months, become more confident and outgoing.

That night I went to bed feeling the happiest I had in a long time. But something told me it wouldn't last, that I had to nurture my own inner conflicts and fend off the demons that would sometimes strike without provocation. But due to the reassuring kindness of Aunt Doreen and Robin Knox, it helped that Susan and I celebrated every birthday and Christmas in Compton just like we did at home. That helped us feel good about ourselves.

Sitting at the breakfast table one morning, a few weeks after my enjoyable birthday party, Doreen said that she had just received some bad news from our mother. 'Children, I'm so sorry to tell you this but your Uncle Benny has been killed in action'. We all started to cry. It had happened on 6th August 1916, during the Battle of the Somme. Life without Benny would be unbearable for my mother, Benny's sister. They and their mother Bessie had been through so much together, especially when their father had walked out on them. Benny was such a colourful character, full of life and hope. When he was happy or excited, he used to rub his hands together vigorously to demonstrate his intense feelings. He was just 29 years old.

It transpired that Benny hadn't been conscripted, but sentenced by the courts to fight in the war effort. Benny and two other local friends had pleaded guilty to stealing a significant number of cigarettes from a warehouse in Chingford. The Judge gave all three an ultimatum: be conscripted into the Army or spend five years in prison. Benny elected to join the war effort, but his two accomplices chose jail instead. Conscription, incidentally, came into force on the 2nd March 1916.

With Benny in mind, I well remember that several weeks later about ten smartly dressed young men marched proudly through Compton village in their smart Army uniforms to fight for their country. The whole village came out to cheer, clap, sing and of course cry for their young sons, who had all been conscripted. Young boys and girls walked alongside the soldiers shouting the names of their heroes, and dogs barked until they were out of sight. Among them were Jake Goodheart's two sons.

Mind you, three young village men had already volunteered to fight in late 1914. A mile down the road, they had met up with other local conscripted soldiers who were equally determined to fight. Two hours later at Stowmarket Station, a full troop train carrying several hundred young men took them somewhere down in south-west England to be trained before experiencing the dirt, grime, chill and terror of war. Many never returned home to their families.

When Susan and I were returning home from seeing the soldiers off, we passed the local shop displaying the *Suffolk Echo*, the local paper, with headlines across the front page - *'Lloyd George becomes Prime Minister as Asquith stands down'*.

On another of our days out together, which I looked forward to very much, David suggested we go fishing in the River Demby, not a mile from Compton. He had fished there many times before, occasionally with his father, and had often been successful in catching roach, dace and bream. He usually threw them back afterwards. We took off from the village and walked along narrow muddy lanes, passing several people whom David acknowledged and holding our rods, tackle, bait, lots of sandwiches and drink.

We sat under a large willow tree that shaded us from the hot summer day, our rods bobbing around in the water. We just sat there talking about nothing as river flies buzzed irritatingly round our faces and tried to eat our live bait. From the bank of the river, I realised, for the first time, how idyllic the area was. Fat cows with black and brown patches on their backs and drooping udders that nearly touched the ground lazily munched the lush green grass without a care in the world. Various birds, including blackbirds, hopped from branch to branch, hoping to pick up a discarded worm or two that we had been using. Coots, aggressive little river birds, were constantly chasing moorhens away from their patches, and a lone swan, using its long neck, dredged the river bed for whatever it could find to eat. We ate our sandwiches and drank lemonade. All was well with the world, until I thought about Benny's death, and of the thousands of soldiers who were at this very moment fighting and dying for our freedom.

All of a sudden, David said to me, 'Have you got a big willy?'

'Pretty big,' was my response, but, I didn't really know. In London some of the boys showed each other their small penises, and one or two had pubic hair. That was about the extent of my sex life. I hadn't seen girls' genitals, not even my mother's bare body. Things like that were not mentioned in working-class home in those days, but of course, with large families living in one room it was inevitable that incest occurred.

David got out his erect penis. I assumed it was a big one. He didn't have any skin over the end of it, unlike mine.

'I've been masturbating for some time, what about you?'

'Yes I've done it a few times,' I said brazenly, which was the truth. With that rite of passage established, both of us starting urinating in the river to see who could reach the farthest.

After several hours of fishing, we had caught, and returned to the river, about five different kinds of fish. Mind you, they were all smaller than my limp willy. It was still warm and humid in the late afternoon sun as we strolled along the river bank throwing stones at anything that moved.

To our right we were startled by screaming or shouting some way off. When we started to walk across the field to investigate, two people, an older man and a young girl, jumped up from the tall cereal crop where they had been lying, adjusted their clothes and quickly walked off in the opposite direction.

'Did you see who that was?' asked a shocked David. 'It was Teddy Flowers, he's about 40, he works for Goodheart, and Mabel Drury from our class. Blimey I'm speechless!' David just looked at me. Mabel, no more than 13, had been in my class for nearly eighteen months and I had noticed that she had grown into a well-shaped young girl.

'I wonder how long she's been having it off with Ted Flowers,' I said.

'Apparently Teddy, and other mature men, have been regularly having sex with young girls,' remarked David.

We decided not to say anything to anyone. You dared not say anything about sex in those days, whatever the nature of the activities. Besides, people had a strong tendency to look the other way, even though any number of people appeared to be at it. That appeared to include Goodheart and his two employees. Was the good farmer lacing his tea, and others, with aphrodisiacs?

It was different for Susan, as she was too young and innocent to understand what was going on around her. But I was sufficiently streetwise from my years in London to understand what was happening to those around me. It was brutal, even though at my age I didn't understand the complexities that caused such behaviour. It set off in me occasional torrents of painful self-loathing. Sometimes I thought my head was going to explode from the deep, dark depression I experienced. Feeling engulfed by my environment, I lay awake at nights preoccupied with nightmares of being stabbed, robbed and ridiculed by the village, as Susan slept soundly only feet from me.

But the problem remained. Who was going to listen to an uneducated working-class kid from poverty-stricken Stepney? I was most reluctant to even think about informing Aunt Doreen, even though she probably realised herself the extent of the abuse being carried out underneath her nose. Understandably, for this was her home and a way of life that very few people could have offered her. It would have been nothing short of financial suicide for her to have come forward to voluntarily discuss information, albeit second hand, with village elders. I knew then, and even more so now, it would have ruined her life. She would have ended up living in some depressing bedsit, at best, somewhere in Central London, at worst living as a residential housekeeper working for a pittance looking after an elderly couple near to death or insanity or both. Compton was no different to Stepney when it came to sexual abuse. Doreen hadn't forgotten what her brother, my father, had instilled into her from a young age: keep your lips closed and you didn't see a thing!

A few months later the so-called 'Land Army' of women started replacing the local men in Compton, Suffolk and around the country who had been conscripted. Local employers managed to keep hold of a few of their workers, but it was women who filled the large gaps and kept Compton, and country productive. As I witnessed locally for the next two years, with my own eyes, women drove large horses to plough the fields to plant much-needed vegetables. They sowed and cut different cereals, pruned fruit orchards, painted large buildings and were as productive as their male counterparts.

Farmer Goodheart, when questioned on the subject, said that women were good, productive and reliable workers. No doubt, in his case, this was a secondary consideration for singing their praises. It was a big step towards the equality that many women sought. It was only in 1914 that the Lords, rather short-sightedly, had rejected votes for women.

World War One had helped bring about female emancipation. That is undeniable. As women at the time said, they had taken over traditionally male jobs and showed most people, especially politicians, that they could perform just as well as men. By the end of World War One over 117,000 women were doing a variety of jobs, from driving trams and working in munitions factories to building homes and maintaining the wheels of industry. In 1918, women over 30 years old only were given the vote, and hard-earned it had been. Many viewed this limited number of women being given the vote for the first time as a Government compromise. But it was at least a positive development from the 1884 Third Reform Bill, in which the electorate was increased to only 5 million.

I personally got on well with those girls, most of whom were women in fact, who worked and lived in Compton and surrounding villages for the duration. The farming and village work was co-ordinated by a Government official who was based in Stowmarket. He saw that the women were treated fairly, had decent living accommodation and had the opportunity to enjoy themselves socially. Most of the residents of Compton treated them well by making food, tea and clean clothes available. Aunt Doreen herself supervised a lot of activities for them. Many of the land girls enjoyed sitting out in the evening, sometimes accompanied by Susan and me, in the fields to watch the German planes flying overhead. The planes made an awful unsettling droning noise as they flew over Britain on bombing raids. No bombs were ever dropped locally, the nearest landing a few miles away somewhere in Essex. But when the siren sounded, we would all run as fast as possible to a large underground bunker that had been built specifically for the war by local men. Other times when we sat on the dark Compton soil, we used to watch the searchlights beaming out from the London skyline trying to locate enemy planes. The most painful sight of all was the experience of seeing London burning after being bombed by German planes. My thoughts would be focused on my family in London and hoping that they were all safe and well.

Through 1917, and well into 1918, the land girls kept Britain alive by their unstinting hard work. Many different women worked in Compton for a few months, and then they were transferred to the places that most needed labour. Information found its way slowly to Compton, and other rural areas, about the slaughter being carried out in Europe. It was the local newspaper that informed us about the third Battle of Ypres had claimed many victims, as did Egypt, Palestine, Gallipoli and many other places. Men died in large numbers - for what? And one of the most significant pieces of war news was that the USA, in 1917, had declared war on Germany; Britain and her allies much needed their support.

I got to know Farmer Goodheart quite well, and he allowed me, with Doreen's permission, along with other boys and girls from school, to help out in the fields assisting the women. We loved throwing the cabbages, potatoes and turnips into sacks, and occasionally at other people, which were then carted off to the local station for national distribution. The fresh Suffolk air and the deep brown earth that covered the land really inspired positive feelings in me. On a few occasions we were allowed to accompany the women on the tractors and lorries to help out at nearby farms, in Ufton, Jakewell and Biddenhow. We were most welcome in rural hamlets and villages, due to labour becoming scarce. People went out of their way to provide us with food, hot drinks and shelter if it was raining. It really was a time when everyone helped each other - a sort of camaraderie had covered the nation for a while.

Throughout their time at Compton and surrounding villages, the women working on the land and elsewhere were great fun to be with. They told wicked jokes and gave us children cigarettes and a few bottles of local beer. One young woman in particular, Joan, slim and attractive, who came from Devon, loved a few beers and a good sing-song. Her personality was infectious. She resided, along with two other girls, in the household of Mr and Mrs Hurst, both former village councillors, public servants and prison reformists. The latter would have sounded like music to the ears of a lot of East End villains.

The land girls, women from various backgrounds, had no inhibition when it came to using the 16th century village pub. Many of the local men, enticed by so many attractive women in their male-dominated environment, lined up to buy them a drink or two, but according to Joan, that was as far as it got. 'It was joking, drinking, cigarettes - nothing else', Joan said emphatically. Even the over-enthusiastic Jake Goodheart couldn't entice any of the girls into his smelly barn!

More devastating family news arrived in one of mother's letters. Once again it was Aunt Doreen who gave us the horrible news that Aunt Jane had been killed in Central London, while she sheltered from hostile bombing. It happened on 17th March 1917, when she was 48. Her sister, my grandmother, Bessie Smith, was inconsolable, not surprisingly, for some considerable time. Notwithstanding the death of her son, the loss of her sister would leave its mark on Bessie for the rest of her life. But in true East End spirit, she kept grafting. 'Fuck em!' she would defiantly maintain about the German bombardment. Naturally, Susan and I were also very upset over Jane's death. We would miss her terribly.

It was the latter that encouraged Bessie, around early September 1917, to leave her job at Bernstein's warehouse and start working as a cook in a large government-owned canteen supplying those war-weary soldiers and civilians with a regular supply of hot, nourishing food and drink. Within weeks she was promoted to supervisor, hardly surprising to me, and stayed until the end of the war in November 1918. Wherever she went, Bessie Smith left her positive and indelible mark on those she met.

With the sad news of the death of our aunt, school was just about bearable until about three months later, when my sinister instincts about Mr Helling were proved correct. While out walking on my own in Box Hill Wood, a small deciduous wood east of the village, I heard various human noises in the undergrowth. Making sure that I remained as quiet as possible, I slowly made my way to the sounds, and, there to my horrible amazement, Mr Helling was rubbing the erect penis of Terence Thatch, a 13-year-old local lad who was in my class. I watched, frozen, for a few seconds, and then ran off back to the village. What if Helling had seen me watching as he masturbated Terence? What would he do to me at school, or if he saw me alone in the village? If I told other people what I had just witnessed, they wouldn't believe me against the word of a mature, educated, local man. For a while I panicked, until I realised that if I said nothing whatsoever about the sexual incident, then no harm would come to me. As with all the other crimes or wrongdoings I had witnessed in Compton, I would just keep my lips firmly sealed.

Not a week later, as David and I walked in local Friston Wood, we witnessed, in amazement, yet more sexual abuse being carried out. This time, the pernicious abuser was none other than Wilfred Tranter, aged 56, married with a daughter and a pillar of the community. He too was a former local councillor, a banker in London and an expert on local history. The boy he was having sex with was John Thompson, aged 14, a pupil at Compton School. On this occasion, luckily, neither party saw us witnessing their sexual activity. David and I were shocked, not just by the illegal and sordid behaviour but the extent of such activity going on in the village, which had become, in my humble estimation, of epidemic proportions. Before the war, I naively thought, perhaps sexual and other abuse didn't exist, but due to the trauma of war, it appeared, it had become an accepted part of country life.

Weeks later, we read in the *Suffolk Echo* of the first daylight raid on London, 13 June 1917, German bombing caused 162 deaths and injuries to about 432 people in various places in the East End. In Poplar, 16 primary school children were killed as they sat innocently in their classrooms. It turned out to be the deadliest air raid of World War One. Aunt Doreen sat crying as she read mother's letter to us about the catastrophe that had befallen the people of Poplar. Aunty was mortified by such carnage, particularly so as she was from the East End herself. She realised that great suffering had to be shouldered by many families, but none would suffer on their own. Many local people, in those days, looked after each other, regardless of the problem.

On the same day, Susan and I, not for the first time, received a letter and a postal order from our great-grandparents, so we could cash them at the local shop to buy sweets to help us forget the suffering for a short while. Tom and Florence Smith, who were now 71 and 75 years old, had both retired after grafting for many years.

As well as both receiving the paltry means-tested state pension, Tom had also paid into a small work pension, and including their own savings, they had sufficient money to live on. Tom still ventured down with old friends to watch the soccer team he had supported for years, Leyton Orient, which was founded in 1881. It was always a mystery to the family why he didn't support West Ham United, the team nearest to him.

'One small consolation, I suppose,' wrote Great-Granddad in his letter to us, 'the war has brought full-employment to London for the first time in ages'. Understandably, though, they did not refer to Jane's death. Mother told me later, that after Jane's death, that Tom and Florence both became more insular and never fully recovered from the loss of their daughter. It must have been very a painful experience for my dear ageing great-grandparents.

After months of difficult behaviour from Mr Helling at school, I nearly bumped into him coming out of the local pub. In a drunken state, he pointed his finger at me. 'Not you again Tatter. You've been a fucking shit head from the first time I saw you. You thick cockney. Don't think you've got anything on me sonny boy, because you haven't. My young friend will vouch to that,' he nastily said, as I ran off, as fast as I could, down to Rose Cottage and safety.

Once again I didn't say anything to anyone. Sadly it would have been a waste of time, even though such a dangerous individual was allowed to roam Compton and other areas unimpeded to force his disdainful, degrading and illegal behaviour onto innocent young people.

Not long after, on November 11th 1918, the German Government asked the British Government for an armistice. The British and her allies had been successful in beating the German aggression. But what an awful price had been paid by the large number of soldiers and civilians who had been killed and injured, many from all those countries which regarded Britain as their mother country. Even little villages like Compton had had their victims. The lives of close-knit families would never quite be the same as they were before the war. Things change, time moves on, but for many parents their fallen sons, heroes all of them, would remain in their hearts forever. Those young men, who gave their ultimate, had died in a hellish realm, mainly in France, to make the world a safer place. I had witnessed myself in Compton the unremitting inhumanity to those less powerful. Violence is an integral part of our genetic make-up. But the ferocity that was let *loose upon the world* in 1914-18 demonstrated how efficient mankind had become at slaughtering its own.

Before those young soldiers, many of them handicapped in numerous ways, started returning home, my parents drove down to Compton to take us back to our home in Stepney. Susan and I had not seen our parents for three and a half long years. When they arrived at Rose Cottage on 15th November, 1918, my sister and I were overcome with happiness at seeing them once again.

'Allo Les and Susan, how are you, darlings?' my mother asked, as she and father hugged and kissed us for several minutes. Along with Doreen, we all cried and held each other. We had lost Uncle Benny and Aunt Jane, which was so painful, but Mother and Father were there for us. Only eight years old, little Susan had grown physically and emotionally in the years away from the security of home. Her hair was longer, darker and thicker than when she had first left Stepney in 1915. She retained her wonderful smile. As for myself, taller, and heavier, with an abundance of maturing hair growing round my genitals, the Compton experience would stay with me forever. It couldn't be any other way. Whatever I undertook from now, it would be informed, I hoped, by those good experiences from my past; this was what I hoped as Father drove us all safely home in a car borrowed from a colleague. Stepney had changed in many ways, like most of the country, which had not escaped the effect of so much suffering and so many traumatic experiences. The world, I realised, is in constant flux.

Chapter Five

Back to the big city

It wasn't easy coming back to my home after my experiences at Compton. There were many times during those first few weeks when I just wanted to scream at the world. When I thought of those young innocent boy soldiers from Compton, indeed, from around the world, I thought, what had we done to each other? Why did we do it? Why? The dead and the wounded, the suffering - it was all so unimaginable that I felt we had lost the one bond we all had: *our common humanity*. I experienced lucid glimpses of hope, hope of a better world, when I realised that my own family and people in my neighbourhood all wanted to make the world a better place. But I became depressed, particularly when I realised the enormous number of dead and wounded from World War One.

According to British Army statistics of the Great War, which I read about much later on to write this book, British soldiers, including allied soldiers from around the world, came to a total force available for deployment during 1914-18 of over 8,600,000 personnel. They served in various theatres of war. Most served on the Western Front, in France and Flanders. The total number of British soldiers who died was around 705,000. That number included those killed in action, those who died of wounds, disease or injury, and those missing presumed dead. Including soldiers from other countries that supported Britain, the overall total was just short of one million deaths. But many more remained unaccounted for.

Over 2,200,000 soldiers were wounded during World War One. Those wounded soldiers returned home to no state provision at all. Ordinary local people opened up their homes to help those forgotten heroes who had fought for their country, and were now in need of support. It was the determination of local people, who co-ordinated various supportive measures around the country, that eventually led to the British Legion for ex-servicemen being founded in 1921, to help all those former soldiers live a productive life from there on.

According to official published sources, the total number of all military and civilian casualties in World War One was over 37 million, over 16 million deaths and 20 million wounded, ranking it among the deadliest conflict in human history. The total number of deaths included about 10 million military personnel and about 6 million civilians. A staggering number of deaths and wounded people from around the world!

Just like Bessie's, an incalculable number of families were never the same again after losing, in some cases, several members from one family. British civilian deaths were at least 107,000 from malnutrition and disease, but that number excludes deaths due to the influenza pandemic. Approximately 17,000 British civilians were killed by military action and crimes against humanity. This hellish nightmare was due to the assassination of one person, the Archduke Franz Ferdinand of Austria, and the subsequent illegal action by Germany.

Within a few days of Christmas, Mother had arranged a family reunion to celebrate: a low-key affair, with sparse resources available to the family. It was so exciting to see our great-grandparents and our grandmother, Bessie Smith. They had, of course, all become older, heavier and slower during those three and half years that Susan and I had been living in Compton. But, it was marvellous to see them, touch them and hear their distinctive voices once again filling the space in our small home at Sandhurst Road.

It was also so good, yet so strange, to familiarise myself once again with the house and garden we had all worked so hard to make our home. When we moved in 1912 the house and garden were a dump, but during the intervening years of the war, Mother and Father had further redecorated it. The whole house was now light and bright. They had bought good second-hand furniture and father had redesigned the kitchen so that even a top chef would have been proud of it.

'Ere we go,' said Bessie in her familiar loud voice, 'all have a tot of this whisky, my darling family'. We drank to better times. When we eventually got round to painfully discussing Benny and Jane, it transpired that Benny's body had not been found, and he had been officially presumed dead by the Army. In 1920, an unknown soldier, for the first time, was buried in Westminster Abbey to symbolise universal peace. For years after, I often fantasized that Benny was that warrior in Westminster Abbey.

Jane was buried in God the Redeemer Church cemetery, not far from where she was born in Barking. Many of her colleagues and former pupils from the school of the same name attended her ceremony. My great-grandfather gave a moving talk about his wonderful daughter, who was now at peace.

At least the Government, in 1919, commissioned Sir Edward Lutyens to design a wood and plaster cenotaph to commemorate all those military personnel who died for their country. In 1920 it was replaced by a permanent structure, built in Portland Stone. Remembrance Sunday was, thereafter, the closest Sunday to 11th November - Armistice Day.

My grandmother didn't sit on her backside once her job had finished supporting the war effort. In March 1919, she had found a job managing a café, just a few minutes' walk from Cable Street. The busy café, providing inexpensive food for poor local people, was open twelve hours a day, six days per week. Mind you, she made it clear from the outset to the Italian owner that she needed time for herself. Living on her own became lonely at times, and at 51 years old, she wanted to spend more time with the boyfriend she had met working in the wartime canteen. Joe was 55, single, short, medium build and a good bloke, according to Bessie. He had lived in Hoxton nearly all his adult life. He had been divorced from Edna, his wife, since 1912. They had two grown -up children, who had both moved out of London to live in one of the new suburbs surrounding the metropolis, after being given the tenancy of new council houses, which provided a better quality of life for their children.

Father had been promoted to deputy head porter at the Ritz Hotel. He regularly brought home stolen food from the large hotel fridges. 'There is more than enough grub for our punters (customers) to eat' said father, with a wicked smile. 'Especially those flashy Yanks. They love eating steaks. Food rationing doesn't apply to the Ritz, yer know. A Yank left nearly a whole steak on his plate the other day. I wrapped it up in paper and brought it 'ome.' Father would steal anything that didn't move.

Mind you, given the chance, so would most people. Mother had found a full-time job packing clothes in a warehouse in Bethnal Green. 'Owned by another Jew but forgotten 'is name. Wages not too bad though, and the place is a lot cleaner. The local inspectors 'ave told the owners to clean up their act,' she said sarcastically. Her head tic appeared to be less troublesome to her, probably because she was occupied with other things. Susan, now aged nine, had been at her new school, Repton, for three months. At the time, things were going well for her, and she had made friends.

As for me, I also had found my first job working in a large, stinking, evil-smelling factory shovelling animal bones into large, sticky hessian sacks. I hated the job from the first minute I set my eyes on the wretched-looking early Victorian building. It was unfortunate that the German bombing hadn't blown it to pieces. The owner, Alex Scott from Aberdeen, informed me and two other young lads just starting work that the bones came from many sources, former war horses, knackers' yards and wild dogs, to be boiled down and used as glue in the paper industry. It wouldn't have surprised me at the time, allowing for my previous experiences, if human bones had also been included in amongst the huge pile of various rotting waste. Unfortunately the waste didn't include our Scottish employer. But I wasn't in a position to be choosy. Besides, it was a pound or two in my pocket at the end of the week.

Most of the other workers, including two former soldiers, were local blokes, other than two middle-aged Africans who had jumped ship in Millwall Docks three years before.

'I'm Les,' I told both black men as we sat drinking our tea.

'Yeah, I'm Luther,' said the taller of the two men.

'And my name is Walter,' said the other.

It appeared that they had sailed from Nigeria, via several countries, collecting various minerals bound for London. Once there, they had taken their pay and a few pieces of clothing and scarpered into the anonymous maze of the East London streets. Employers, government officials, or whoever didn't give a damn who you were or where you came from. War had been very expensive for Britain; so as long as you could work, and the cheaper the better, you were welcome. If you found a job, then you kept it, even if it was cleaning shit out of cuckoo clocks, as my father used to joke.

After the post-war boom of 1919-20 had ended, British unemployment rose sharply, and would stay high until World War Two. The unemployment problem was particularly depressing for those many servicemen, our heroes, who had returned from the Western Front, where huge numbers of our soldiers had died, to find very few jobs on their return. Although, I didn't ask my two colleagues about their war experiences, they must have felt so worthless, after years of horrible war still fresh in their memories, to be given such a demeaning job as filling up bags with bones. That's all the soldiers had seen for four bloody years: human bones, broken, twisted, bent, snapped in pieces, blown to atoms, bloodied bones in rat-infested rainwater. Bones, bones and more bones!

A few months later Aunt Doreen wrote to my mother. She said Susan and I had done well at Compton. This wasn't true. We had both been polite to local people, studious at school and adapted well to village life, she said. All bullshit. Everybody was so sorry to see us leave for London. More bullshit.

I did, however, feel moved when mother told me that Farmer Goodheart had lost his eldest son on the Western Front, that evil place where thousands of young men had lost their lives in the mud, blood and stench. Apparently, four other local young men had laid down their lives and several others came back home with various wounds to convalesce at home or, if you were too damaged, in a local asylum. What was most surprising was the revelation that Robin Knox was not an architect, but worked for the government as a spy. That was the reason he was absent from his home for long periods of time. Who can you trust, I thought, in a world where you said one thing, yet did another? I was beginning to grow up!

In June 1920, at the grand old age of 15 years, I found my first girlfriend in the local pub, a real dive called the Locomotive. Mind you, most pubs round the East End were pretty awful places in those days. As the pub owners needed the money, they never asked your age, they sold alcohol regardless of how young you were. Connie wasn't exactly bright, but she was all I could find. Mind you, I was no film star. I had asked other local girls if they fancied going to the cinema, or having a beer, or having sex in the park. None of them said yes to any of my suggestions. So I was lumbered with Connie for a while, but she always turned up on time, and enjoyed buying us both chips and coke at least twice a week in Jake's café in Shadwell, where she lived with her parents and brother. Not an inspiring social life by any means. Connie worked in a large factory making hats for the export market. Well, that's what she told me. But as she was a little absent-minded, they probably ended up in North Scunthorpe.

One day I asked Connie, 'what do yer think of sex?'

'Not for me,' she quickly responded. 'Me mum told me

to be careful about men who want sex before marriage,' she reminded me, just in case I got other ideas.

'Don't yer fancy a bit of sex with me, Connie?' I bluntly asked. Her large mouth was still crammed full of chips.

'No I fuckin' don't,' she eloquently responded.

As young teenagers do, we quarrelled, we laughed, and due to the lack of money, we walked for miles around East London visiting many cafés along the way. I found most of them full of people, many of them unemployed former soldiers who were down on their luck. For the price of a cup of tea, and a few cigarettes, the owners let them keep warm inside for a few hours rather than throwing them out into the cold.

It was tragic to watch young men who had fought for their country and other younger and older unemployed men wasting their lives looking at four walls. Some of them, you could tell, were sleeping rough, most stank and hadn't washed or shaved for some time. Used by the Government to fight and kill other human beings, they were now thrown on the scrap heap. It made me think more deeply; why, I thought, had well over half a million Brits been killed during the war, yet two years later many had nothing to call their own in a land fit for heroes?

I carried on working for another eighteen months or so at the bone factory, where the stench overpowered you and human dignity was non-existent. Of course, I needed the money so that I could help out with family bills at the end of the week. Mother and Father didn't earn a great deal. As unemployment was high, you just put up with what employers threw at you. They knew you had nowhere else to go. Take it or leave it. So much for a country fit for heroes.

I read in the local *Stepney Gazette* that many former soldiers, depressed and embittered by what they had returned home to, grouped together and embarked on walking the various byways and tracks of Britain. They thought it would keep them healthier and dignified, and they hoped along the way to meet former colleagues. For some of those former soldiers, who had been traumatised by war experiences, it was an ideal opportunity to think about their future away from the demands of everyday life. They were supported by former colleagues. They hoped to find temporary or casual work with accommodation on farms, building sites, anywhere, as they walked about the countryside, the place they had fought and died for. Those brave young men, not frightened of attrition, gathered ever-growing support from other former soldiers and various people who were sympathetic towards their vision of self-sufficiency. So began a culture of walking as an alternative way of life, not just for former soldiers, but numerous others: tramps, the unemployed, the homeless and the mentally ill also took on the challenge.

One small consolation for the local unemployed, if you could call it that, was that in 1921, the Government increased benefit payments for the one million jobless in Britain. But the number of jobless people would grow much higher in the years that followed. At one stage it rose to over three million trying to find a job. The war had cost Britain dearly, not just in the number of men dead and wounded but in financial terms. It was not surprising that various hunger marches took place over the following years.

Out of the blue, so it seemed, Mother received a letter from the Peabody Trust, offering her a tenancy of one of their flats. She forgot, prior to moving to our current home in Sandhurst Street, that she had in fact made several applications to different sources to be housed. Peabody had just completed a large social housing development, comprising 60 flats, in Shadwell, and asked Mother if she was interested in moving.

In excited anticipation, my parents went to view the flat they had been offered as their new home. Even Bessie was impressed by the size of the two-bedroom flat, the large communal garden and the number of shops within a short walking distance. My parents were hesitant about moving home once again, but although 59 Sandhurst Street was a house with a garden, the Peabody offer was a new flat that would meet their needs as they grew older. Being aware that slum clearance had just started and an offer like this might not come around again, they decided to move. Mother was, nonetheless, nervous of the upheaval she would have to experience. Above all she loved the security of her own home, especially now the war was over and she could plan for the future.

With the tenancy agreements signed, my parents moved into their new flat, 4 Belfield Terrace, Roper Gardens, Shadwell, on 20 January 1922. As usual, Father, with the help of three dubious-looking characters, moved all their furniture in a small lorry to their new home, a new smartly-decorated flat, with a small balcony overlooking the communal garden. They cried with joy. Mother insisted that even if she were offered Buckingham Palace, she would still remain at Peabody, hopefully for the rest of her life. I was so pleased for my parents and for Susan, who was now 13 years of age and would soon be earning a living.

The Housing and Town Planning Act of 1919 (the Addison Act), all my family were interested to read in the local paper, was seen as a watershed in the provision, not before time, of council housing. At last, with the close of the Great War, a new social attitude had focused the Government's attention on a national responsibility to provide homes. Not before time working class families, some at least, could forward to being re-housed, But it took many years before some councils around the country got their financial act together.

Chapter Six

On the road with Sammy and Percy

The time had come for me to move on from the bone factory before it sent me insane or moronic, as I couldn't take it any more. Taller now and thin as a rake, with a mop of thick brown hair, I collected together a few warm clothes in my rucksack and my cherished war medal, and without any real notion of where I was going, I walked out of my parents' new flat. All I knew was that I had to get out of London for a while, mainly due to the continuing dark and depressing thoughts I kept having, but also to see how others lived.

Those painful inner experiences had first started rearing their ugly head when I had lived in Compton, or was it Sandhurst Street? Ever since, intermittently, they have been there banging away at me. There was no real explanation as to why they first started. As I didn't want my parents to worry, I left a brief note on the kitchen table explaining my departure. With a few pounds saved from my wages, I walked out of Belfield Terrace. It was about 12.30pm, a dry overcast day.

My mind was in turmoil as I took the packed, smoke-filled 22 bus to Kings Cross station. I stood on the pavement outside the busy station, not knowing where to go. I felt hopelessly lost amidst the noise of vehicles, trains and faceless people.

On impulse I bought a single ticket to Thirsk in East Yorkshire. Someone had mentioned Thirsk in a newspaper article I had read only last week, in connection with the moors nearby. It appeared that someone had got lost there, and was eventually found in a bad way, several hours later, by the police. Sod it all, Thirsk was to be my destination.

I was quite flabbergasted when the porter told me the journey would take over five hours. The only other time I had ever travelled by train was during the war, to Stowmarket, which took less than two hours. Don't worry about how long it takes, I kept reminding myself, get on the fucking train.

I sat on a crowded platform seat to eat my smelly cheese sandwiches. There were young families, couples and people on their own. Some read the *Evening News*, with the headline, 'Unemployment rises again this month'. Some smoked, while others looked straight ahead, probably, like me, listening to the deafening sound of the station Tannoy system announcing departures and arrivals of trains.

The huge steel engine, pulling ten varnished teak carriages, slowly pulled, steaming and hissing, out of King's Cross station at 4.15pm on that warm March day in 1923. From the back of the train, I gradually made my way along the corridor to near the front, where I found there to be fewer people. I found a compartment with only one person in it.

'Good afternoon young man,' said the middle-aged man courteously.

'Hallo there. Nice day, ain't it?' I replied.

After placing my knapsack in the overhead luggage rack and taking off the thick, warm, grey overcoat my parents had bought me last Christmas, I sat on the seat furthest from the other passenger. I felt safer.

It wasn't until we had been at least twenty minutes into the journey that the well-dressed, dark-haired man asked me if I would like a cigarette.

'No thanks,' I said.

'Do you mind if I smoke?' he asked. I didn't mind at all, besides it was a smoking compartment.

'Going very far?' he asked.

'No not really. Thirsk,' was my nervous, half-hearted reply.

'On holiday are you?' was another of his well-spoken, probing questions. I told him that my parents had been killed in Poplar during the devastating first daytime air raid on London. With no family left in London, I was going to stay with a friend of my father's, who lived a few miles from Thirsk.

'I'm awfully sorry to hear about the death of your parents, young man,' he said. 'My name is Toby

Wainwright. Here is my card with my telephone number. Please contact me if you ever need any assistance,' he said, smiling with a glint in his eye. At that moment, my mind took me back to decadent Mr Helling reminding me what glances like that could mean.

Halfway into my journey, I walked to the restaurant car, several carriages from where we were sitting, to buy tea for the affable Mr Wainwright and me. I noticed that the train had become occupied by many more passengers, some standing in the corridor talking and admiring the rural scenes, who must have boarded during the last three station stops. We sat there in silence drinking tea. Mine tasted more like warm kitchen slops.

As dusk descended and the temperature dropped, my co-passenger closed the small windows, which were slightly ajar, and pulled the white cotton curtains. 'I shall be getting off the train at Tenby station in about fifteen minutes' he said, smiling. 'My housekeeper will be there to drive me to our home some ten miles away. It was very good meeting you.'

He stood up like a soldier to button up his grey pinstriped suit, pulled on his gabardine jacket and locked his black briefcase. He shook my hand, slid open the door and walked rather briskly down the corridor, ready to descend on to the station platform. From what I could see of it, from the obscurity of my compartment, Tenby station looked very small and dimly lit, with several small flower beds and a ticket office. As he walked hurriedly out of the rural station, I thought that Mr Wainwright, who had his own telephone number, must have lived a comfortable life. I wondered what he did for a living. And more importantly, why did he give me, a young uneducated cockney from London, his personal details?

Now I was on my own in a warm, quite dirty, yet comfortable compartment. The only time I ventured out was to the toilet. My anxiety level rose considerably as I thought of the daunting prospect of arriving all alone at Thirsk station. Where could I go in a place full of unknown people?

An hour later the ticket inspector, a fat, surly bloke with no teeth, came round to inspect my ticket. 'On yer own son?' he asked me.

'That's right,' was my brief reply.

'Been to Thirsk before?'

'Yes, many times. 'Ow much longer does it take until I get there?' I asked the inspector, whose stomach bulged over his London and North Eastern Railway supplied trousers.

He looked at his pocket watch. 'About another thirty minutes,' he said. He left and closed the door. I pulled the curtains apart and all I could see through the window was a vast black of nothingness for many miles around. I became even more frightened and concerned. Where I was going to sleep, I didn't have a clue. If this had been the East End there would have been plenty of beds for a night's kip in the Salvation Army or Rowton House, but I was miles from nowhere.

One thing for sure came to my mind; I would have to use all my wits, if I was to stay safe away from the prying eyes of the police, or anyone who would know I came from London and was homeless. The aftermath of the war was still uppermost in the minds of people. Nearly every working-class family had lost a family member, or had one wounded. Recession was rampant throughout Britain. Unemployment was constantly rising. The last thing local people needed was a young homeless scrounging tramp from London. But where else could I have gone? It was out of short-sighted impulse that I had come to Thirsk in the first place.

I felt helpless and depressed. No doubt these locals would be similar to those people in Compton - full of animosity towards a young bloke viewed as a self-server, whose only motivation was to steal their hard-earned chattels.

The train pulled into Thirsk station around 9.30pm, and I sat in my compartment for a while to let the other passengers go ahead of me. When I stepped down onto the concrete platform, I felt cold, lost and all alone in an uncaring world. Why should others care, I thought to myself, about one young person with nothing to offer but trouble?

I looked around at the huge iron framework that held the station together. It was such an impressive sight. Not long ago, people of my great-grandparents' generation would have seen huge stations, like Thirsk, being built around the country. Although they did very little for poverty-stricken East Enders, Victorian wealth certainly built a transport infrastructure that was the envy of the world.

After a brief view of Thirsk station, I was accosted by two tramps begging for money, so I made my way out of the station. Before I set off, I made sure my uncle's medal was safe in my inside pocket. That medal represented, for me, bravery, honour and freedom. Qualities I certainly didn't possess. The wet dirty Cambridge Road outside was nearly empty, except for a few passing cars and a parked lorry delivering coal to a pub called the Railway Arms.

Two hundred yards down the road, I ventured into a café full of tramps and homeless people, who appeared to be in a similar predicament to me. It was a small dirty café, ill-lit, and full of old tables and chairs that had seen better days, just like most of its customers.

'Tea please governor,' I said to the old man serving.

'Here yer are young lad. That will cost you two pence,' said the old chap, who had snot running down his nose. 'Aye, yer a long way from London young lad,.

'I lost me parents in the London bombing' I lied. 'Got nowhere else to go, so I thought I'd try me luck in Thirsk.'

'Fuck all 'ere for yer boy,' he said. 'Most of the collieries and factories 'ave bin laying of men due to a surplus of coal, and as fer accommodation, forget it boy, many locals are living in near squalor. Local council's built a few 'ouses but things are grim.'

I found a vacant seat near six old tramps; they were all smoking and drinking tea. All of them stank like Farmer Goodheart's cowsheds. Their faces, I assumed, hadn't felt water for some considerable time. They didn't have thirty teeth between them, but they were friendly. Sammy, a tramp wearing an ex-army greatcoat, offered me a kerbside twist (a discarded cigarette) to smoke.

'How's it going young feller?' asked one of the other tramps, whose name was Percy.

'Lost me parents during the war,' I said, my standard reply. It transpired that Percy and the five other tramps in the café that night had all fought in World War One on the Western Front. Most of them looked years older than they actually were. Trench warfare, mayhem, death, the thousands wounded, rats, lack of food and fear had affected them all. After being demobilized from the Army, they had returned home, like so many thousands of other soldiers, to find there was very little for them after their years of slaughter and suffering. So Percy and his five friends in the café took to the roads, not only to recover from their war experiences but to try and find work. Most of the blokes in the café did not come from Thirsk. Tramping the byways and tracks of Yorkshire and other places had brought them inadvertently together. They all agreed that walking, begging and sleeping rough was hard most of the time, but it also brought support and camaraderie.

Another former soldier, Harry, who had lost his right eye fighting on the Somme, told me that if I was homeless, then I was welcome to kip with the six of them in an old deserted warehouse on the edge of town. I gladly accepted their kind offer, conscious of the fact that they had all experienced trauma during World War One.

An hour later, the seven of us walked out single file from Bob's café, just like prisoners being released, and continued along the Cambridge Road. Most of the shops and houses looked grim. We walked for a further mile or so in torrential rain, passing many more shops that appeared to have ceased trading as they looked empty. I was prepared for a cold wet night due to the fact I had the good fortune to have put two thick jumpers into my knapsack.

As we tramped along the road, I realised that so far I had not seen any bombed buildings, but nearly everything appeared to have black coal dust stuck to it like glue. Perhaps the Germans didn't think Thirsk was important enough.

'Turn right ere,' said Jake, whose old clothes were by now soaked, like the rest of us. To the onlooker, we must have looked a desperate sight at 1 am, tramping through the driving rain, talking and singing as if we didn't have a care in the world.

A postman on his bicycle said 'Good morning lads' as he passed us like a drowned rat on his way to work. I remember Bessie telling me that postmen, for the first time in 1880, began to use bicycles in the East End. We all walked down an alley, climbed through a hole in a fence and into the premises of J. Payne & Co, Building Suppliers.

The warehouse had been empty for some time. There were several holes in the roof and side walls, but that hadn't deterred these tough blokes from sleeping here the past year. As we entered the wet, damp, dirty building, I was taken aback by several wild cats that ran screaming past us. Using an old paraffin lamp for a light, Percy led the way to a small room at the back of the old warehouse. Once inside, I was amazed to find several old mattresses covered with many thick blankets. There were old wooden chairs, a table and even a worktop. The tea, and other items, were boiled or cooked on a wood burning stove they had built. What resourceful people, I thought to myself. There I was in my new home and I had no rent to pay.

Fred, pointed to where I would be sleeping. 'That'll keep yer warm son. Eh what's your name anyway?' he asked.

'I'm Les Tatter. I came up by train from King's Cross today. I'd only been half an hour in Thirsk before I walked into that greasy spoon café back there,' I explained.

'Percy told me yer lost yer parents in the London bombing during the war?' asked Sammy, another tramp. 'That's bad fucking luck son'.

'That's right, on 13 June 1917, the first daylight raid of the war. 162 were killed including 16 children. Bastard Germans!' I said angrily, I had no option, I thought, at the time but to give them a load of porkies about my parents.

About ten hours later we started to reappear from under our worn-out but comfortable blankets. I awoke feeling warm, relaxed and secure. What a stroke of luck it was meeting up with these men. Although I had only known them for a few hours, they came across as genuine people who knew what it was like to suffer extreme deprivation.

After a few minutes that rancid smell from the night before hit me again like a cannonball. God, how the stagnant air reeked! It was no wonder the cats did a runner when my six fellow tramps appeared.

The light of day revealed the true reality of my fellow tramps - for that was what I had become, a tramp. Mind you, compared to the rest, I smelt and was dressed like a middle-class choirboy, but it wouldn't last. Unknown to us all, Harry and Sylvester, two other tramps, had just returned from the High Street armed with milk, bread and wood they had stolen from two shops. 'Fuckin' easy to steal round 'ere,' said one-eyed Harry.

Both Jake and Harry came from Darlington, and had known each other as navvies repairing local roads before being conscripted. 'Darlington's full of families shagging each other if you ask me,' said Jake, a short, thin chap with shining blue eyes who walked with a stoop. 'At least three girls I knew had children by their fathers.'

In contrast to Jake, Harry was over six feet tall and stout, with hair like the mane of a wild horse. He had been brought up in children's homes, where he had personally experienced sexual and physical abuse by staff. But he wasn't bitter, just bad-tempered at times when others rubbed him up the wrong way.

Jake had boiled the water by burning logs in an oven he had made himself, and made tea. The fresh bread had been spread with butter that Fred had pulled out of his knapsack. I wasn't sure I wanted to eat the butter, because it resembled motor oil.

'How long you had that Fred?' I asked. He was a short, fat, toothless, friendly bloke from Manchester.

'Not long Les. About three weeks. The cold air keeps it fresh yer know,' he remarked.

'Up my fucking arse, more like three months,' groaned Harry.

All seven of us sat round the blazing fire drinking tea; some were smoking and the rest were eating various oddments they been carrying for a few days. As I didn't want to be poisoned, I ate the fresh dry bread. No wonder some of them had lost most of their teeth. Mind you, that may well have been the consequences of what they were given to eat during the war.

In the warm afternoon daylight, the size and extent of the damage to the warehouse was fully revealed. It must have been over a hundred feet long and fifty feet wide. One end of the roof had caved in and most of the broken windows had probably been vandalised by local kids, who at times were told by the tramps to stay away from the warehouse. All the kids did was shout abuse back. On two occasions the police had visited, but they were sympathetic towards the tramps.

For the next few months most days followed a similar pattern of survival. We split into three groups and went on stealing sprees around Thirsk town. Two of us came near to being caught by the police and shop owners. My partner in crime, Harry, and I were assigned to target food shops, of which there were plenty. We stole bread, cheese, cold meats and milk. Between them the others brought back wood, second-hand clothes, fruit, tea, coffee, papers and so on, and items we needed for everyday living. Being young and seeking sympathy from local people, I begged on numerous occasions, not just on the main road, but in the poverty-stricken working-class areas on the outskirts of the town. Although they had very little themselves - most lived on national assistance - their kindness really moved me when a few families asked me into their slum homes for tea and bread.

Most of the time it was the elderly people who gave me a few pennies or a bag of food. One dear old lady of about 80, who was a regular church attendant and often observed carrying her bible, wanted to invite me back to her home for a meal. She looked down at me sitting on the pavement dressed like a workhouse urchin.

'You come back to my warm home young man for a hot meal, with Jesus as your guide,' she said. 'If you repent your way of life, I shall give you a bible of your own.'

On another occasion I was accosted by a well-dressed drunken middle-class bloke carrying a bag full of bottles of alcoholic drink. He was so drunk that he was listing from one side of the pavement to the other like a battleship in a storm.

'Hallo, young man, would you like a drink with me in my home? It's very comfortable there.' He smiled and winked at me, no doubt after one thing.

That same afternoon, a young patrolling police officer stopped in front of me. 'You are young to be begging' he said. Once again, as many times before, I gave him the same old spiel about my parents being killed during the war. After that explanation, he continued patrolling.

In the evening I walked back to my 'hotel' in the warehouse holding various goods I had acquired from my daily begging. Just before entering the alley leading to my abode, on the corner of Maybury Gardens, a newspaper shop placard announced that the British Broadcasting Company has been founded and they had opened a 'Radio Service'.

After a while, I wondered what Thirsk was really about. Was it just like any other place in Britain? On the outside people appeared relatively decent. They said hallo, good day and good morning. People smiled, nodded and gestured. Regarding the seven tramps traipsing round their town, given the opportunity, the people with money and security would probably have kicked them out as soon as possible, even though those so-called tramps had fought for their country. Less than five years on from that mayhem, people had now forgotten all about those brave men who were supposed to inherit a land fit for heroes. Not surprisingly, all most people thought about was surviving from day to day. Reality, it appeared, what was in front of your eyes as you counted your money, ate your food, if you had any, and kept warm in front of a warm fire with coal provided by miners working miles underground for peanuts. Reality for most was the cost of someone else's loss. Reality was a double-edged sword. Believe nothing you are told, and only half what you see.

Probably most people in Thirsk, like most other people, didn't actually enjoy living where they did or with the person they thought they loved. But anything was better than living on one's own with little food or being a degraded homeless person who owned nothing whatsoever except the clothes he stood up in, which applied to many local unemployed working-class people. During wartime people rallied to each other's assistance. Positive emotion for the benefit of humanity has, in most poverty-stricken areas, been long forgotten. The name of the useful game, if you have money, is sex; it has always been a bargaining tool, used to advance those who wield the most potent power, to grasp what is available for their use only. Giving sex freely to those with that power will offer you potential opportunities that can help you live a better life. Call it love and all manner of earthly and spiritual resources shall be forthcoming, but only if you play the game skilfully. Woe betide you if you get caught faking the game. Banishment awaits, minus your dignity, to those who are so stupid, immature and naive as to think others haven't read their scripts.

These were the thoughts and feelings I experienced when the dark demons descended upon me. Most of the time I kept them at bay by ignoring their intrusion, but occasionally their negative feelings overwhelmed me.

When I was in Thirsk, there was a mix of middle and working-class people. To the north-east of the town, stretching all the way to the sea, were bleak moors, hills, forests and a few collieries. There had been a cattle market in the town since around 1750. Many small farms that once thrived now stood deserted. It was the collieries and factories, a few miles out to the north and west of the town, that once provided the bulk of the work for most working-class men. Many of the collieries, apparently, are now unproductive, due to cheaper coal being imported. Plumes of dirty smoke could be seen belching out from the tall factories. And if the wind happened to be a strong south-westerly you could also smell the acrid factory smoke engulfing Thirsk. Others men worked in forestry, or building desperately needed council houses to replace slum clearance, or at the Garnside Power Station some ten miles to the north-west. The famous - or infamous - Eagle Hotel (it all depends how you value decadent behaviour) used to be the central meeting place for the more affluent farmers. Once they had sold or bought their livestock, they drank and ate to excess for several hours. Sammy informed me that there had been many a fist fight between drunken farmers fought outside the hotel. Apparently the police used to throw them into the cells to sober up.

Chapter Seven

Mucking out

A few months later Sammy, Percy and me decided to try our luck in another area, Slinton, four miles to the south-west of Thirsk. It was suggested by Sammy, who had visited the place some three years before on one of his many wanderings. Taking a track at the back of the railway station and alongside the coal depot, the walk into Slinton, allowing for a smoke, eating sandwiches and a lie-down in the September sun, took no more than a few hours. Lying there I thought about my family, as I did most days, and wondered how they were all coping financially after the war. I thought about the senseless work in the bone factory, and the sympathetic feelings I had for the two soldiers who had worked there with me.

But looking at the wild orange common bird's foot trefoil which carpeted most of the walk lifted my spirits.

On arrival in Slinton, a hamlet with one small early 19th century pig farm and three labourers' cottages, Sammy took us to the derelict barn where he had dossed for a few nights. He was pleased to find that the large hessian sheet he had left there was still in a fit state to use as cover on one side of the old 18th century building. That old barn had certainly seen better days before we arrived, but the friendly farmer gave us various used materials so we could make it habitable. From then on we were on good terms with John Dunn, who, along with his wife Alice, had farmed at Nine Elms for many years. He found us regular work around the farm, for which we were recompensed with large regular meals, well cooked by his old, thin, but active wife.

In the evenings we sometimes spent time in one or other of the farm labourers' cottages smoking and, drinking home-made cider, which was powerful enough to knock a horse over, and joking with the workers and their wives. During the drunken bouts, I often fancied making love to Tom's buxom wife Ingrid, who with elephant-sized thighs, looked and spoke as though she had been socialised by the animals. Drinking with Tom and the other farm labourers gave us the opportunity to sleep in front of their cosy warm log fires, instead of freezing in the old barn, which housed rodents, feral cats and numerous birds. Mind you, all three workers' houses had depressing dark brown walls, and there was a constant lingering rancid smell of tobacco, alcohol, human sweat and excrement. It wasn't for the faint hearted. All the workers, their wives and children had lived there, it appeared, contentedly for years.

Occasionally Tom drove pigs to the nearby Thirsk market to be sold, which gave me the opportunity to post my first letter to my parents in nearly a year. Other than the market, the workers' lives revolved around the farm. Most of the adults and the three children appeared to be semi-illiterate. Life, I assumed, must have been terribly boring for them, but I found them really decent people, who, I think, enjoyed our company while it lasted. It seemed like another planet living in Slinton, compared to the noisy and crowded way of life I had been used to in London.

John Dunn and his wife were both born and brought up in Newcastle. He and Alice moved to Thirsk in their middle 20s, when they were given the opportunity to farm Nine Elms, which had been left in a run-down state by the previous farmer. The Dunns had worked hard to rebuild Nine Elms into a small productive farm. 'It's been a hard life, but a good one,' John said to me one night over a pint of his home-made beer. He also told me that they did not wish to bring children into such a violent world.

During my regular mornings work mucking out the sties, as the pigs sniffed and snorted round me, John asked me about my past. 'What's a young lad like you doing up here all the way from London, Les?' he asked.

I gave my usual response about my parents being killed in the war. That was one occasion when I wished I had been straight with John. What was the point, I kept asking myself, of continuing to lie about my past? It was something I had to confront sooner rather than later.

Tom and the other two workers, Amos and Henry, and their wives were all born in Thirsk. They all told Sammy, Percy and me various stories, usually influenced by alcohol, about watching German planes flying overhead in the night sky, but no bombs were ever dropped, they informed us, around Thirsk or outlying areas. Mind you, a lot of their stories had to be taken with a pinch of salt. Amos, who was built like a highland bull and as thick as two short planks, reckoned that one night during the war he had witnessed a round spacecraft land not a hundred yards from Nine Elms Farm. Allowing for his mentality and the ten pints of the gut-rot cider he drank nearly every day, his story is hardly surprising. He was, though, a good, charitable man, who, given the opportunity, would usually help you. With enough cider and encouragement, he would undress to his filthy black underpants and throw a 56lb iron weight an amazing distance.

Just three weeks before we left Nine Elms, I was thrilled to receive a letter from my parents, as John had allowed me to use his address. I told John to expect a letter from my brother. Not surprisingly, Mother was angry that I hadn't waited to explain to her and father what I was experiencing at the time, instead of running away from home. She emphasized that she and father would have supported me. Everyone in the family had been constantly worried about me, especially as I had not written for over a year. Anyhow, she was now mightily relieved that I was well, working and travelling around Yorkshire, although I did not mention my associates were tramps or the thieving we had done. All three of us were gentlemen of the road, and that made me feel good about myself. Life was teaching me a thing or two.

Mother now worked as a cleaner in Bellfield Terrace. She loved it there and found everyone friendly. Father was ensconced at the Ritz Hotel as deputy head porter, but unofficially he removed more food from the tables for his own use than the waiters did. Susan had found a job working in a clothes factory near Poplar. It was work that at least gave her a regular income. She loved living in the Shadwell flats, as did my parents. Bessie was well and enjoyed running the café near Cable Street, where she kept everyone in check like a bullish field marshal. Most surprising of all was that Bessie and Joe were still an item.

The last paragraph of the letter was bad news; both great-grandparents had contracted an illness. Florence, aged 82, had been diagnosed with lung cancer and Tom, 78, had been medicated for a heart condition. The wheel of life was moving once again. I wrote back to Mother immediately, expressing my deep concern for my great-grandparents. I explained that my two friends and I were moving on from Nine Elms Farm to work elsewhere. Once I got another opportunity, I would write to her again.

We had decided to move on from Slinton, even though we had really enjoyed our time living and working with decent people at Nine Elms. All the farm workers were characters in one way or another, especially the powerful Amos, who could lift a pig above his head.

'It were also good ter see pigs livin' their short lives foraging in the fields fulla cowslip, buttercup, winter cress and hedge mustard', Percy remarked.

We didn't want to return to our other friends back in Thirsk, because Sammy had another interesting idea about walking east across the North York Moors to another village where he had briefly worked, called Sinnington. Besides, I had on two occasions visited the other four tramps in the warehouse when Tom and I had been at Thirsk market. Each time I gave them a large parcel of food that we had made up for them at the farm. They would survive.

After a goodbye party the night before, Sammy, Percy and I departed early one morning from Nine Elms on 12th June, 1924. Only three days after my 19th birthday, but I looked forward with excitement to the world that awaited me. With knapsacks full of food and warm clothes, we walked briskly along well-worn local stony tracks, just as I had done with David Cecil, full in places with mauve ground ivy, heading for Oldstead, a small hamlet, on the western boundary of the North York Moors.

Halfway through the eleven-mile journey we found a small patch of shaded grass away from the intense summer sun to eat our much-needed food. We soon attracted crows and rooks, as they bobbed around us waiting for handouts. Both types of birds are aggressive, and if hungry, will come menacingly close to get food.

'Where you from Sammy?' I asked my short, slim friend, who had a raucous laugh. He constantly chain smoked if given the opportunity, and would drink anything that smelt of or resembled alcohol.

'I was born in Northumberland, but when I was a kid of about five, my parents first moved ter Penrith, then ter Ripon ter work in steel factories,' he explained. 'At the age of six I was abused in a children's home. When I was about 17, I left home fer good. I've lived in many different places, but I'm really a wanderer. I don't belong anywhere really. That's the way I like it, Les'.

He lit up a kerbside twist and took a few swigs from a cider bottle. Walking had made him into a wiry, strong and self-sufficient man. During his 40 years, he had travelled several thousands of miles, either on his own or with other like-minded people. I liked Sammy, and during our time together, I thought I got to know him quite well. That's if it's possible to really get to know someone, anyone, which is very doubtful. We all have inside us an utter darkness that refuses to let many of us emerge, most of the time. My other self made sure that part of me remained hidden to most people, especially when I was asked personal or confusing questions that frightened and panicked me into being somebody, or something, else. I often fantasised about being a red admiral or peacock butterfly, then I could grow wings, become independent and free and fly away to any place I choose, usually a safe place where no one, except a few chosen people, could find me.

Sammy went on to explain to Percy and me about his painful, frightening experiences of being gassed in the trenches during the battle of the Somme. 'Aye, I lost several close comrades. They were blown to bits. Arms, legs and blood every fucking where. Many of my comrades were severely wounded and had to be taken back to Britain. Many had limbs missing. 'Orrible gaping fucking wounds in comrades' heads, their backs, stomachs. It was a fucking nightmare,' explained Sammy, near to tears. So moved was I that I pretended to go for a crap behind a tree, but instead I cried, thinking about those young, innocent lads who never returned home to their families. It was the unknown walkers like Sammy and Percy that made up the bulk of those former soldiers, walking, for numerous reasons, along hidden byways to find their inner peace and sanity.

We all sat there in silence, pondering, no doubt, on what Sammy had just told us, until it was agreed that we should continue our walk to Oldstead. The same stony track from Slinton took us over the shallow flowing Cod Beck River, then three miles more of walking through scrub, bracken and ling until we entered the village of Thirkleby. It was a quiet, still place, with an inn called the Jolly Farmer, post office, church with spire and several early Victorian cottages. It reminded me of a place time had forgotten. We wondered if all the inhabitants had died of a mystery disease, or whether they were frightened to come out to speak with us. We didn't see anyone. After ten minutes we took the hint, and carried on walking the last two miles over rough terrain into Oldstead. We were in for a shock. When we arrived it was even smaller than Thirkleby. Had all the village people, similar to the last place, known we were coming and hidden, hoping we would soon move on again?

We sat on the only village seat, which was very old and had seen better times, to rest our weary feet. When

I took off my boots to air my feet, an almighty smell hit our noses. The Nine Elms pigsties smelt of perfume compared to my stinking feet. My second-hand socks were about ready to disintegrate.

'That's a great way of meeting the residents,' said Percy, who very rarely wore socks. Percy, now 36 years of age, was short and bald and had a disproportionately fat belly for his size. He was born in North Wales, where his father worked as a farm labourer. In common with most people, they had always experienced very hard times there. He had three sisters, who were all older than him. When he was young, being so light, his ambition was to be an apprentice jockey. He wrote to a Newmarket horse trainer requesting an interview for a job. He never got a reply. Instead, he moved to Liverpool, where he found work in a factory making lampshades for the export market, until he volunteered to join the Welsh Guards to fight on the Western Front. Like many thousands of others, he was bombed and gassed and suffered shell shock for a while. Since being demobbed, he had not met any of his family, although a friend had got a message through to his parents to say he was well. After a year of utter poverty in Manchester, he couldn't find a job, and slept rough most of the time; he starting walking, hoping at some stage he would find work. That's how he met the other tramps. He loved the open road, the wandering on foot, that tramping gave him.

We were sitting on the seat, airing our dirty feet and eating the last of our cheese sandwiches, when a frail old man using a walking stick approached us. He looked like a walking ghost. His hair was chalk white. He was very thin and his old skin just about stretched over his spectacled face. He had sunken eyes and bony hands. It was difficult to know which was the oldest, the village seat or the old man. He appeared out of nowhere, it seemed.

'Good day gentlemen. I hope you are all well?' he asked. His teeth were stained varying shades of yellow and brown. At around 80 years old, he reminded me of a biblical figure I once saw in a schoolbook that Miss Cohen had given us.

We explained where we had come from, and said we were looking for some temporary work and shelter for a few days or longer.

'My name is Mr George. Come with me to my house for tea and sandwiches, and I'll see what I can do for you all,' he said, pointing at a large detached house only fifty feet from where we sat. He lived in a most beautiful early 19th century Gothic-styled house. There were two large gardens, front and rear, planted with many different late spring/early summer flowering plants. It was the large mass of daffodils at the front of the house that caught my eye. There must have been hundreds of them. And in the middle of the front garden stood a large flowering gorse bush standing well over six feet tall. Being a wild flower bush, I imagined he had acquired it from a woodland margin or heath locally. It was obvious that Mr George's garden had been professionally cared for over the years.

'Looks if the old boy 'as a few quid,' observed Sammy, as he nudged me in the ribs.

We marched in single file into his large kitchen, where we were introduced to his housekeeper, Mrs

Bainbridge. She was dressed in an appropriate black uniform and aged about 50, tall, well-built and stern looking, like an upper-class nanny; the sort of person who constantly reminds you that you are from of an inferior class. Even at a first glance, I observed, she reduced Sammy and Percy to the lowest form of life.

'Tea and sandwiches for all of you?' she asked.

The large well-decorated kitchen was at least twice the size of my parents' living room. It had a wooden table and six chairs in the middle. We were never invited into any of the other rooms during our time at Moorlands, the name of the Mr George's country pile.

My two friends and I sat opposite the old chap across the table talking, eating and drinking tea. I assumed our host had once been a horse rider or owner or something similar, as there were four framed prints of various coloured horses by the artist George Stubbs on the kitchen walls.

'I have lived here for forty years and I've loved every minute of it,' he said. 'When I was younger, I used to walk on my own for miles across the moors, sometimes twenty miles in one day. Alas, due to my age, I'm now unable to do so.' He had noticeably become rather sullen. Minutes later he remarked, 'Make the most of your time boys, because life is nasty, brutish and short.'

We each in turn told Mr George a little about our lives. How much of what we were prepared to communicate to a total stranger can be left to the imagination. My two tramping friends did recount their experiences of being on the Somme, unemployment and walking around the country looking for work. I did not mention the fictional deaths of my parents, but I told all three men about my experiences of London being bombed, my time in Compton and working in a mind-numbing bone factory before I left home in March 1923.

The old man, fixed his eyes intensely on the table for a few minutes. Then he got up, with the aid of his stick, and said he could help us. It transpired that the other three large Gothic detached houses in the village - there were no other buildings - had been designed and built by one of Mr George's forebears during the reign of William IV. 'Who in the fuck was 'e', commented Percy.

'If you are interested, boys, this is what I propose,' he said. 'I need the gardens, and some adjoining land, of all four houses to be maintained. You can sleep in my warm barn down the bottom of the garden and my housekeeper shall prepare your food each day. There will be no payment involved'.

After a brief discussion, we agreed to the old chap's proposal. We weren't in a position to refuse, of course, and he knew that. But we had got ourselves a decent place to kip, eat and do a bit of work into the bargain.

Like three tramps being led to the workhouse, we walked in single file escorted by the upright Mrs Bainbridge, who swung her arms, according to Sammy, like a soldier, until we reached the barn. It was small, clean, warm and tidy, and ideal for our few needs. In no time at all, we had made our beds from hay and various blankets that lay in one corner.

'We'll all be as hot as toast tonight,' said Percy, who wasn't used to such luxuries. Mind you I was still cautious of both men, as they wouldn't blink an eye before stealing all my belongings when I was asleep; they had been taught to survive.

There was even a tap with cold running water where we could wash ourselves, including our stinking feet. If there were various rodents in the barn, I surmised, no sooner had they smelt Sammy's feet than they would be gone in a flash.

Thirty minutes later, Mrs Bainbridge brought us three large bowls of hot soup, half a loaf of warm bread and a jug full of tea. We tucked into our food, and didn't come up for air until it was all devoured. Before falling off to sleep that first evening, I thought of Mrs Bainbridge and the fear I recognised in her eyes. I felt she suffered from the fear of loneliness, something I experienced most of my young life. It is a fear that has the potential of taking over the inner lives of any unsuspecting soul.

Perhaps her fear had been brought about by living on her own. Although we never found out, we wondered whether she had had a husband who was killed during the war. Or had he died naturally, had she been divorced or had he walked out of the marriage? Now that she was cooped up with Mr George, enjoyment didn't exactly appear to be a way of life.

After eight hours of sleep, I was the first out of my bed of straw. I washed my face in cold, invigorating water and had a quick look around outside before our breakfast. Except for the occasional high-pitched screams of swifts, all was silent as I looked across the soundless lonely moors to the hills north-west of Oldstead. Some way off a solitary kestrel hovered for a few seconds, until it made a powerful aerial dive upon a little rodent minding its own business. To the east were various lush green forests of oak, beech and elm. The whole magnificent natural picture in front of me was something I would continually experience for the next few months, and I would sometimes, when not working at Moorlands, make the occasional trip into the heart of its dark interior.

Many wild animals roamed round the hills, forests and moors looking for food and shelter; roe deer, rabbits and foxes, to name a few. Various birds and rodents, would make tentative raids to nibble the softer domestic plants at Moorlands. It was during this time that the newly-formed Forestry Commission started planting thousands of fast-growing conifers. Supplying the Great War with timber had depleted Britain of most of its indigenous trees. It was certainly a nature lover's paradise my friends and I had found to work, eat and sleep in for the duration. Mind you, Mr George and his friends did not have a sentimental view of their near surroundings. Over the years they had shot rabbits, and most other wild animals, for sport. Vermin, the locals called them.

After our breakfast, Mr George put the three of us to work sawing three long slim elm trees into small pieces to keep the homes resourced for cooking, hot water and fires. We were never allowed inside any of the houses, except in Mr George's kitchen to eat our food, as they no doubt thought we would steal anything in sight. How right they were! The other three houses also had housekeepers, who used to show their faces occasionally when requiring wood, fruit from the orchards or vegetables from the small allotments we tendered. They were, of course, instructed not to waste their owners' time speaking to reprobates like us.

One did, however, speak to me on several occasions when out of sight of the owners where she worked and lived some one hundred yards away. Geraldine Gould was only 25 years of age, not unattractive, short and well-built with long brown hair tied into a ponytail. She was about as thick as I was, but kind, and we enjoyed the occasional cigarettes we had together behind the barn where I slept. Unfortunately, she refused my sexual advances. Even in the 1920s, you could still be sacked for talking to someone beneath your social status. She had got the housekeeper job through reading a magazine, *Countryside Vacancies,* in her local library. Although the position was similar to in-service before World War One, she could go home some weekends or weekdays to visit her family. If she had had a car, she would have had the opportunity to drive home every evening. But purchasing a car, for someone like her, was no more than a dream.

After World War One, many of the owners of large estates were unable, for numerous reasons, to keep them going. Many were sold off to institutions, and many were left to fall into disrepair. In Britain, the economy experienced a decade of deflation and stagnant growth. Hitherto cheap labour had been plentiful to run those opulent grand estates, where pampered lives and privileged families were sustained by armies of cheap skivvies. That had all but finished. Yet a lot of those working-class people who depended on in-service work now found themselves amongst the ever-growing number of unemployed people.

Everyday life was basically the same at Moorlands: work, food and sleep. The first three weeks were taken up sawing and cutting the various dead trees that had been lying around the gardens of all four houses, for some time. Mr George had a regular load of large logs and smaller trees delivered by James Beckinsale, who owned a farm near Ampleforth. The latter was a prosperous place with several farms, large houses, an inn and a private school. Several times after helping Mr Beckinsale we used to drive into Thirsk to collect a month's supply of groceries for the four houses of Oldstead. A huge amount of food was consumed by the small hamlet. On two occasions the farmer allowed me to post a letter to my parents and visit the tramps at the old warehouse. There were only two of them left; Harry and Sylvester had departed a few weeks previously with the intention of walking west to Ripon, and then, hopefully, to the Dales. Jake and Fred looked underfed; in fact they looked thin and malnourished. All I could give my two remaining buddies was a few warm blankets I had stolen from Mr George's barn. I also gave them a few pounds of fresh fruit that had been stored in the same barn. They too thought the right time had come to move on as local shopkeepers, police and the public were giving them a hard time. I wished them well, and I never saw them again.

Once Beckinsale treated me to a Thirsk special, a fried meal consisting of food produced locally: eggs, bacon, liver and sausages, the best meal I had had since leaving London. For a while I regained my confidence in humanity. 'No bombs landed round 'ere, but plenty did along the east coast due to ship building and armaments factories,' was Beckinsale's reply to my question about German wartime bombing. He explained to me that the large scar on the side of his face and neck, had been sustained in 1899, during the second Boer War. His painful war experiences and a hard, single life making a living rearing a few hardy sheep next to the North York Moors had made him, understandably, a stoical man. He didn't speak more than 500 words whilst in my company.

There was a period of seven days when all we could do was keep dry inside our living quarters, alongside the rodents. When it rained on the moors, it sounded as though a monsoon had come upon us. All manner of weather hit the place: snow, hail, sleet, fog, mist and frost. The moors were always beautiful, but never more so than after bad weather, when the sun shone on all life.

Percy in particular, couldn't stop walking around the barn during our confinement. The war had left its mental, as well as physical, scars on him, as it had done on thousands of soldiers. Due to mental problems after the war, he had two short spells as a voluntary patient in his local asylum. 'All they gave me was this fuckin' awful jollop to drink' muttered Percy, whose hands, the size of shovels, started shaking. 'Tasted like vinegar, it did. The food weren't bad, but there were some terrible cases in there from the war. Shell shock it was called. Fucking terrible. I wanted out.'

It was during this forced rest that Percy showed me the tattoos he had had done after the war. On the top half of his right arm was a skull and crossbones, with the inscription *'born to lose'* underneath. On the other arm was a tattoo of a standing soldier holding a rifle, with another inscription *'never again'*. Life is shit, I thought to myself, as Percy walked out into the torrential rain for some solitude.

My dark days had returned once again during the past few weeks. My other self had started to reassert its dominance over me. I knew what was happening to me, but could do very little to stop the 'black dogs barking,' as I called them. I looked at my two tramping friends, or whatever they were called, and thought they were out to get me - to do me in, beat me up or something more sinister. I kept checking that they hadn't stolen my rucksack, with its sparse contents inside, the only possessions I had in the world, except for the medal I kept in my inside shirt pocket. I wasn't sure at this stage whether it was a knapsack or rucksack. My rucksack was different to the other tramps, whose knapsacks were given to them after the war.

I was becoming very confused about what was going on around me. Yet again I felt myself bottom of the heap, just as when I had been young, scratching a living working for that old bastard Mr George. He must have had a fortune; he owned one large house, probably other properties as well as a car, and gods know what else, yet he treated us like animals. Everything in all four wealthy houses was out of bounds to scum like us, we were restricted to his kitchen. We ate and drank from different cutlery and crockery from those used by him and his kind. In all the time we worked our guts out for him, he never once asked us whether we would like warmer clothes or comfortable boots to combat the bitter winds that flew at you across the moors like an Arctic storm.

Many times during my stay at Moorlands, I was really tempted to steal money, food or clothes from Mr George's house. I occasionally mentioned it to Percy and Sammy, but they weren't that keen. Sammy was correct when he said, 'how much can we carry on foot? How far would we get before the police pick us up?'

When I didn't feel well, I did act irrationally. In one of my most intense, fearful, lonely times, I thought of stealing Mr George's car, stealing his money, and driving away with Geraldine beside me. It was during these acute phases of gloom, darkness and depression that the splendid mental pictures of the colourful peacock butterfly, with his strong wings of freedom, helped me overcome, somewhat, my dark thoughts.

However, later in a more rational state of mind I asked Mr George if my parents could send me a letter using his house as an address. He agreed, which was very reassuring as it provided some sort of emotional contact to my parents. There were times when I missed them so much that I felt like crying, which I did on occasions when on my own. The malaise that had somehow taken over me was at times unbearable. It was the main reason for leaving home, or rather running away from parents who were decent, caring people and, no doubt, if they had known about my problems, they would have supported me. Although London was my home, if I returned, there would be very little work for me due to my age, lack of skills and the rising unemployment.

At other times my main preoccupation was the idea of suicide. The deeper I went into myself, the more of a reality such terror became. On occasions, I was preoccupied thinking about the nasty methods I would use to end my life. Everywhere around me. Life was shit; a deep descent into hell and obscurity seemed a relief from my daily torment. As the last war had demonstrated, life was short, and full of suffering and torment. You didn't have much to live for. If you were very lucky, after the age of 70 you lived in a cold room at home, usually alone all day, as those looking after you had to work. The government had taken the best of you, and for recompense they gave you a miserly means-tested pension. It was at such moments, when my feelings were so intense, that I usually resorted to the fantasy of being as free as a butterfly.

My darkness lifted, somewhat, when I received a letter from my parents two months later. 'Our dear darling Leslie, we miss you so much...' the letter began. Tears came to my eyes when I read that my great-grandfather Tom Smith, aged 79, had died of a heart attack, peacefully in his sleep, three months previously. He had had a wonderful local church ceremony which was attended by his family and many former colleagues. He was buried in the local church next to his daughter Jane.

I felt so bereft that I hadn't seen or written to him and Florence for at least three years. It confirmed my previous thinking that life is not worth living. My dear old Tom Smith had done his bit, as they say, from cradle to the grave. In that cheap coffin, his flesh, organs and blood would rot until only his old bones remained for the worms to crawl over.

In some detail, Mother explained that she was well and still worked as a cleaner. Father had been sacked by the Ritz for stealing food, which was no surprise, but had found another job as a lorry driver delivering coal to local people. Now that she was approaching 60, Bessie had found a part-time job working in a Hungarian bakery in Whitechapel, where she made customers laugh from morning to night. Good old Bessie, I thought, what a character. Unlike me, she didn't let life, with all its misery, hardships and suffering, get to her. My great-grandmother's lung cancer had deteriorated and she had lost weight, but at the age of 84, she clung to life for all it was worth. Susan, now 17, was also well; she had found another local job as a machinist, making various women's clothes for the fashion market. Good luck to them all.

On my last trip to Thirsk with Farmer Beckinsale, I posted what would be my last letter to my parents for some time, as Mr George had already informed the three of us that we were no longer required. I thanked them so much for writing, but had to explain to my parents the position I was in and that I hoped to write in the near future. 'Well done lads for all the good work you have done here in the past 14 months' said the half-smiling Mr George, whose bony face had, since we first arrived, deteriorated into a near skeleton. 'Good house and garden maintenance. Your well-developed vegetable garden and fruit orchard are productive. Here's two pounds each, a bundle of sandwiches made by Mrs

Bainbridge and three large bottles of beer to quench your thirst as you travel.'

'Hooray!' I shouted. We were back on the road once again.

We walked east along a narrow well-worn sheep track heading for Nawton, a small village on the southern boundary of the North York Moors. It was about a ten-mile journey and full of interest. Mr George had given us the address of a farmer friend of his in Nawton who could find us some work. How time had flown, I thought to myself, since we had first entered Nine Elms farm.

It was a hot August day as we made our way along narrow roads and tracks (former byways for cattlemen) to our first stop, Ampleforth. With more than twelve hours of daylight on our backs and alcohol and sandwiches to nourish our fit bodies, we found walking the five miles easy. In turn we were treated to the delights of lapwing, curlew, redshank and large flocks of red grouse, who were all feeding on the abundant wild food. If we could have caught the buggers, it would have given us a limitless food store. Large areas of sessile oak could still be found on the south of the moors, but the Scots pine, even at this stage, was the dominant species, although few in number.

We were quite apprehensive about what affluent Ampleforth would make of us as we entered their village, sat down on their charming small green, full of roses, to wash our feet and pollute yet another pond full of ducks and geese. There we lay on the warm lush green grass soaking up the early evening sun. We had finished the alcohol and sandwiches a mile back in the shade of Burtis

Wood, where Sammy, incidentally, had eaten raw wild mushrooms with his sandwiches. Sammy told Percy and me that the edible mushrooms were called chanterelles.

'They grow in damp places, they do, usually underneath mature oak trees,' he explained. 'Being on the road nearly all me life, the land's taught me about its ways and bounties that help yer survive. Most people will give yer fuck all.'

With the money that Mr George had given us ready to spend, we walked the fifty yards into the local 17th century inn, the Japps Cross. Apparently John Japps was a notorious local highwayman who had robbed many a local person of his money. The inn was a tatty old place full of dirty old chairs, tables and floorboards. They were only fit for the blazing log fire which burned in front of us. The bar reeked of masculine sweat, infused by cheap tobacco and ale. It was the only opportunity working men had to have a beer together away from the beck and call of their employers and families.

'Three pints of ale, please governor,' Sammy said to a surly-looking old man with grey mutton chops and a pipe sticking out the side of his wide mouth.

'There yer go boy,' said the barman, as he placed the beer on the bar. 'That'll be one shilling and sixpence for 'em all. Yer been tramping the roads lads?'

'Yep, apart from the young un. Me and my friend 'ere been tramping those byways since Armistice Day in November 1918,' was Sammy's response. 'We came home to fuck all after fighting for our country on the Somme. A terrible injustice, that's what it was, to all those brave young men that died and those that came home to bloody nothin', so we tramp roads to try and find work.'

'Sorry to hear that lads, we all owe you a great debt for what you did in winning freedom for Britain. We all thought the first Labour Government to be elected the year before last, led by Ramsay MacDonald, would change things for working people, but they lasted only a few bloody months in power. Conservatives got back in didn't they?' said the barman.

For the next three hours the three of us drank several pints of ale bought by local farm workers. They were exempt from war duty as their employers needed them to work the land, producing much-needed food for the country. Before we left the inn, the three of us being well drunk, the governor of the place, Arthur Balding, gave us a pile of lamb sandwiches, a large home-made cake and three large bottles of cider to take with us. We felt that God had smiled down on us once again as we walked down the road singing at 10.30. We had nowhere to sleep, but it was a warm night and ideal for sleeping under the stars. We left Ampleforth - I'm sure they were glad to see us depart - and took an old droving track with a signpost pointing six miles to Nawton.

'That's too fucking far to walk tonight lads,' said Sammy, who could usually walk for miles. 'Let's walk a couple of miles and sleep outside Sproxton.'

Less than two hours later we found a patch of short grass under a large beech tree, where we bedded down for the night. Thousands of midges kept me awake for a while, as they buzzed and darted around my head trying to eat me alive. The other two were asleep in seconds, snoring and farting like the wind section of the Salvation Army Band.

The noise of squabbling rooks above woke me at around 6 am. It was another warm summer day. I had a hangover from all the alcohol I had drunk the night before. I took off my trench coat and two thick jumpers I had worn during the night and dipped my head into a nearby cattle trough. The cold water brought my faculties back to life again. Sammy and Percy were both awake and smoking the fag ends they had taken from the pub ashtrays in Ampleforth. They looked a desperate sight as smoke billowed around them.

Sammy started drinking the remainder of the cider the inn governor had given us. After a night out on the beer my two partners had never looked so disreputable. At least in Oldstead their dirty protesting bodies experienced a few cold strip washes. Mind you I was no artists' model myself. In two years, I had grown a little taller and heavier, but nothing like Percy's bulging edifice, which housed enough food to have fed Farmer Goodheart's prime Jersey cows for a week. Sammy on the other hand, regardless of what he ate or drank, remained slim and wiry.

We all eventually sat down on the warm earth, devoured the few sandwiches that were left for our breakfast and discussed where we were going.

'Let's try that farm in Nawton, you know, the place the old boy in Oldstead told us about,' I suggested. 'We might earn a few bob.'

At that moment the realisation that my two companions were in truth heroes struck me forcefully; they had fought for my freedom and the freedom of my country, and I was grateful. Wherever we went, no one knew, except for a handful of people, the horrors they had experienced and the sacrifices they had made. Feeling humble, sometimes I felt inadequate when in their company.

Over the last few days I had felt the darkness, anxiety and fear returning to haunt me yet again. Where it came from I never knew or understood. Was it something I had inherited? It was at these times that space was my only salvation from the feelings of despair and loneliness that threatened to engulf me. I had often wondered whether my mother's behaviour or personality was related, in some way, to my own experiences. From her earliest days, Mother had been a loner, preferring to read or take various bus trips around London on her own. She had rarely associated with boyfriends or girlfriends. My father was probably her one and only lover, who then married her. Later she had contracted a tic movement of her head. Most people thought that a sign of nerves, as they called it in those days. However, we were very much like any other family in poverty-stricken Stepney. People were preoccupied with getting through the day, earning a few shillings, buying food for the family, rather than trying to analyse things they didn't understand.

'Let's go straight on ter Sinnington, lads. It's about twelve miles,' said Sammy, who had originally suggested it way back at Nine Elms Farm. 'We can easily walk that in a day, and we might get some work there for God's sake.'

We started walking around 8 am, following a Roman road that stretched across the beautiful, lonely moors full of ling, bracken and large gorse bushes, whose yellow flowers smelt of fresh coconut. From time to time, I noticed clumps of blue cornflowers bobbing about in the light breeze. At times we were accompanied by birds of prey which were hunting rodents. As we were about to cross the first of three rivers, the River Rye, about half mile from Nunnington Village, we frightened a large flock of red grouse to flight, they had been hiding amongst the thick ling undergrowth. The red grouse are a widespread resident of hilly, ling-clad moorland regions.

Having no food, we were fortunate, several miles on, to buy bread, cheese and milk from a smallholder in a little hamlet called Trowbridge.

'Good day to thee,' said the smiling, elderly toothless lady, who lived in a rather small stone cottage that had plumes of smoke billowing out of the chimney. She made us a large pot of strong refreshing tea, just what we needed after walking several miles through the ancient peat bog. This type of bog sustains, amongst others, sphagnum moss, cotton grass, bog rosemary and dragonflies. Mrs Briggs told us, that she and her late husband had been living in Trowbridge for forty years. 'Aye I still work the smallholding on my own,' she said. The woman must have been at least 75, but she was slim, wiry, had long grey hair and was upright as a lamp post.

We paid the good lady for her hospitality, and moved on laden with enough food to last the day until we arrived in Sinnington. We walked along in single file, as plover and wheatear flew overhead, with the summer sun beating down on us, with not a care in the world. Yet from time to time, I thought about how my family in London were making ends meet. Especially my mother, as she cleaned the staircases of the flats where she lived with my father and sister Susan. Was father still carrying those heavy coal bags for a living? And I thought about my dear young sister Susan grafting in some dark, cold factory for 10 or 12 hours a day, her eyes fixed on a loud machine making clothes for the rich middle classes.

Wading across the river Dove, we saw a solitary merlin drinking the clear, cold water. The next river we crossed by a small bridge was the shallow River Seven. Sandpipers darted just above the water trying to catch flies as we continued walking along the well -trodden Roman road until Sinnington came into sight. Feeling hungry, and with a good day's walking of many miles behind us, we decided to eat our much-needed food on Sinnington Common.

'I kipped 'ere about six years ago with two old soldiers, Bobby Askew and Charlie Crook,' said Sammy. 'We did a little work in the village, about a week's work for a surly old bastard farmer who gave us little food but expected us to work all day. In the end Charlie told the old git to stick his work up his arse.' He went on to explain that in days gone by Sinnington Common, in the summer months, used to be full of trampers, waiting for the nod from the local orchard owners ready to pick the abundant apples and pears. The work lasted for about six weeks, and then the lads used to move on.

We awoke to a chilly early September morning. You could have heard a pin drop, it was so quiet and peaceful. As I lay there, wrapped in all my thick warm clothes, for it is cold even on summer nights on the moors, I thought about the various people I had met, or observed, so far on my journey from Nine Elms. They appeared to be a rare, interesting breed of people, whose main quality was resourcefulness. There they lived in a barren landscape, trying to eke out a living from the ever-encroaching North York Moors; the horse and plough were used mainly in the southern parts of the moors. It would be the same story in Sinnington Village. Generally these people were tough, hard-working, resilient, independent folk who were determined to leave their land in a better state for those who followed. I concluded that they were just like East Enders and people around the world who were trying to survive in a hard world, made harder by the vagaries of the Great War. Yet there was something about those people living on the North York Moors that was unusual and unfathomable.

Sinnington was like most of the places I had visited or seen on the North York Moors, with old stone-built 18th century cottages, a shop that sold nearly everything and an inn, the Wayfarer. The only difference from the other villages was the large 17th century stone-built church, with a tower, which dominated the small bustling village. Its Christian presence seemed to have been the main focus for the generations of people who had lived there. As in other villages, the church would have been the inspiration and guidance for families who worked this hard landscape.

Full of optimism, but dressed in dirty, smelling rags, we walked into Sinnington hoping to find work, accommodation and food. In a small allotment, large white butterflies flew round cabbages that sparkled as the sun shone on them. Oh, to be a butterfly, I thought to myself again, and have the wings of freedom to fly away whenever one chose to!

Only two cottages down, there were white mushrooms growing on a compost heap. Sammy had seen them before, but they needed to be cooked, he said, otherwise they leave a lasting bitter taste in the mouth and sore arse after bouts of diarrhoea.

'Good mornin' gentlemen, how are ye on this warm delightful day?' asked an old man across the garden opposite to us.

'We're OK. We've been on the road for some time governor. We're lookin' for some work and accommodation. Do yer know of any?' Percy asked the chap.

The old chap, Mr Hague, who told us he was 80, was tall and well-built with a stoop from many years working on the land. He wore the obligatory cap, as most men did around those areas. He invited us into his fertile vegetable garden for tea. When we were ensconced on his patio chairs, eating his home-made cheddar cheese sandwiches, the old chap explained how he had worked on the land since he was a young boy of 12 in Guisborough, north of the moors, where he was born. Since his early days he had worked as a ploughman, cow-hand and pig worker, all at different North York Moors farms. He and his late wife had moved to Sinnington thirty years before to work for a pig farmer, John Brake, who had since died. Mr Hague had retired only ten years ago, and he received a small state pension, enough to pay the rent on his cottage, which was owned by a cattle farmer, Ted Slate.

'They were tough times lads, I can tell you. Look, go up to Briar pig farm, ask for Captain Booker, the owner, and tell him I sent you along for some work,' Mr Hague insisted on telling us, after we had the cheek to eat all his bread and cheese.

Like three lost souls just come in from the wilderness, and smelling not unlike the residents of Briar Farm, we walked through the village to the farm some hundred yards away. We spoke to a plump middle-aged man wearing a cap, leaning on a large wrought iron gate.

'Mr Booker?' I asked.

'Yeah I'm him,' he said rather abruptly.

'Mr Hague sent us. He thought you might 'ave a few days' work and accommodation for us,' I explained to the ruddy-looking farmer.

'I need tons of pig shit shovelled from my yard onto a lorry,' he said. 'If you can do that competently, I also need someone to clean the inside of my large hay barn. There's about seven to ten days' work for you. If you're up for it, then you can sleep in the barn. I have plenty of rugs, and I'll feed you three good meals a day. Also, if I like the work you're doing, then I shall give you a few jugs of my home-made beer.' That was the non-negotiable way Captain Booker hired us for a few days.

Donned in protective overalls and boots supplied by the farmer to protect our own filthy rags, we started grafting an hour later. We stood for a few minutes looking at a huge pile of stinking, steaming pig-shit, which somehow we had to load onto the back of his dilapidated old lorry and dump it on his fields.

'We might as well get shovelling or otherwise this bastard will tell us to piss orf,' moaned Percy.

We shovelled and shovelled for the next four hours, until the farmer came out with three large jugs of ale, cheese and warm bread. That was manna from heaven as I was nearly on my knees after non-stop work. For one so young, I felt unfit.

As we sat down to eat and drink, I felt a growing affiliation with the moors. It was as though I really belonged to this place, yet at times it was menacing; strange, yet oddly reassuring. Other times my feelings frightened me and warned me not to venture any further into its clutches. The moors had this mesmerising effect on me, especially when I felt, or I thought I felt, depressed, fearful and hopeless. Many times when I was with my tramping friends, I wanted to break with them and walk the cold, lonely moors on my own. My instinct held me back from wandering into dangerous places that could have caused me terrible problems, or even death. Even so, I did venture out twice on my own, to Hood Hill when working for Mr George. Why was I so preoccupied with loneliness?

We were all woken early next morning by the farmyard cockerels making a hellish cacophony of noise, prompting us to start the day. Sammy reckoned that the farmer had placed the birds there deliberately to get us out of bed early. Given the opportunity, I would have gladly strangled them all. We all had bodies that were stiff and aching from the previous day's graft. All I wanted was the sanctuary of my warm hay and blanket bed. My mind went back to the secure bed I had slept in at my parents' home, when mother used to bring me tea and toast before I slipped into my clothes.

My little reverie was abruptly ended when the farmer came into the shed with a tray full of tea and bacon sandwiches. 'Off with cocks and on with socks. Here you are lads, your grub before a good day's work,' remarked Captain Booker, who probably thought what useless specimens we all were. He was about 50, and I realised that he was the right age to have fought in the Great War. Something I should investigate.

The thick bacon sandwiches and hot tea kept the three of us shovelling the proverbial pigs' gold until midday. Each time we loaded the farmer's lorry, we spread the contents all over his three fields. He maintained that his free-range pigs, a common sight in this part of the world, put on weight more quickly due to the extra nutrients the shit gave the grass. Mind you some of them were a large size, especially the fat sows, which regularly gave birth to twelve offspring. At times, with a little imagination, I could have sworn that a lot of those growing piglets resembled their owner!

After four days of continual shovelling, the end was in sight. That afternoon Percy complained of a painful stomach he had had for two days. Now it was so acute that the farmer drove him immediately down to the village to see Dr Hardcastle.

'Where are the pains? How long have you had them? What have you eaten lately?' the doctor's questions kept coming, which confused poor old Percy. The doctor prodded, poked and felt the area of concern. Mind you the huge stomach that Percy carried around with him could have housed anything, after years of eating food from numerous sources known and unknown. That included the swill they gave the soldiers to eat on the Somme.

An hour later, our tramping friend returned to where all the action was, as Sammy and I had nearly completed removing the foul stuff onto the lorry, which Sammy drove precariously to the field and back each time. Mind you I was well prepared to jump out quickly just in case Sammy lost control of the vehicle and drove into the farmer's house or barn.

'Some people would do anything to shirk work Les,' said Sammy, mocking Percy for going to see the doctor.

'Fuck you Sammy, I felt fuckin' terrible. The old boy gave me this bottle of jollop to take three times daily for three days. I've had a couple swigs already, and I feel a lot better, but it tastes like sewage water,' explained Percy.

Later that day, around 6 pm, farmer Booker brought a huge tray to the barn consisting of four large bowls of steaming broth, half a loaf of bread and four large jugs of his home-made ale. 'You've done well so far lads. Cheers,' he said, raising one of the four jugs to us. We did likewise. We ate the good food, drank the strong beer and generally talked shop amongst ourselves, until Sammy asked the captain about his background.

'Were you in the Great War, governor?'

'Yes I was, but I didn't see any action, except when I was shafting a local girl called Mabel. I was stationed at nearby Thirsk training camp teaching young officers who thought they knew everything. That's how I ended up here at Briar Farm after the war. With my savings, I managed to get a small mortgage on the old Georgian house, this large barn, many sties for the pigs and five acres of land.' I was surprised that he would tell us his own personal history.

'What about you lot?' he asked in a military tone of voice and grinning attitude of superiority. Sammy acted as our spokesman, as usual, going into detail about how he and Percy had fought on the Somme, had been bombed, gassed, nearly poisoned and starved, and had both lost many friends in the thick mud and blood of the Western Front. Sammy also explained how I had lost my parents during the German bombing of London, and why I had taken the train north to Thirsk, where the three of us first met.

At first Captain Booker looked flabbergasted by what he had just been told. His face was visibly moved by all the painful details, of which he was obviously unaware, like most people who hadn't fought on the Western Front. After minutes of tangible silence, Sammy remarked, 'they call this a country fit for heroes, but the only thing we and many other former young soldiers could do was to take to tramping round the country hoping to find work, accommodation, and our sanity, along the way'.

Farmer Booker returned five minutes later with four more large jugs of ale. 'Well I'm so sorry about what happened to all three of you. For once, I'm lost for words to convey my feelings,' said the big farmer. Being single, he did all his own cooking and cleaning, along with the everyday responsibilities of running a large and successful pig farm. He was also a local councillor, and determined to make Sinnington a better place for business and local people. I could only admire the way the farmer conducted himself. His background was fundamentally different to the three blokes now living, temporarily, in his barn. From a middle-class educated family, he had been given all that was needed to be successful in a hard world, at a time when the British economy would stagnate for years to come.

Yet I loathed the power he, and people like him, had over most other people. Middle-class and working-class people had their lives predestined by birth. I was once again reminded of my former class friend David Cecil, whose walking companionship I had enjoyed. No doubt his father had made sure he went to university to study for one of the professions and a good comfortable life beyond. Our paths, of course, would never have crossed if it hadn't been for the intervention of the war.

We had all but given up shaving with cold water. All three of us had beards, although mine was no more than a sprouting of bum fluff. Sammy and Percy were used to wearing beards for long periods of time during their various wanderings. We let our hair grow long, but managed to get it cut when convenient, as at Nine Elms Farm. At times my two friends resembled religious hermits coming out of the wilderness after many months of solitary retreat. Although the other two had lost most of their teeth fighting on the Somme, I had managed to keep cleaning mine even though I had lost a few more since arriving at Thirsk station. My teeth were black and white and deteriorating. But we were fortunate when the farmer Booker gave the three of us some really good, nearly new, expensive clothes. After discarding most our own filthy clothes, fit only for the fire, we looked like three dapper men ready to hit the highlights of parochial Sinnington. Can you imagine toothless Percy dancing with the mayor's wife, and breathing from a belly full of rotting flesh all over her painted face?

Chapter Eight

The Monastery

Three more days' work followed cleaning dead rodents, cats and pigeons out of his barn, and that brought an end to our work at Briar Farm. The farmer gave us a large pack of various sandwiches, home-made bottles of beer and one pound each to help us on to our next destination, Pickering, on the southern boundary of the North York Moors, some four miles from Sinnington. The farmer informed us that compared to most places on the moors, Pickering was a relatively large town with a church, three inns and many shops of various descriptions, including a farrier, market gardener, tool merchant, doctor's surgery and many private and public cottages and houses. Just outside the town, he went on, were various cattle, sheep and pig farms where it could be possible to get some work. Five hundred yards further on, farmer Booker said, was a stone-built Cistercian monastery, a place where monks had worked and prayed since the early 19th century. The original monastery, which stood on the same site, was dissolved in the 16th century by Henry VIII. The Cistercians, the stricter part of the Benedictine faith, were founded in 1098.

During several of miles of enjoyable walking amongst the bracken and ling, we stopped several times for food, drink, or a sit down for a cigarette before sleeping through a very cold night in the church garden shed at Pickering. Hours later, looking over the top of a creosote-stained tarpaulin, we were surprised to find a young man standing there oiling a small lawnmower.

'Good morning lads, I didn't expect to find you all cuddled up like there like three large dormice,' commented the short, stocky man in his early 20s, dressed in a thick black overcoat and wearing a cap.

'Yeah, we've bin on the road for ages' I explained. 'Recently we've bin workin' in Sinnington for Captain Booker for a few days. Good bloke. We found this shed late last night. Too bloody cold to sleep out.'

'Yeah, I've 'eard of 'im. I'm Bernard, the church gardener,' he said.

'Know where we can find some work and somewhere to stay round 'ere?' I asked Bernard.

'You can try the monastery up the road. They 'elp walkers and trampers,' he said.

After hearing that, we got our few things together and headed for the monastery, hoping that the men of God could save us from another night of sleeping out in freezing temperatures.

Sammy and Percy pushed me forward as I reluctantly walked up to the large green front double doors of the monastery. I banged the ornate metal door knocker. Several minutes later a middle-aged man, with a shaven head and wearing a white habit answered the door.

'Good morning young man, and what can I do for you?' asked the short, smiling monk.

'Good mornin' governor. Sorry sir, me friends and I are lookin' for some work and accommodation. Yer see we've bin walking for many days across the moors and we're tired and 'ungry. Could you 'elp us sir?' I apologetically asked the friendly monk, who wore sandals.

'Come in the three of you, and we'll see what we can do. But first I will have to ask my superior, Father John-Paul.'

We sat on three wooden seats just inside the main doors, in a quiet and austere-looking room. The only other object in the room was a framed picture of Christ hanging on one of the bare light brown walls.

The monk returned about ten minutes later with another hairless monk.

'Hallo gentlemen. Welcome to Heythrop Monastery,' he said. 'My name is Father John-Paul, and I am the Abbot. My fellow monk here is Father David. He has told me what you are seeking. If you're interested, you can help out the other monks here by working in the vegetable garden and orchards. You can sleep in a small dormitory we keep for lay visitors. And you are welcome to eat at set times with the religious community here. What do you think about my proposal?'

Without thought I said, 'that would be great, Father. Thank you,' and all of us smiled in unison at the fortunate offer. Everywhere was silent, outwardly austere yet peaceful. I had only been in the place a few minutes, but I felt somehow safe and secure, if the first impressions of the monks were any guide.

Father David took us to the kitchen to meet three other monks, Brothers Arnold, Colin and Bentley, who did most of the cooking for the community. All the three monks appeared to be in their 60s, but looked younger than my two friends.

'These three men are here to live and work with us for a time,' he said. 'Brother Colin, please could you give them breakfast, and afterwards, take them to meet the other Brothers out in the orchard?' requested the softly-spoken Father David. He left the room, saying we would meet him another time.

No sooner was he gone, and feeling famished, we started eating rapidly from large bowls of steaming porridge placed before us. This was followed by several slices of buttered toast and mugs of hot tea. The aches and pains of my body from last night's sleep in the ice cold shed started to subside. I felt human once again. I could now start to take in my surroundings, and ponder on what the Abbot expected of us. Likewise, Sammy and Percy showed their pleasure at being fed and watered.

'God must 'ave known we were coming 'ere,' Sammy said, followed by one of his raucous laughs. Quiet man

Percy didn't comment. His mind was probably reliving life in the trenches.

For the next five hours, except for a brief lunch break, the three of us worked in the large orchard assisting three other shaven-headed Brothers. It was enjoyable work in an atmosphere of near silence, which I soon found suited me very well. One of the Brothers, Luke, taught me how to prune various fruit trees and soft fruit bushes. We took the rubbish on a wooden barrow to the end of the garden to be burnt on a large roaring fire. Embers shot into the autumn sky as the notorious North York Moors rain started to gently fall onto the yellow/red flames, rain that nurtures all that lives on the moors. Deep green moss had covered the old red brick walls that surrounded the monastery.

While my two friends worked in the garden with the two other Brothers, I enjoyed throwing the fallen golden and brown leaves onto the fire. The peace and solitude became so palpable that for a short time I thought time had stopped, so intense was the experience. Luke and I stood in silence watching the flames leap and dart out of the fire, as the burning wood crackled under the heat. It was time for us all to clean the tools and take them back to the wooden shed that stood in the bottom right-hand corner of the garden, next to the compost heap. After that work session, Luke explained that most of the time the monks enjoyed manual work in silence. Actually most of their everyday activities were spent in silence.

We followed the three Brothers into a small, colourful utility room, adjacent to the kitchen, to wash our hands for the 6 pm community evening meal. On two of the otherwise bare green walls were framed pictures of Jesus Christ and Mary embracing Joseph. Underneath both were written: *We surrender to God. Our vows are of poverty, obedience and celibacy in an environment of solitude, silence and prayer.*

Just before entering the yellow-painted dining room, which had various icons displayed on the walls, the three Brothers stood next to each other and said some kind of prayer. I felt moved by their commitment to God, but I couldn't help looking out of the corner of my eye as I noticed Sammy and Percy both had a smirk on their bearded faces. The three of us sat at the end of a large wooden table, as two of the younger shaven-headed Brothers served the food.

We ate our food of soup, broth, bread and tea in complete silence. Such a contrast to the unruly cafés in Cable Street. It was a well-cooked and enjoyable meal in an atmosphere of calm reflection. None of the monks looked at each other, or around them. They were completely focused on eating their food. After the meal was finished, we helped the monks wash the old crockery and cutlery before they retired to their own rooms for prayer, reading and an hour of social friendship with fellow monks. None of us trampers had been in this type of environment before, but after a while, it was an experience I actually began to find reassuring. But it was early days.

Later that evening, Father David informed us that Father John-Paul would like to meet us informally in his office.

'I hope you enjoyed your first day working at our

monastery,' said Father John-Paul. 'The three Brothers found you all hard-working men. As you have realised, we spend most of our time in silence, but of course we have to talk sometimes, although we try to keep it to a minimum. I hope you find the dormitory comfortable.

He turned to me. 'Leslie, do you remember our first meeting? We were in the same compartment aboard the Thirsk-bound train on 9th March, 1923. I gave you my business card, with the name of Wainwright on it. I use that name when carrying out accountancy work on behalf of the monastery. The address on that business card, you may recall, was in Tenby. That is the community where we train our younger monks who are starting out on their spiritual journey.'

He had looked so different in the train wearing his smart suit and polished shoes and carrying a pigskin briefcase. Due to my painful experiences back in Compton, I had assumed, wrongly, that Mr Wainwright, as he was then, had ill intentions towards me. Back in the warm comfortable dormitory, I eventually found his dog-eared card down at the bottom of my damp rucksack.

Over the next few weeks we gradually immersed ourselves in everyday life at Heythrop, working, eating and sleeping. Without prompting from any of the religious community, there were occasions when I, and sometimes Percy, but never Sammy, joined the monks to pray, sing and listen to bible readings, usually given by Fathers John-Paul or David. Understandably, Sammy didn't want anything to do with religion after his terrible experiences on the Western Front, where many soldiers were shot at dawn for cowardice as the 'dog-collared men,' as he called them, stood, watched and said nothing about such barbarity. 'Fuck em all! They all need shooting as far as I'm concerned. Hypocrites, that's all they are,' Sammy raged about those he thought had done great injustices to many innocent shell-shocked men.

Fortunately, I had no experience of army or religious injustice. I did, however, have experience of religious people in the East End. They came across as condescending, arrogant, middle-class young people who had just graduated from their ivory towers of Cambridge and Oxford. Having no experience or understanding of everyday life, especially in poverty-stricken areas like London, they would preach to people about living a good, productive and honest life. Many times as a young boy I remembered my grandmother Bessie telling the religious people what to do with their lives as they weren't needed, nor wanted, around Stepney. Furthermore, Bessie and many more local people were outraged by what Engels had to say about East Enders, who thought the 'inhabitants passively submitted to their fate'. Many East Enders, included the dockers and Jewish radicals, saw to it that the locals kept fighting for change. But the anarchist writer John Mackay was correct when he called the East End the 'empire of hunger'.

None captured the terrible poverty of the East Enders better than Jack London, one of my heroes, in his book *The People of the Abyss,* published in 1903. London experienced the squalor of living in doss-houses, workhouses and everyday life on the streets, where he saw first-hand the hellish conditions that more than a million poor endured. His book, and a great deal of this book, give voice to the poverty and suffering experienced by East Enders in the following quote:

WAGES

Some sell their lives for bread,
Some sell their souls for gold,
Some seek the river bed,
Some seek the workhouse mould.

Such is proud England's sway,
Where wealth may work its will,
White flesh is cheap today,
White souls are cheaper still.

FANTASIAS.

Every month at Heythrop Monastery, the monks had what was known as a friendship meeting, where you could talk about yourself in a supportive and sympathetic environment. Three months later, all three of us attended one such meeting. On this occasion, all nine monks who lived there were in attendance. After three monks had talked about various issues, Sammy, rather bravely I thought, began talking about his life; he said that he felt unloved by his parents, who were constantly moving around trying to find work. He had a younger sister he rarely saw. The authorities had placed him in a children's home when he was about six. There he was sexually and physically abused. Those painful experiences, Sammy said, had made him stand up for himself, and taught him to be self-sufficient and hard.

At that stage, I observed that Brother Luke was visibly shaking. As I got to know him, I understood that the shaking was his sensitive response to suffering. It was rather moving listening to Sammy, and it was the one and only time I saw tears roll down his cheeks.

'What a brave and resilient person you are, Sammy' said Father John-Paul, who was also physically moved by what he had just heard. 'My heart, and no doubt the whole community's too, go with you.'

After that, without any prompting, Percy launched himself into a brief story of his awful experiences; he was semi-illiterate, having received little education. His father was an alcoholic who used to beat him and his mother regularly. His father had been to prison many times because of his violent conduct. He ran away from home many times, only to be returned by the police. Percy's first job was delivering meat for the local butcher, who used to sexually abuse him at the end of the day when the shop was closed. Neither man spoke about his wartime experiences as soldiers. When Percy had finished talking, Fathers John Paul and David both paid tribute to the strength and resilience of my two tramping friends. I spontaneously got to my feet and put my arms round both of them, recognizing the immense suffering that they had both endured.

When it was my turn to talk, all I wanted to do was apologise to my two tramping friends and the monks for deceiving them because of the overpowering sense of guilt I had been shouldering ever since I had left London. I told them I was sorry that I had lied about my parents being killed during the war. I explained to them that by lying about such an immensely emotional matter as losing one's parents, and being a vulnerable teenager, I had hoped people would feel sympathy for me and give me food, clothes and money. I hoped the monks and my two tramping friends would understand that I had left London to try and better my life. It had been painful, I explained, to leave my family behind in London and travel to Thirsk, where I was unknown and unsupported. My quest was to try and discover what I could achieve with my life. From my seat, I also conjured up enough courage to ask Father John-Paul for permission to enable my parents to write to me here at the monastery. It would be reassuring for my parents to know that I was safe.

Without hesitation, he granted my request. 'Thank you Father. All you monks are so thoughtful, knowledgeable and kind,' I said in a moment of utter deference to my seniors.

'Thank you for those kind words Leslie, but we must remind ourselves what Tolstoy said, *'we can know only that we know nothing. And that is the highest degree of human wisdom'*. That was the learned sage's response.

Brother Luke and I worked regularly together in the productive orchard and allotment. He informed me in his usual calm and mindful manner that the monastery tried to be self-sufficient in growing fruit and vegetables. Most seasons they produced enough for the community to eat fresh wholesome food daily, but the little meat and fish the monks consumed was delivered by the local butcher's shop, Sperrings. During my working time with Brother Luke, I got to know very little about him as the monks were more focused on their relationships with God than with people. The monks swore an oath of allegiance to their God Almighty and found it unhelpful to keep being reminded of their previous lives. I found that difficult to understand, and assumed they were running away from real life. I didn't know anything about Luke except that he was about 30 years old, of average height, slim bordering on thin, intelligent, and always helpful and kind. There was a constant smile on his thin pale face which irritated me from time to time. Was Brother Luke repressing his feelings so that he could practise a religious life without being burdened by his past experiences? I suppose to a certain degree that is inevitably the case for most people. One didn't know anything about him, so it would be unreasonable to judge. If his actions were any sort of guide to his future intentions, then he appeared committed to the spiritual life. And that I admired about him unequivocally.

It was the cynical side of me that questioned his motives for being attracted to the one God. The same God, presumably, that did not intervene during the carnage of the Western Front, and did nothing about the bombings in Poplar where so many innocent men, women and children were slaughtered. The same God, presumably, who does nothing to help alleviate universal human suffering. Admittedly, coming from an inexperienced understanding of life, I none the less assumed all gods to be a delusion. Yet there was something I had felt at Heythrop, something I had not hitherto realised; that fundamentally there was, or could be, a purpose to life. I didn't feel frightened all the time by the false belief that these were unknown persons who would rob or even kill me. For some unknown reason, I was reminded by what Mrs Lane had told our school class in Compton, '*A sip is the most that mortals are permitted from any goblet of delight*'. Perhaps I was being reminded, yet again, not to expect too much from people because they are unable or unwilling to deliver.

Two weeks later, early one morning, a monk slid a letter under our dormitory door. In excited anticipation, I opened a letter from my parents, the first one I had received for some considerable time since living in Oldstead. All my family sent their love to me, and were glad I was living in a monastery. I was saddened, but not surprised, to read that my great-grandmother, Florence, aged 85, had died from lung cancer a few months previously. She was buried next to her lifelong partner, Tom, in Barking.

At least she was now free from pain and suffering. What a life she had lived and experienced; those poverty-stricken days in the East End of London, where streets of women tried to earn some money as prostitutes to feed their young vulnerable children. Many others had no choice but descend into the twilight world of crime, as the wealthy of London did nothing about the extreme poverty except make money off the backs of those in dire need. Yet Florence and her God-fearing parents managed to eke out a living amongst the maelstrom of human degradation.

My parents, Susan and Bessie were all well, which was so good to know, as living hundreds of miles away, there was nothing I could do to support them. As unemployment grew in Britain, my family held onto the jobs they'd had for some time.

Now that I felt somewhat grounded at Heythrop, I immediately replied to my parents explaining my continuing tramping from Oldstead to when we had arrived at the monastery. I told them I felt safe and secure there; that the monks were good people, and all had led many different kinds of lives before committing themselves to a spiritual life. The last time I had written to my family - or when I received their letter, I can't remember which - I became depressed again. My 'other self', as I named it, appeared to take over my whole existence. Deep dark feelings smothered my everyday life for the next week or so. So intense were the feelings that I felt useless, hopeless, not worthy of anything good happening to me. At times I felt like killing myself. Other times I felt like running away from human existence and hiding on the moors, so great was my assumed failure. I thought I must change my name and travel to another part of the country where I wasn't known and start again.

After a week of hating myself, and everyone else, Brother Luke must have realised something was unwell with me. 'I've noticed during the last few days, Leslie, that you have not been yourself. Can I help you?' he asked in his usual concerned manner. It was the first time I had discussed, in detail, my depressive problems with another person.

Brother Luke discussed my painful mental problems with Brother Bentley, who as a former mental hospital nurse had gained some understanding of depression, if that, indeed, was my problem. 'Good morning Leslie. Brother Luke told me about your mental problems, and he thought I could help you,' explained Brother Bentley, a short, slim, intelligent man, aged about 45, from Glasgow, who still loved football, even though he had been living at Heythrop for ten years. His one passion was Celtic Football Club.

After I had explained my background in East London, the London bombings, the sense of loss at not being with my family, travelling to Thirsk and tramping with my two friends, Brother Bentley arranged weekly meetings where I could discuss various issues with him. At the first hourly meeting, he explained that he thought I needed spiritual healing based on Christian faith. He said I would have to let go of my previous life, to a certain extent, if I was to benefit from our time together.

'How can I do that?' I asked, rather confused by the word 'faith'.

'Faith is an intangible word to understand. We must place our trust in God and that we will be healed by his presence in our hearts. We must invite him in and believe that Almighty God can cure our lack of faith. You see, we don't love ourselves enough, and the consequence of that can be mental and/or physical illness'.

Not really understanding or believing Brother Bentley's explanation of faith, I none the less continued to meet with him for the next few months. During this time I had many bouts of depression, when my other self took me over. At times I thought I was living someone else's life, so great were my delusions.

This was the case regardless of whether I wrote or received letters from my supportive family, who were by now interested in my activities at Heythrop. For the first time in over three years it was good to receive regular letters from my parents, grandmother Bessie and Susan. They were proud of the way I continued to grow up and accept responsibility, although they were all desperate to see me once again. But still my inner torment continued unabated. After a couple of months of healing sessions, I explained, as much as I could, to my two friends the inner turmoil that I had been experiencing for many years.

In hindsight, my depressive episodes possibly first began when we moved into Sandhurst Street in 1912. Subsequently, I had often thought that living in the bedroom where a murdered person had lived before me could have brought on my depression. But equally, my mental problems could be explained by other circumstances involving something entirely different. At those times of utter darkness I kept returning to the notion of freedom that butterflies inspired in me. Especially the elegant, multi-coloured Duke of Burgundy, and the large white butterflies whose graceful flight reminded me of what it would be like to soar way above the ground.

Sadly, my two friends Sammy and Percy had decided to move on from Heythrop monastery, and make their way over the rugged and beautiful moors to the east coast. From what I had read, I realised their walk was over dark soft peat bogs that had developed over thousands of years. Over gorse, low-lying bracken and prickly thorn, in some places were in abundance. And in other places, oak, birch, beech and conifer allowed them dry cover if they decided to sleep out under the stars, something that was not unusual to my two tramping friends. From the coast their goal was to walk north to Robin Hood's Bay. That would be a journey of about 30 miles, and no doubt one they intended to enjoy. Being resourceful men, they could work, sleep and eat using their wits and cunning.

'I'm gettin' too fuckin' domesticated, Les boy!' roared my dear friend Sammy, as he pointed at Percy's big belly. We need to get back on the road and lose some weight.' This elicited a wry smile from Percy, whose hair was very long, although on top he was completely bald.

'That's right Sammy. The spiritual life has made me fat,' said Percy, as we all embraced, sadly, for the last time. That would be the final time that I was to set my eyes on two great unsung heroes. I would cherish forever the times we spent walking, working, talking and stealing together. No finer men exist in the whole of Britain. With tears streaming down my cheeks and their rucksacks piled high with food and drink needed for their journey, I said goodbye, on the outskirts of Pickering, to two great men of the road.

Every evening when I went to bed and every morning when I woke up, I thought and dreamed of my friends wandering life's byways somewhere. If you saw a cloud of smoke it would probably be Sammy chain-smoking kerbside twist. Bombed and gassed, yet wiry, strong and full of a powerful life force, Sammy kept going regardless.

Percy, similar to Sammy but minus the slim body and toothless mouth, would use his coal-shovel hands to keep himself fed and warm. Both men had written, or rather I did it for them, their names and year of their births on the walls of what became, for many months, a warm and cosy dormitory. Many other visitors had also left their details for others to enquire into. I was reminded every morning when we woke; Sammy, without fail, would salute and say 'good morning governor' to a framed picture of Jesus Christ on the inside of the front door.

There was a loud knock on my wooden dormitory door. As I opened it a short, rotund man of about 60, with a large bushy moustache and wearing dark blue overalls, greeted me. 'Good morning Les, I'm Robbie,' said the smiling old chap in a broad Yorkshire accent. 'I've been the part-time maintenance man 'ere at the old monastery for many years. So many years that I've lost count son. I maintain whatever needs maintaining. Be that inside or outside of the monastery, but anything too big they send for a local building contractor. Also I help to look after the old stone and brick walls and I can prune the trees if needs be.'

We walked round the monastery and gardens together, constantly stopping so that Robbie could explain various things to me in detail. Half way round, he explained that the reason for the conducted tour was for me to familiarise myself with the layout of things, as the Senior Father wanted me to be responsible for some of the maintenance. I was rather taken aback by my new assigned role at Heythrop. My mentor continued to explain the whereabouts, wherefores and wherewithal of what needed attention now and what was needed in future.

As we continued walking, I noticed that Robbie had a slight limp. It was from an accident, he explained, when he had fallen off a hay rick when he was young.

'When we were kids, all the local boys and girls used to 'elp the farmers load the 'orse drawn carts with freshly-cut hay,' he said. 'He gave us a penny each, the old miser.'

'Did any bombs drop round 'ere during the war?' I asked him.

'None dropped on Pickering, although several bombs dropped on the fields and moors. One bomb dropped on the late Farmer Adamson's cowshed and flattened it,' he recalled.

Apart from occasionally visiting the village to buy or collect something for the monastery, or to visit Robbie's nearby cottage to borrow building tools, my everyday life at Heythrop was as regular as dawn and dusk. I would get out of bed around 6 am, quickly get my clothes on, as there was no heating, wash in cold water and run over to the warm dining room for breakfast by 8 am. There I joined the monks for breakfast in silence. However, they had been praying, chanting and reading since 5am in the small chapel next door to the three dormitories where the nine monks slept. They prayed, whenever practicable, three or four times daily, seven day a week. The community consisted of Fathers John-Paul and David and Brothers Luke, Bentley, Colin, Arnold, Simon, Joseph and Ian. I motivated myself to join the community for prayer at least once a day in the evening, when at the end of the day's work, I felt more relaxed, having thought I had achieved something, not just for myself, but for the community. That indeed was central to the spiritual lives at Heythrop, where prayer helped the individual achieve eternal salvation, and at the same time work for the betterment of others.

However I often thought, when praying in the chapel with the monks, how surreal my experiences were, standing in complete silence, sometimes for an hour, not really knowing or understanding what it was all about. I assumed that the test of faith challenged all the monks to live a more committed religious life, having taken their vows of poverty, obedience and celibacy. Only much later did I learn that every monk will end up in the monastery's communal coffin. For the monks being interred, this is not the end of their lives, but the beginning of a new spiritual journey that extends, Father David explained, 'into the afterlife where they meet their God Almighty'. Sod me, I thought, I hope he doesn't send me straight to hell.

Taking into consideration my background, where, except for a nominal service at school, religion had played no meaningful part in everyday life, this was something of a revelation. Even though I welcomed, at times cherished, the peaceful, friendly environment, and respected the monks' lifelong religious commitment, the intense atmosphere made me feel, at times, deeply insecure. An insecurity that had been with me, probably, since my youngest days in East London.

After mentioning this to Brother Bentley, a meeting

was arranged for me to discuss my problems with Father John-Paul. We met on the beautiful sunny summer morning of my 21st birthday, in the small monastery flower garden. The fusion of colour brought about by the multi-coloured roses and gladioli was, I hoped, an auspicious sign for a bright and intense conversation with the Father.

'How can I help, Leslie?' were the reassuring words of the senior monk of Heythrop Monastery.

'Well Father I'm concerned about the long time I've spent away from me family. It's over three years now. I feel I should be 'elping out by bringing in money to the 'ousehold. And there are times when I love being 'ere, but I gets confused about the religion sometimes,' I tried to explain.

'Well Leslie, first of all, I admire the way you have handled travelling with other, more experienced men. You have looked after yourself, and for one so young, you've adapted well. Regards missing your family, it is understandable and natural that you want to see them again. I hear you write and receive regular letters from your family? Now the religious problem that you experience here at Heythrop again is very understandable. I remember that after my first three years training to be a monk here, there were times when I was confused and doubtful and lacked conviction in my religious practice. There are occasions even now, after many years of religious devotion, when my faith is surely stretched to the limit.' We started walking slowly round the garden together. A puff of wind slightly brushed his white cotton habit.

'I have a suggestion to put to you. Why don't you travel home and visit your family? Once you are there, you may want to stay with them, and put religion at the back of your mind. If on the other hand, you feel unsettled in London for any reason, you can come back to Heythrop for a while.' His understanding of my personal problem had given me the opportunity to look deeper into my options.

Chapter Nine

Home truths

With my feelings a lot clearer, I decided to travel back to London and visit my parents. It was something that had been on my mind for some time. I was excited, yet at the same time nervous about meeting my family after being away for so long. No doubt they had all aged and matured, especially Susan, since the last time I had seen her when she was a schoolgirl. Now she was working, finding her way in the world, and according to Mother, had a regular boyfriend.

Since childhood, Susan and I had not played an important role in each other's lives. We hadn't spent much time growing up together although, of course, we did live in Compton. Because she was five years younger than me, I tended to play with boys my own age, both at school and where we lived. That meant we met only in the evenings at home for tea, or during school summer holidays. But, of course, we used to fight and quarrel like cats and dogs just like most growing children in the back streets of East London. The little I knew about Susan was that she had grown into a strong character. Now I was returning home, it was my intention to spend more time with my sister and develop a good sibling relationship.

After another enjoyable evening meal with the monks in silence, Father David announced that I would be departing Heythrop monastery to visit my parents. All the monks embraced me and wished me well. Early next morning, with the sun shining, Brother Joseph, whom I had exchanged no more than a few words with during the past year, drove me in a small grey car to Thirsk railway station. I didn't remember much of the Victorian railway station that I had arrived at on 6th March 1923, but I will never forget the café I went into, a few hundred yards down the road, and the good friends I went on to walk the moors with. That experience has left an indelible mark on me.

During the two-hour journey to Thirsk station, Brother Joseph told me about his life before taking the five years of vows which led to being a fully-ordained monk. Now 40 years of age, He had lived at Heythrop for more than 15 years. 'The past 15 years have been most fulfilling, now that my life has a purpose,' he said. He was born into a working-class family in industrial Blackburn. His father had worked in a factory for most of his life, and his mother was kept busy at home bringing up five boys. Brother Joseph first worked in the same factory as his father, but disillusioned with that, he left home and wandered aimlessly around the country before being caught stealing food from a shop in Nottingham. The courts sent him to borstal for one year and there he acquired bricklaying skills, which he subsequently used to earn a living, until, as he put it, 'he found God'.

I had seen Brother Joseph many times at Heythrop, yet I had always assumed, quite wrongly, that he must have come from a middle-class family, been well educated and lived a comfortable life. How we project our own misleading ideas and feelings onto our fellow men! Brother Joseph left me with a powerful metaphor, which can be interpreted in many ways, when I asked him how and why he changed. His response was: from his background you had to stand back and think about what you needed and where you wanted to go, or otherwise '*it is like changing tyres on a moving car*'!

During the rail journey from Thirsk to London, my mind was totally preoccupied with meeting my family once again after being away from home for more than three years. The only times when I was fully aware of my surroundings was at ticket inspection, buying tea and using the toilet. Otherwise my thoughts continually kept returning to my parents, Susan and Granny Bessie. I felt like some lost sailor who had travelled the world seeking riches, and was only now looking forward to falling into the arms of his loved ones.

I stepped down from the train on to Kings Cross Station platform, to be engulfed for a minute or so by steam pouring from the large superb-looking engine. How clever some people must be to have the knowledge to design such a beautiful specimen, I thought. Once it had cleared, I briskly walked past passengers alighting from the dirty stationary carriages until I eventually saw my parents, fifty feet away, waving at me from behind the ticket barrier. My family and I hugged each other for some time, laughing and joking. The train announcements made conversation difficult.

'You alwight son? Good ter see yer after all this time,' said my smiling father, who was well dressed in a blue serge suit, but looking older and heavier. 'I borrowed me friend's car son, it's just round the corner,' he explained, as we all walked the two hundred yards or so to where the black car was parked.

'Ow yer keepin', Mum, Susan, Bessie? I missed you all very much. You look dressed like a millionaire dad. Orf the back of a lorry was it?' I asked my father, who at the same time nudged me the ribs.

'Ow you keeping Leslie?' both Mother and Bessie asked.

'I feel well mum. And it's good to see yer, Bessie and Susan,' I said with a smile.

'Gawd you've shot up son, and put on weight. Three years ago you looked like a mortuary specimen,' commented Bessie, who hadn't lost her sense of humour.

'What's in the rucksack son, gold?' Father said, taking the piss out of my tattered old rucksack, which had seen much action.

Back inside my parents' comfortable Shadwell flat,

mother had made sandwiches and a marzipan cake, my favourite, and bought several bottles of beer. She was really making a fuss of me being home. Her head tic, or spasm, I noticed, had become more pronounced. But it was good to see the old home once more, I thought, and after travelling for so long without a bath it would be good to slip into the hot water and sleep in a warm bed with sheets washed by my mother.

We laid into the beer, devoured the sarnies (sandwiches) and scoffed the sexton blake (cake) till none was left.

'Fancy fish and chips. Les boy?' asked Father. I declined his offer. It was sufficiently enjoyable just to sit with my family, what was left of it. Later we drank tea in a quiet and peaceful atmosphere. However, after a few hours, I became aware that I felt awkward sitting there with people, I thought, I really didn't know. Of course they were my decent and supportive parents, grandmother Bessie, and attractive sister Susan. Yet somehow, I felt an emotional distance between us. I had been away for three years, much had changed, including myself, and it would take time to develop deeper feelings for them, I tried to reassure myself. After so many lonely, difficult days spent in different places on the North York Moors when I had craved their company, now that we were in the same room things felt rather more confusing. But I had to give myself the time and space to settle back into a way of life that, not too long ago, I had run away from. Yet I had learnt, somewhat, not to deny my feelings: I felt alienated from those people who loved me.

After a few days of sleeping long hours, moping around the house and eating infrequently, I persuaded Susan to come out with me for a few hours. Whether I remained living with my parents or not, I was determined that while I was here, I must spend some time with my sister, even though my mental state was becoming fragile. At Susan's suggestion, we walked down Shadwell Heath Road and into a newly-built pub called The Green Man. We took our drinks and sat in a quiet corner of the brightly furnished pub.

'Our first time together in well over three years Les. What 'ave yer bin doing in all that time?' inquired Susan, who was now 16, well-proportioned, and looked sexy in her new dark blue coat and skirt.

'It's a long story sweetheart and I 'aven't got the energy to tell yer the whole of it now. I cut some capers with two former soldiers I met in a café in Thirsk, Sammy and Percy. That's where I went on the train from London.'

'We wondered where yer went Les. I was the first to read the note you left for Mum and Dad.'

'Well, after gettin orf the train in Thirsk, I went in this café and met five or six former soldiers. Decent blokes like. I stayed with 'em in a disused warehouse for some time before Sammy, Percy and me went walking and got jobs living on a farm. Great fun it was. Then afterwards we went tramping for miles and stayed at a few places. It was a right laugh most of the time. The other two were good geezers. Tell yer the rest another time'.

'What is this monastery stuff then, Les?' Mum said you've bin livin' with a load of monks,' said Susan with a broad grin.

'Yea that's right. I enjoyed it most of the time. Can't yer imagine me with a shaven 'ead and white robe, looking like Moses trying to find the bull-rushes?' Susan laughed loudly.

She had found a new job, three months before my return, working for a shipping company, Davies & Co, as an office assistant in nearby Wapping. They transported steel around the world. No doubt some of their metal had been used by our enemies to make weapons to use on our lads during the war. Her work entailed sending electronic fax messages to various companies informing them of delivery dates. Not exactly mind-blowing work, but she received the same wages for working nine hours a day, in a clean warm office, as she did working in a factory for ten hours a day in a dirty, noisy environment. Since leaving school two years before, the only work she could find had been working in factories, but now she hoped to improve her job prospects at her new employers.

'I like the work there, Les. The workers are friendly, and we often go to the pub for our dinner break,' said Susan, who appeared more confident and assertive than when I last saw her. I was also pleased that my sister had found a decent job that didn't involve working on large, mind-numbing, oily machines for long, monotonous hours, like most of her former schoolmates. In those days women took those dreadful jobs because within a few years, or even less, they were expected to be married with children to bring up. Besides, it was difficult in those days for working-class women to remain single; all respects go to my Aunt Jane, who was single all her adult life, had a decent job, and lived on her own for the last few years of her life, until she was tragically killed.

'How long you bin courting Cyril for?' I asked my sister.

''Bout six months. He's a decent bloke. He works down the gas works as a stoker, and lives in Limehouse with his parents and six brothers and sisters. Some of 'em is a bit scatty. 'Is old man is a drinker and beats up 'is mum a lot. Sounds familiar, I thought. We meet about three times a week. He's met Mum and Dad a few times.' Susan didn't show too much enthusiasm for her latest boyfriend. As she was bright and presented herself well, I felt she was frustrated with a boyfriend who lacked the wherewithal to enjoy life, but she was not yet 17.

The inevitable subject of our parents eventually came up for discussion. Much as I loved and respected them, I had had mixed feelings towards them since returning home. Still a young man, and with the last three years of experience behind me, I tried to explain to my sister what I thought about them.

'They've done a lot for us by keeping us safe in all the places where we've lived. But they 'aven't showed much initiative over the years, 'ave they? All they've done is unskilled work, instead of trying to better themselves.' As soon as I made that comment I realised how ungrateful I was being to the two people who had fed and clothed me for the first and most important years of my life.

'They didn't get the opportunity Les to do anyfink else,' said Susan, understandably defending her parents.

'They married young, had us two kids and just worked to keep their 'eads above water. As you know life is tough for those right at the bottom of the heap'.

'Ave they still got the same jobs? Mum cleaning the stairs at the flats, and Dad delivering coal?' I asked, knowing what Susan's reply would be.

'Yeah, they're still at it, bless 'em'.

With that we put the subject to rest, as I didn't want to upset my sister. Within the next few months, although it didn't apply to Susan, women aged over 21 would be able to vote in general elections for the first time. Women had demonstrated during World War One that they were as capable as men when it came to thinking for themselves.

Weeks passed as I continued living with my family in their newly-decorated, comfortable Peabody Trust flat. Instead of carrying out the work themselves the Trust gave grants to their tenants, who could then choose their own colour scheme. It was father who motivated me into action by encouraging me to decorate the flat a light lilac colour, while the family were out working. For a few days I was engaged in vigorous exercise and mental concentration as I moved from room to room, leaving behind me each time finished work which, even by my own estimation, was well accomplished.

Acutely mindful that I was reaching the end of decorating, the dark mental states that had been hovering around the past two weeks started to take hold of me once again. My other self forced its way into my inner life, with little respite, for the next few weeks. So intense did the dark feelings of hopelessness, guilt and anxiety become that after a spurious excuse to my parents, I walked out of my home, accompanied by my rucksack, not knowing where I was heading.

I walked and walked for miles along main roads, local roads, paths, alleys, parks until I somehow arrived in Aspen Street, not a hundred yards from Euston Station. I sat on the pavement not knowing what to do. Within half an hour about ten tramps had asked me for money, cigarettes or alcohol. Their plight was all too familiar to me. As I raised myself from the damp dirty pavement, I got into an argument with a tramp who was drunk and wouldn't leave me alone. 'Fuck off, you prick!' I shouted at him. He eventually shuffled his decrepit body down the road to the next unsuspecting person waiting for a bus.

I felt frightened and alone in a heartless city that didn't give a damn about the likes of me and the large number of tramps drinking alcohol who were scattered around the station. I moved on, and walked down a narrow dark street parallel with Euston Station, where tramps sat on the pavement sleeping, smoking and drinking. 'Give us a fuckin fag,' one tramp shouted at me. 'Got any spare change sir?' shouted another, as I continued walking. Somehow I felt I was heading straight into the bowels of the earth's cesspit...

My eyes opened, and I saw a brownish flaking ceiling above me. I stared, trying to understand where I was. Anxiously, I quickly got out of the bed, and realised that I was in a large dark dormitory with long rows of beds either side. When I stood up, I noticed that most of the beds were occupied by old men sleeping. Some were snoring, others shouting and swearing incoherently. Most of the men had tied their wretched clothes and boots to their dilapidated iron beds, hoping they wouldn't be stolen. The dormitory stank beyond words. Natural light shone onto the disgusting, filthy sheets and blankets that I had been sleeping in for God knows how many hours. I felt I had been sent to hell for all the terrible thoughts and feelings I kept experiencing.

My nightmarish world continued; I panicked, not knowing where I was and how I had got there. Rapidly putting my shoes back on, and with my rucksack in hand, I walked towards the door, but found it locked. I gave it several loud bangs, hoping to draw attention to someone to let me out. After about five minutes an unkempt middle-aged man opened the dormitory door. 'What's this fucking noise? It's only six in the morning. Can't yer sleep?' he angrily asked me.

'Sorry mate. I gotta get out of this place before I suffocate,' I blurted out, as I rushed past him and ran down two flights of stairs, through the front door and out into the wonderful fresh morning air. I stood there for minutes taking in gulps of air. When I looked at the name of the Victorian building I had just escaped from, I realised that I had booked into one of the many cheap dirty lodging houses that existed in London at the time. What had my life come to?

Chapter Ten

The adventures of a costermonger

For the next few weeks I found decent inexpensive accommodation at the Rowton House in King's Cross. Rowton Houses were a chain of hostels built in London by the Victorian philanthropist Lord Rowton to provide decent accommodation for working men in place of the squalid lodging houses. For a small charge, I got a cubicle to myself where I could remove my clothes and boots at night without worrying that someone would steal them. There were also clean bathrooms where one could wash after a day's hard work. For a further shilling or so, one could upgrade to a special room, which was similar to hotel accommodation. It was reassuring that I had managed to save over a pound from the various monies we were given at Oldstead and Sinnington.

I felt safe and secure knowing that most of the staff, on the whole, diligently oversaw the well-being of the working-class men in their charge. The only objection men had to the regime at all Rowton Houses was the strict discipline. There were rules against cooking, drinking alcohol, non-smoking in bedrooms, playing cards, sexual activity with other men and so on. Personally, I understood why such rules existed in large hostels, where men, some of them tough characters, from many varied backgrounds, had to live together in some sort of harmony. Mind you, if you played your cards right, so to speak, alcohol, and other banned items were available to buy from staff and residents. During the various times that I used several different Rowton Houses, I only witnessed a handful of fights caused by men fuelled with the demon alcohol. These places were unlike cheap lodging houses which were frequented by alcoholics, people with mental illness, idiots, sexual perverts and many other tortured souls. I had to live in Rowton House, because I had nowhere else to go. My parents' flat wasn't big enough for four grown people, and besides, I didn't have a friend in the world who I could ask for help.

Although I felt like phoning Father John-Paul to ask if I could visit him at Heythrop Monastery, I realised that I should try and find a job, anything that could help me pay my way. With that in mind, I thought of a local costermonger, Billy Wendle, who was a good friend of my father's. They had worked together in various markets, and Billy had served plenty of prison sentences for stealing, fraud and causing affray.

My father arranged for me to meet him a few days later in his local pub, the White Swan in Wapping. Incidentally, in those days, anyone and everyone could be found in their particular pub. It was a sort of business address. More villainy was carried out in pubs than in any other place.

'Awight son. Yer dad told me you're looking for some collar [work]?' asked the pugnacious-looking Billy Wendle, a tough-looking bloke, short, fat and balding with several scars down his right cheek. Not the kind of man you took the piss out of unless you hated yourself.

'That's right Billy. I can turn my 'and to most things,' I said, hoping that was what he wanted to hear.

'You will fuckin well 'ave to in this game boy,' he said, as he looked at me through piercing brown eyes that frightened me. 'Right, OK Les boy, you can start tomorrow at 7 am. Be in the Black Boy café in Wapping High Street'.

The next day, as arranged, I met Billy Wendle, accompanied by other costers, in the smoke-filled café . Once there he read us out his verbal riot act. All the other seven workers were young local lads looking for a few shillings to buy their way into decent accommodation, just like me. Half of them had experienced children's homes, mental asylums or prisons. One chap, Lucky Collins (unfortunate first name), had been in all three institutions by the age of 21. During Billy's thirty-minute pep talk, or rather more eloquently, 'you do it this way you cunts,' Lucky had not only stolen my cigarettes but had the audacity to steal the scarf I had left at the back of my chair.

In a nutshell, this is the way it worked as a costermonger: I would hire a handcart from Field-Marshal Billy. Other workers also had the opportunity to choose a handcart, a market stall or a large wheelbarrow. 'What's all important lads is yer don't forget to wear your neckerchiefs round yer scrawny fucking necks. And also I want you all to 'ave a loud sing-song or chant so customers know you are around selling the goodies. Understand, you bunch of cunts? And one last important thing, be aware of the old bill [police], they enjoy nicking us the bastards,' screamed our leader, mentor and potential executioner.

Police hostility was not surprising, as from mid-Victorian England onwards, it appeared that costermongers, who were unlicensed, seemed to be everywhere under-pricing their goods and services, sometimes to the detriment of established local businesses. But grist to the mill for the costers in using their initiative by make a living, albeit a tough one, out on the dirty streets of London. I was now one of them.

Fate paired me with Lucky for a few weeks, until we were competent enough to venture out on our own. We took turns in pushing, or sometimes pulling, our eight-foot long cart full of fruit, vegetables and other items around the neighbourhood shouting, singing, chanting or swearing, trying to sell our goods to hard-up local women. Other times Billy gave us something different to sell. Lucky being well known as a rogue round the Wapping area, people came and bought our goods, which were cheaper, and inferior to those in the local shops. That irritated the shopkeepers, who, given the opportunity, would tell us to 'fuck orf'.

On one occasion, just off Wapping High Street, a decrepit old butler (are there any young butlers?) shuffled out and bought many pounds of fruit and vegetables from our cart. Because the goods were too heavy for the old man to carry back to the large detached house on his own, Lucky carried it straight into the house for him. Minutes later he emerged from the house with a smile on his freckled, devious face.

'Step up the pace Les, and take the next left at Vine Street,' instructed Lucky as we both pushed the barrow, like demented undertakers, out of sight of the house we had just served. Hidden by a row of terraced houses, Lucky brought from underneath his overcoat a gold case full of Havana cigars. It could have been a fake, but how would two buffoons like us have known any different?

'That must be worth a nice few bob Les,' said the amused Lucky, as we stood talking like two conspiring gangsters 'You'd better hide it somewhere Lucky, because when the 'ousehold find it missing they will phone old bill and they'll soon find out we've bin there for fuck sake,' I said, worried.

Lucky ran down the road, hid the case somewhere, and was back in a few minutes. As we continued down the road singing and chanting trying to sell our goods, I asked Lucky, a lanky, scruffy person, who he thought would buy such a valuable item. 'Most of the people you know 'avent got a pot to piss in, 'ave they?' I reminded my partner.

'Leave it to me. I'll knock it out [sell it] to someone,' said my incorrigible co-worker, who would steal a post box given the chance.

On another occasion, as the wind and rained lashed around us, a well-spoken middle-aged lady came out from her mid-terraced, brightly-painted house and invited us in for some much-needed shelter. 'Come in' she said. 'You look like two drowned rats standing out there exposed to the elements. In a moment, I shall buy some fruit and vegetables from you, but first a cup of tea is in order.' She went off to the kitchen.

'Some decent stuff 'ere to nick,' Lucky whispered to me.

The woman was back in five minutes with tea and cake for us all. 'I'm Mrs Duckett, I teach English at St Edward's primary school in Poplar. My husband is the headmaster there. We moved up to London from Surrey at least fifteen years ago, and as we liked it so much, we put down roots,' Mrs Duckett explained, as she started to pour the tea out in a room full of expensive furniture. She was rather tall for a woman, had long grey hair and walked with a noticeable limp.

'Could I use your toilet Mrs Duckett?' asked Lucky.

'Upstairs, my dear, last on the right.'

As Lucky ascended the thick carpeted stairs, I knew there was only one thing on his mind: to steal anything, even a bar of soap if needs be. We thanked Mrs Duckett for the tea and scarpered.

Back on the streets trying to attract local people, we continued singing the praises of our inferior goods as we pushed our handcart round the local estates. We stood on many different street corners, opposite houses only fit for slum clearance, hoping to make a few shillings from mainly unemployed people.

'What do yer think about that, Les?' asked Lucky as he pulled out a jar of French perfume from his grimy pocket. 'I can knock that out (sell) for a nice few bob in my local pub.'

'Why the fuck steal that from a decent old woman who was kind to us?' I asked, irritated by his behaviour.

'No worry Les, those people are well hung [rich]. They won't miss a jar of fucking perfume. If they do, that's too bad,' said Lucky rather aggressively.

After serving a few customers, my mind took me back to my days at school, when, according to my teacher, I showed enough promise to be able to get a decent job. Now look where I was, knocking out mouldy vegetables and rotten fruit not fit for human consumption. And working with Lucky, who didn't exactly inspire, it made my depression darker, deeper and more painful. On the pretext that I had diarrhoea, I used to sit on a public toilet seat for at least ten minutes at a time, so that I could get a brief respite from my colleague's petty attitude. It was comforting to know that in two weeks I should be working on my own; that's if I didn't end it all by jumping off Tower Bridge in the meantime.

Bessie had arranged, via my mother, to meet me in a pub, the Lucky Traveller, just off Stepney Green Road. I was pleased to have written on several occasions direct to Bessie during my tramping on the North York Moors, and she wrote all the gossip back to me, but I hadn't seen her for some time due to living in Rowton House.

'Allo grandma, 'ow are you luv?' I said humbly to Bessie, mindful that I hadn't attended her parents' funerals.

'About bloody time we 'ad a talk together young man. Instead of gallivanting all over the place, you should 'ave been with yer family 'ere in London. They've missed yer sweetheart.' She smiled sarcastically.

'Sorry Bessie, there were many times when I wanted to come 'ome, but things stopped me,' was my pitiful response to a woman who had heard it all before.

'What stopped yer then, Les?' Bessie demanded. She pushed the question several times until I had no choice but to respond accordingly. I started explaining about my early days, when as a young lad, I lacked confidence, and how I was frightened of most people, especially the tough lads at school who used to beat me up. When that happened to me, Bessie used to come along to the school and explain to those tough lads in no uncertain manner that if they hit me again, she would knock their fucking heads together. After that, I was very rarely picked on, but afterwards not many people wanted to play with me, except, nutty Rodger, who was as stupid as a box of spanners.

I tried to explain to Bessie that she was a confident person who wasn't easily frightened, unlike my mother and me. Bessie wasn't too pleased when I suggested to her that the reason Mother was a loner and had gone everywhere on her own until she met her husband was that she had felt undermined by her controlling manner. My mother explained to me on many occasions that she thought Bessie was a tough, domineering person.

Besides, I suggested to Bessie, I thought that was the reason Mother developed a head tic later on when she was a young mother.

'It was around the age of 12, that I started experiencing these dark, powerful, depressive feelings,' I said quietly and guiltily to Bessie.

'Why didn't yer say something to me boy, or your parents?' she said rather curtly.

'I apologise Bessie, I thought everyone in the family would laugh at me for seekin' attention for something that didn't exist,' I cried helplessly. I regained my composure and continued. 'Ever since the depression, if that's what the problem is, it's been a heavy burden for me to try and sort out. The dark moods, feelings of being unworthy of anything.' I explained that this had seriously affected my employment prospects, which explained why I had had only had one paid job before I ran away to Thirsk. I said I felt so inferior around girls that only one girl I took out ever invited me back to her room, but I had declined because I didn't understand what was expected of me. Afterwards, I had made an effort to keep out of her way until she had found another boyfriend. The main reason I had gone to Thirsk, I said, was that I realised no one there would know me or recognise me. Even though there were times when I had enjoyed travelling with Sammy and Percy, at other times my depression had been so overpowering that I had wanted to run away and hide on the moors, hoping no one would ever find me alive. Suicide had been uppermost in my mind when depression had taken hold of my inner life.

Tears came to my eyes once again. 'Other than explaining all these repressed feelings to yer Bessie, the only other people who know about my mental problems are Father John-Paul, and another monk, at the monastery,' I sighed in emotional relief.

After telling this anxious and intense story, I went up to the crowded bar to purchase two more much-needed drinks.

'I didn't know anything about this son,' said Bessie, shrugging.

I went on to explain how I had been living at Rowton House, which was better than most hostels, but did little for my self-esteem. At least, I explained, I had a full-time job, as a costermonger, selling goods around the streets of the East End.'Perhaps you stuck up too much for us Bessie. When we started to grow up we thought you would always be there for us,' I said rather humbly.

'I only did what I thought was right at the time Les,' replied Bessie. As we prepared to leave the pub, I could see she had been moved by the painful experiences I had told her about.

For the next year or so, I managed to make a living selling my wares to supportive local working-class people. Most didn't have very much money, and they were hard taskmasters to do business with, although fair. During all this time I lived at Rowton House in Whitechapel. Earning a regular income allowed me to have a cubicle to myself, a good soak in a bath when required, wash my clothes, and eat good food in the hostel or in inexpensive cafés. Since explaining to the family, especially my parents, how depression took over my life from time to time, my relationship with them had improved. It also helped that I was living elsewhere, as there were only two bedrooms, and Susan was now at an age where she needed a room of her own. But I regularly visited my parents for an evening meal, when I had the opportunity to give them free fruit, vegetables and other goods.

My parents continued to work hard, especially my father, but I noticed that years of delivering coal, for twelve hours a day in all weathers, had taken its toll on him. Although only in his middle forties, he had regular pains in his back and arms, which probably came about from lifting two-hundredweight sacks of coal. He was a tough father and a survivor, and I am indebted to his memory.

Then I met Betty Walsh, who worked in one of the many local cafés I frequented in Cable Street, Stepney. She was a gregarious person who was always running about with plates of fried food for the many men who used those places. Other than that, she washed up and kept the place clean and tidy alongside her two colleagues. Bossy yet humorous. The owner, Alfie Bass, a former East End tearaway, was supportive and paid them a decent wage. Mind you he wanted his 'pound of flesh'. The so-called working men's cafés were on the whole, in those days, clean warm places where you could buy a full plate of well-cooked food without breaking the bank. But some of the cafés didn't half pen and ink (stink) after the local dossers had been sitting in them all day. They usually opened at 6 am and closed invariably around late evening, with staff working two different shifts. Those women earned their wages and, afterwards many of them went home to feed their starving families.

'Nine hours a day of graft is enough for me,' moaned Betty, the only daughter of Irish parents. 'That fuckin boss pushes me to the limit, when I tells 'im he needs another worker, he says he can't afford it', moaned Betty. She was no film star, but at 27 she was a kind, friendly woman who loved a beer and a good laugh. What first attracted me was her long, thick red hair, which shone like stars. She tried to kid me that consuming large amounts of draught Guinness and eating well-cooked bacon hocks had brought about her only redeeming feature. But looking at a photograph of her Dublin-born grandmother, I realised where her appealing appearance came from.

In November 1928, Betty and I started living together. We rented two small rooms in a large detached Victorian house, not far from her parents' flat in Bethnal Green. We shared bathroom/toilet with three small families, all from Scotland. The children were usually noisy, and the husbands invariably drunk. Not a house full of bliss, I can assure you. We also shared a small garden full of brambles, nettles and lots of dumped rubbish belonging to other people. Similar to Sandhurst Street, our house was at the end of a terrace. Our recently-painted furnished rooms were nothing to shout about, but they were better than the other rooms, which were apparently full of damp and mildew. That must have been uncomfortable for the families, especially the children. However, many of the slums had been, or were in the process of being, knocked down and replaced by new council houses which were being constructed over most of Britain. But a lot of councils were slow to even get started by blaming the lack of money for the problem.

After a long week's graft trying to earn enough money to keep our heads away from the workhouse door, the one enjoyment that Betty and I usually looked forward to was a long walk round our local Queen Victoria Park. That wide open space was full of large London plane trees and beds of many varieties of blooming flowers, depending on the time of the year. In season most of the treetops were occupied by territorial rooks guarding their flimsy nests of twigs. The deafening noise they made fighting among themselves for scraps of food could be heard some way off. The wildlife in London was such a contrast to that on the North York Moors.

Families who came from different countries would play together and squabble on the swings, kick footballs and try out their new roller skates. Invariably children ran back to their mothers nursing bleeding arms or sore knees. At the end of our enjoyable walks, we usually stopped at the park café to buy a mug of tea and a bacon sarnie in a friendly atmosphere of good humour with other locals. Some of them recognised Betty from the café. Most Sundays, Pearly Kings and Queens used to dance, sing and frolic among the crowd. It was a grand atmosphere, as people would join in singing with the Pearlies leading the way. One of the Pearly Kings, Billy James, who was 90 when I knew him, was a local character full of fun, charm and devilment. He came from a long line of Pearlies, as did most of them, going back through London history.

I particularly looked forward to walks with Betty, as they distracted my thoughts from the depressive, darker side of my mind as we enjoyed each other's company in surroundings we both loved. It was the same when we were at home together. She enjoyed reading passionate novels. Betty was an easy-going person who did her best to make do with the little she had like most people in those days. Despite all our faults, we got on well together. For the first time in my life I felt more relaxed, and my confidence and self-esteem started to grow. Betty Walsh made a contribution to that, and I am eternally grateful to her.

It was some time before I had the courage to explain to Betty about the nature of my tramping days, and how they had been exacerbated at times by depression, but by other factors too. She was sympathetic. After visiting them a few times for dinner, and going out for a few beers together, I gained Betty's parents' confidence sufficiently to explain my past. They were interested in my travels, and hoped my depression would improve in time.

'You need to drink a few more pints of Guinness, my son,' suggested Mr Walsh.

Things were looking up for me: I lived with a woman I loved, I had a regular job, and my relationship with my family had never been so supportive, while most of the time, my depression was not taking over as it had done before. Yet I still experienced a frustrating inner need to achieve more, a yearning to do something different with my life. It was an intangible feeling, a longing for something that I felt was beyond my capability. Perhaps it was just that; feelings that most people have, without any real direction or point. In essence, I felt I was wasting my time when I could be engaged in something more constructive

With that in mind, I impulsively walked into a phone box in Millard Street, Poplar, and phoned Father John-Paul at Heythrop Monastery. *(The red telephone box was introduced in 1924 and was designed by Sir Gilbert Scott).* As the phone continued to ring, my anticipation and excitement grew. It felt like a lifetime. At last, 'Hallo Father John-Paul speaking,' said the voice I longed to hear.

'Allo Father, it's Leslie speaking. 'Ow are you?' I asked, full of nervous energy.

'Hallo Leslie. I'm well thank you. How lovely to hear from you. What are you doing with yourself?' he asked.

'I'm a costermonger, sellin' goods in East London. I'm living with a woman called Betty. She is a really decent person Father. She works in a café, that's where I met 'er,' I enthusiastically explained.

'I am so pleased to hear your life is going well for you Leslie.'

'Can I come up to Heythrop and stay for a few weeks?' I said eagerly, hoping that he would agree.

'Yes of course you can. When would you like to visit us?' he asked in his usual clear, peaceful voice. As I had to discuss my intended visit to Heythrop with Betty and my employer, the loveable Billy Wendle, I made arrangements to inform the monastery at a later stage.

Although I was somewhat anxious and guilty about discussing my visit to the monastery with Betty, I nonetheless managed to gather enough confidence several days later to ask what she thought about it. At first she was reluctant to agreeing, due to the concern that I could lose my job, but after much soul-searching, she agreed that I might benefit from living and working with the monks I had got to know quite well.

'The money I've saved will cover our rent for a few weeks,' I said. 'Besides if we are really stretched for money, I can always sell my forebear's medal.' Deep down I knew that would never happen, unless it meant saving us from living on the streets or in the workhouse. 'I want yer to enjoy yourself there Les, as yer did before,' said Betty, who by this stage, although she didn't say, must have felt rather insecure.

It was during the fortnightly costermongers' meeting in the George pub in Limehouse that I broached the idea with Billy Wendle of taking time off work.

'You want to visit a fucking monastery for a few weeks, son? You gone orf yer fucking rocker! The next thing you'll be tellin' me is yer've become a monk with a shaven head. Now, now Les boy. The way you're going you'll end up in the laughing 'ouse, or even the 'ouse of correction. 'Ow many weeks you want orf?'

Billy wasn't used to new ideas, especially not ideas about visiting a monastery to work with reclusive monks, miles from civilisation. Besides, according to my employer, the working world ended at Upminster. It was embarrassing discussing something so personal in front of all my fellow costermongers. None of them actually understood what monastery life meant. All they did was take the piss out of me. As for Billy, he was as sensitive as a concrete building. From his tough, no-nonsense background, you just came out with it, regardless of who was listening.

He agreed I could take three weeks maximum off work. These were the times when I just felt like walking away from it all and travelling up to Heythrop, or wherever. If needs be, I could very quickly get back tramping and meet up with the men of the road. It was now that I realised I had the inner resources to travel, to live elsewhere and not be overwhelmed by different conditions. But the most important thing that worried me was my respect and concern for Betty, as I didn't want her to suffer due to my irresponsibility.

A few months before my departure for Thirsk, working-class people were jubilant over Labour's victory in the 1929 General Election, its last short-lived victory having been in 1924. Once again, James Ramsay MacDonald would be Prime Minister, but for only two years. The minister advising MacDonald on rising unemployment was Oswald Mosley. In 1932, Mosley formed the British Union of Fascists (BUF). The Fascist party changed its name in 1936 and again in 1937, but it was essentially the same political party. Anti-fascists, including my family and hundreds of local people, were determined to prevent the BUF from marching through Cable Street, Stepney. These parties were dissolved in 1940.

Chapter Eleven

The call of the Monastery

When I informed my family of my intentions to visit Heythrop they weren't too happy about my decision, but I was on the Thirsk bound train two weeks later. In contrast to the last time I had embarked on this journey, when confusion had masked any idea of what I was letting myself in for, this occasion would be entirely different.

As small suburban stations flashed by on the non-stop express train, the new house building I witnessed was mostly a blur, as I tried to remember the time I met the smartly-attired Father John-Paul, who was reading correspondence taken from his posh suitcase. My first thoughts about him, understandably at the time, were not very complimentary. His flashing eyes told me one thing only: sex. But how wrong and misled I had been due to my experiences with Mr Helling and others in Compton. All I could see now was a positive, clear vision of Heythrop Monastery and the monks within its sturdy walls. Surrounding the old building was the rugged beauty of the North York Moors and its wildlife, from the smallest germinating seed to the largest living organism, the Scots Pine. It was as though the moors were calling me back to walk and find its hidden treasures. Nearly every time I thought about the moors, my mind instantly conjured up those two resourceful wandering tramps Sammy and Percy, who had taught me so much about life under the stars. I wondered which journey fate had sent them on.

The Kings Cross express arrived on schedule. The large steel Victorian station clock had just passed 2 pm. It was a bright and sunny day. As I gathered my faithful old rucksack from the overhead luggage rack, I was full of optimism, tempered by some anxiety, but feeling that my life was making progress. Walking down the long platform, I remembered the tramps begging for money the last time I had been here.

Brother Joseph was waiting for me at the arranged place next to Smith & Son. We hugged each other. 'Hallo Leslie, how good to see you after such a long time. What have...'

'Sorry Brother Joseph for interrupting you,' I said happily. 'It's so good to see you again. I'm well thank you and really lookin' forward to staying at Heythrop Monastery with you and all the monks.'

'The car is parked just round the corner,' said the affable Brother.

As we walked out of the station, a large white butterfly landed on the lapel of my old coat. It stayed there for a couple of minutes before flying off. Was the butterfly trying to tell me something? I realised that it might symbolize the latent potential within me to find my own wings of autonomy, and fly free of the shackles that held me back.

The journey to Heythrop was an enjoyable one; Brother Joseph had brought along a flask of tea and sandwiches for us to have in a small hut near Plimpton, sheltered from the biting wind that comes off the moors even during summer.

'This is such a lovely spot, I thought it would be a good idea to stop and have our food,' he said. 'Besides, we must make the best of what our dear Lord God has given us, Leslie.'

'Yeah, I agree. It's wonderful to sit 'ere quietly overlooking the moor and the forest, while we eat our cheese sarnies,' I said, full of hope and optimism for the days ahead.

We ate in silence and looked at the wild, colourful summer kidney vetch bobbing around in the wind. How could such a small plant, I thought, survive in these harsh conditions? Yet they not only survive, but flourish to provide food for various living creatures. Pondering on my own limitations when compared to a small insignificant flower, we were joined by a lone golden plover eating seeds from nearby grassy patches.

'Recently, Leslie, I have been reminded of what the

Roman poet Juvenal had to say about the influence nature has on all things,' said Brother Joseph. *'The grape gains its purple tinge by looking at another grape'.* We can interpret that in many ways, of course, but for me it's the word 'tinge' where God is influential'.

I didn't understand what he had said about God's influence, so I remained quiet, not wanting to repeat my ignorance yet again. But I did ponder for some considerable time and thought about Brother Joseph's motivation for living at the monastery. Some time later I recalled the interesting explanation he had given me three years previously for living the religious life.

An hour later we arrived at the monastery, which looked majestic in the late afternoon sun. Being rather sentimental, I had always viewed the place as a haven of peace and simplicity, detached from a world of strife and suffering. The evening meal being an hour away, I walked to the dormitory where I had last slept three years before. The rancid smell of Percy's feet still seemed to linger in the air. It reminded me to look at my fellow tramps inscribed names and dates they had left on the walls, along with many others, whom I didn't know by name, but their spirits would remain *ad infinitum*.

Lying on my sleeping bag on one of the three single beds, I noticed that three more framed pictures of Jesus, Madonna and child had been added to the room since the last time I was here. From my earliest days in London churches, schools and libraries, I had seen many pictures and images of Jesus and other Christian iconography. They meant very little to me then. Here, of course, at

Heythrop there were numerous pictures of religious figures to remind you of the significance of the place, and the reason for being there, although I gave little thought to their meaning. It wasn't until I saw the newly-installed framed picture of Jesus Christ opposite my dormitory bed that I realised, for the first time, how the power and beauty of the Jesus figure had begun to affect me. Slowly yet surely, the influence of the religious figures made inroads into my dim consciousness and repressed feelings. Whether that awareness would endure or not, only time would tell.

I made my way to the dining room to eat my first meal with the monks. They were the same monks sitting there eating the splendidly-cooked vegetable flan whom I had seen when I had departed in July 1926. I felt anxious about being in the monastery, yet at the same time reassured to be among men I felt safe with, even though I did not know them that well.

In certain respects it was quite odd sitting in silence for over an hour with nine monks. Not used to such silence, I tended to fidget and to look about me to see if others were doing the same. They all looked peaceful and untroubled by the world going on around them. If they required food, the monks would give a slight nod to one of the brothers who came round armed with tasty, wholesome dishes. From the moment you entered the dining room to when you departed, everything was calmly carried out mindfully. There was no noise and no hurrying. At every meal, various monks would lay the table, serve, then clear everything away to be washed and make their way back to their own rooms.

As I was leaving the dining room, I had a brief conversation with Father John-Paul, who welcomed me back to Heythrop Monastery. In his usual unflappable manner, he remarked, 'You look well Leslie. I hope your stay with us will be a happy one for you. Brother Joseph thought you would enjoy working with him tomorrow in the garden. So after he has finished praying, and had his breakfast, meet him down near shed at 9 am. And remember, *'God gives every bird his food,* but *he does not throw it into the nest'.*

'Thank you Father,' I said. I walked back to my room feeling confused, yet again, by words of religious wisdom, which I assumed were intended for me to work out and interpret, not just during my time at the monastery, but elsewhere too.

After a near sleepless night worrying about Betty's well-being, my family, my job and hoping I had I done the right thing by coming here, I was pleased to meet Brother Joseph in the garden early next morning. As I was aware of his background, which was similar to mine, it was not surprising that Brother Joseph was the one monk I had the most confidence in.

'Good morning Leslie, I hope you slept well on your first night back at Heythrop?'

'Sorry Brother Joseph. No I didn't sleep at all well worryin' about various people at home, so I'm pleased to see you,' I said quietly.

'I'm sorry to hear that Leslie. I hope things will settle down for you. As our dear maintenance man Robbie has retired, it leaves us with more work to do in the future, but I'm sure we will all cope. Robbie has been a great supporter, in many ways, of Heythrop, for twenty years or so. Now that he is over 70, he has earned a well-deserved rest. Robbie is a very religious man and often prayed with the community here. Even though he is ageing, I hope he can visit us from time to time. We plan to pick him up occasionally from his small cottage in the village and drive him here for prayers, hymns, psalms and readings. Those practices have always been an integral part of his life. I remember Robbie saying only several weeks ago in the garden here that God gave him great spiritual company 24 hours a day. He had never realized before, although he does now, just how profoundly alone upon this planet we all are'.

That word 'alone' was at the forefront of my mind again. Sometimes it made me feel so insecure that I often thought I was floundering as the days passed by. Upon hearing or thinking about that word, I would sometimes descend into depression, secrecy and guilt. Feeling the odd man out, I had to try to find a balance in my life.

On a warm late September day, as a breeze crept in from across the moors, nearly all the vegetables had been picked, Brother Joseph and I proceeded to dig the soil and prepare it for another season. It was enjoyable digging in silence, except for the occasional curlew landing on the overturned soil to devour a wriggling worm. To add to this preparation, we added a whole lorryload of recently-delivered pig manure from Farmer Booker. He, like Robbie, was an ardent supporter of the monastery, and again like the latter, very rarely charged for his much-needed services. It was Captain Booker who had delivered several loads of bricks and other building materials over the years to help keep the monastery in one piece, although it was the monks themselves who had done much of the building and rebuilding, with professional skill and dedication.

After lunch, we continued as before digging in barrow-loads of 'brown gold', as the captain had called it, into the dark, well-maintained earth which had been mulched by many monks for over a hundred years. The sky turned an ominous dark grey. Father Joseph could tell that the heavens were about to open and nourish our garden, and he directed us into the small shed for shelter. Minutes later rain fell, like a monsoon in India, creating a large puddle all over the garden.

'God answered my prayers,' smiled Brother Joseph, who appeared to love every minute of his waking life. If only, I thought, my life was full of love and faith, just as Brother Joseph's appeared to be. He must have been completely committed to his religious life.

On my own in the dormitory, I had read chapters from two books about the long arduous process to which a young aspiring monk has to commit himself. 'How did yer first start being a monk? I mean, what did yer 'ave to go through Joseph, to get this far fifteen years later?' I asked him.

Although silence was an integral part of religious practice, Brother Joseph realised that I had a craving to understand how a monk's life works.

'Well Leslie, I shall have to be rather brief,' he said. 'A new monk starts as a postulant for six months, followed by two years as a novice, after which you take your first vows. My first vow was for a minimum of three years, after which I could have left, but I chose to take my vows for life. Brotherhood is central to a monk's life. Although I didn't, most have a calling or vocation from an early age to live entirely for God. Once you are living in a monastery, you settle into a routine. You don't worry about social life, or even the future. But it must be remembered that it isn't easy, even after 15 years, to live with men from different backgrounds. Families seldom visit us, but I write monthly to my family as I am still interested in what they are doing with their lives.'

Was I any wiser after Brother Joseph's explanation of his religious growth and development? I would have to keep asking questions, reading books and, most importantly of all, practice along with the monks and when I was on my own.

Because of numerous toothaches and associated problems, Father David arranged for me to visit the local dentist in Pickering. As I hadn't seen a dentist for ages, my teeth were in a very bad state. Even as a youngster, I didn't brush my teeth regularly, although mother did buy some kind of paste that I thought was more of a hindrance than a help. She bought anything down Cable Street market that was cheap, regardless of its effects on your teeth. Some Indian potion or lotion she once brought home made my gums bleed for weeks, and was so smelly it would have been refused as food even by a hungry pig. Mother was so gullible when offered anything cheap. Compared to most of my friends at school, whose mouths resembled Bazalgette's sewers, my teeth were relatively healthy. Mind you, lack of hygiene generally, and short-sighted government policy didn't actually help working-class kids to cherish their teeth. Yet environmental health did improve. But after years of abusing my teeth, they were now in desperate need of attention before they all dropped out. The piano keyboard came to mind when assessing the appearance of my 'Hampstead Heath' (teeth).

'Well Mr Tatter, you haven't looked after your teeth have you?' snapped the dentist. Mr Hutchinson was about 60, tall and thin and sported a large moustache underneath his abnormally long nose. He had been the dentist in Pickering for many years. Locally known as 'the butcher', he had lived in a large stone-built detached house at the western end of the village ever since he moved in with his wife and two daughters. Many avoided his practice but instead took their chances in one of the local pubs to secure pain relief, rather than having to undergo his brutal use of drills.

'The only effective dentistry I can do for you is remove the offending decayed teeth and make false teeth for you,' he said. 'There are about six altogether. At least you'll be able to eat more effectively in the future. Do you understand?' he smiled scornfully.

After an hour of torturing me in his dental chair, he had extracted the aforementioned teeth and measured my mouth for false ones by stuffing into my numbed and battered mouth a gadget filled with white paste that tasted like oil. 'Return in three weeks for your false teeth to be fitted,' he said. He added, 'make sure you clean your teeth in future'.

With my mouth feeling bloated, I walked through the village looking at the various shops and different faces that I was seeing for the first time. Buxom, noisy middle-aged women, most of them carrying baskets, lined up outside the village butcher's shop. It appeared that Edward Cracknell, an ageing, slim, red-faced man wearing a white boater and gown, was the women's choice when it came to buying the best cuts of meat. I watched captivated by the way he threw large pieces of meat onto a cutting slab, similar to the treatment the dead receive in a mortuary, and within no time at all, had served three contented customers.

At the end of the village, discreetly hidden from view by a beech copse, was a large, dilapidated, detached Georgian house, with the front covered in dark green ivy and yellow honeysuckle. The small gold-lettered sign stated that it was a local council home, Moorfield House, for people with mental and physical handicaps. Instructed by a male nurse, four men were cleaning the brick-covered drive with brooms and shovels. They all looked awfully stigmatized, even for those unenlightened days. All four men had had all their hair cut off, and their clothes appeared to be unsuitable even for an institution. They stood there resembling the desperate-looking East London tramps who wore Hessian sacks to cover their bodies and newspapers round their feet to keep warm.

'Can I help you sir?' asked a middle-aged male nurse, who had seen me observing what the men were doing. 'No thanks,' I replied, and quickly walked back to the monastery, feeling rather low and despondent about the short straws some people have drawn in life. Their lives were more worthless than mine. They had no power or control over their pathetic lives, but their protectors could at least have dressed them decently, I thought to myself.

The three-week holiday I had agreed with my employer was coming to an end. During that time I hadn't contacted either Betty or Billy Wendle, although I had promised I would. I anticipated what was awaiting when I eventually decided to phone both of them. Everyday life at Heythrop was interesting, intense and different from my mundane life in London. The strict routine there, for whatever reason, appealed to my personality. It was secure, regular, peaceful and based on shared brotherhood of purpose. During the last three weeks I had had small bouts of depression, but nothing like the deep, dark feelings that sometimes overwhelmed me when I was least expecting them.

On some mornings I was sufficiently inspired to join the monks at 5 am for prayers in an environment unlike any I had ever experienced before. No words exist to describe the intense feelings that took over my being for a while. It was as though I was tapping into a deep core of my being that had never changed. I felt I had fallen into a spiritual void where anything or everything was possible. The whole experience was inexplicable. Mind you, who really knows what happens to the individual when they removed themselves, if only for a few minutes, from their habitual conditioning?

So engrossed was I in religious life that it wasn't until another twelve days had passed that I felt duty bound to contact Betty and my employer. Sitting in Father John-

Paul's small, brightly-painted office, my knees trembled as I phoned my employer in London.

'Where in the fuck 'ave you bin? I said you could 'ave no more than three weeks' holiday, but it's now nearly five weeks. Why didn't yer phone me, yer prick?' he roared.

'Sorry Billy, I forgot to. I also forgot to phone my girlfriend Betty, by the way,' I humbly explained.

'Anyway your job has bin taken by someone else. You 'ad yer chance son. Good luck Les,' were my employer's last cutting words to me.

Fuck me, I thought, once again unemployment was staring me straight in the eyes. No money, no food and how was I going to pay the rent? I was in big shit again.

Recovering my thoughts after being sacked, I sat in the Father's large leather black seat, anxious about what Betty would have to say when I phoned her. I realised, of course, that I should have contacted her at least two weeks earlier to explain myself. Here I was, sitting in the seat of the big white chief of Heythrop Monastery, wishing it was me who had his power and influence. Another predicament loomed large for me.

Anticipating the worst, I picked up the phone and rang Betty's place of work.

'Allo, could I speak to Betty Walsh please?' I asked Alfie Bass, the café owner.

'Is that Les speaking? Hold on son and I'll get 'er for yer,' he said. After a few tense minutes, Betty eventually picked up the phone.

'Where in the fuck 'ave you bin?' she demanded. 'I've waited ages for yer to contact me. You've bin away five weeks and I've 'eard not a dicky bird from yer. I couldn't wait any more for yer, as I was running out of money. So I'm back livin' wiv me parents. I sent your clobber to your parents' gaff [home] in Shadwell. You 'ad your chances Les. Goodbye, and don't contact me again.'

After that shattering news, I recalled, with bitterness, what Mr George at Oldstead had impressed upon Sammy, Percy and me: 'life is nasty, brutish and short,' he had sternly remarked.

That evening, still reeling from the two injurious blows to my feelings, I sat opposite Father John-Paul in his office, which was adorned with imposing iconography.

'I can imagine how you feel Leslie, after breaking up with your partner and then losing your job, all in one day,' he said. 'All the monks and I are, of course, here for you. We will, of course, support you. As you sit here so sadly, I am reminded of the first line of Blake's poem 'The Little Lost Boy'. The first line reads, "Father, father! Where are you going?" God the Father is always here for you, and everyone, especially those experiencing a hard time. How do you feel at the moment?' He sat there with a warm, reassuring face, reminding me of the love he and others had for me in an uncaring, materialistic world.

'I feel so worthless, useless, and unwanted,' I muttered, as I cried helplessly into the strong arms of the Father. The scene was reminiscent of Jesus, dressed in his white robe, holding a poor wretch unto his body. Only a few days before I had felt on top of the world, and life had taken on an altogether different meaning, but now I felt at rock bottom, weak and unable to carry on. My stupidity had let me get carried away from everyday practical reality. There was a saying my father had kept reminding me of: *'be practical, earn a few bob and keep your head above water'*. Through my own incompetence, my world had collapsed.

Departing from the office, I was presented with a small crucifix and chain, a symbol that would constantly remind me, the Abbot remarked, that God is always with you.

The next few weeks I spent mostly in my dormitory alone, except for taking meals with the monks. Father John-Paul had insisted I attend meals, where I would receive the love and support of others. It would reassure me, he said, that I was an integral part of Heythrop Monastery.

During the following days and evenings, various monks came round for a brief chat, to give me books to read or just to show me a tender, smiling face of support to help my recovery. My depression had returned with a vengeance. Every day I fought with dark, deep moods that unceasingly tormented me, even in my sleep. During these episodes I had new experiences that frightened me to such an extent that sweat would pour, so it seemed, from every part of my thin body. The dormitory room felt as though it was closing in on me. Terrified that it would squash me to pieces, I often ran outside for safety. I was so petrified that I occasionally slept in the garden shed, where I felt safe, until I returned to the evil-smelling dormitory. Where the smells came from was a mystery, although with hindsight they probably didn't exist.

With almighty effort I tried to stay in touch with the piece of me I recognised, knowing that if I failed then all hell could be let loose upon me. About ten days into my lonely existence, although I was well supported, I began to experience, usually in the evenings, what could be described as a vague sense of omnipotence. What I mean by this is that I felt I had enough power and authority to take over the role of Abbot at Heythrop, due to the ever-growing incompetence of Father John-Paul. It had been so ordained by God himself, who, incidentally, had appeared in my bedroom several times. Most of the time I was incapable of trying to understand my delusions. They became a continuous flow of unguarded thoughts and feelings. It was as though I was being dragged along by an uncontrollable torrent of water, and at times I became submerged in a world of despair and hopelessness. When I re-emerged for a while I thought desperately that suicide was the only way out of my living hell.

My other self, as I usually called it, was dominant during my weeks of self-imposed exile as I hid in my human-made cocoon. It was my protection against the outside world, which threatened my very existence. First Billy Wendle, then Betty, had denied my value as an individual human being, one who had his own personal thoughts, feelings, dreams, aspirations and ideas. I didn't want to be tightly wrapped in my self-made cocoon, but I was incapable of growing those metaphorical wings of independence that could have set me free like a soaring colourful red admiral.

With my childhood experiences in mind, it was not surprising that I had retreated into my own world for safety. As a child, I had found being with other people, unless I knew them well, a fearful ordeal. Usually Bessie, but others also, came to my rescue when I was unable to cope. As I approached my 25th birthday, I now realise how that kind of protection had become detrimental to my emergence as a mature person. But how many people do fully emerge and become free during their lives, I wondered?

In the last week of my inactivity, I had intense thoughts about projecting violent feelings and desires onto my parents. I wanted to blame them for everything that had happened to me. At the time, I didn't realise how delusional and irrational it was to burden my parents with all my self-imposed problems, inadequacies and failures. Most parents inflict some harm on their children, although in most cases not deliberately; however, they are to some extent responsible for the way their children succeed or fail in life.

One night in particular the murderous feelings I had for my parents held no bounds. Not only were they responsible for being unable to look after me and Susan as children, they were guilty of killing my great-grandparents in the most gruesome manner possible. In my deluded state, I thought that one night my parents had broken into their grandparents' house and while they slept, robbed them of all their savings. Afterwards my mother, only three feet away, had shot them dead. I also had sexual fantasies about having a relationship with Susan. During the last few days before I returned to reality, I used to lock the dormitory door, as I was frightened that I would be attacked.

Joseph was the only monk I allowed in, to deliver my meals, and as I became healthier, we begun to discuss my various feelings. It was at this stage that I started to re-emerge into a normal world based on reality. It had been a terrible ordeal for me; the shock and anger at losing my partner and my employment had been so traumatic that the only safe thing for me was to withdraw into my own inner space and time. The whole experience had been frightening, painful and confusing, yet somehow I had tried to make sense of some of my childhood repression, recent experiences and the motivation in returning to Heythrop Monastery.

Due to my seclusion, Christmas had passed unnoticed. Thick deep brilliant white snow covered Heythrop, Pickering village and the mysterious moors, where thousands of wild animals were doing their utmost to survive the winter freeze. Feeling that life had more to offer than simply suffering all the time, I sat relaxed and confident, eating my breakfast of steaming porridge with the friends who had supported me through a challenging time. All around the breakfast table were men of different ages and backgrounds, yet they all shared a faith which demanded vows of poverty, obedience and celibacy. In many ways I felt privileged to be among these humble men, who wore their white distinctive habits at all times to demonstrate their purity of heart. Although I only knew scant details about one or two of them, they had all given up the worldly life, for whatever reason, to carry out the work of God, consisting of prayers, hymns, psalms and readings. The dining room iconography, with its many framed images of Jesus, Mary, various disciples and crosses, had taken on a more significant meaning and role for me. Those images encouraged me to look beyond my own needs, if I was to develop a more mature understanding of myself and the world I lived in. But I realised that things weren't that straightforward, and that it would take many years, all my life even, to come to terms with and to make sense of a living, practising faith.

Within a few days I had joined several of the monks for the winter indoors maintenance of Heythrop. With very little to be done outdoors, other than repairing a few broken roof tiles or clearing the fallen autumn leaves, it was time for the monastery to have its yearly painting and decorating programme. At this time of year some of the older monks used to carry out less vigorous activities like repairing furniture and habits. They gave the windows, curtains, carpets and other things their yearly wash and clean. Some monks were skilled at repairing bibles, books and iconography. Other monks wrote religious books, papers and treatises. One monk in particular, Brother Colin, who had been at Heythrop Monastery for over 25 years, was experienced at keeping well-organised financial ledgers up to date, not just for Heythrop, but other monasteries as well.

The non-growing season also gave those monks who usually worked outdoors the opportunity to polish up their culinary skills in the kitchen. Many times Ian, Joseph, Luke and I spent enjoyable periods in silence preparing and cooking community meals for the smiling, grateful monks, who certainly appreciated them, if spotless clean plates were anything to go by.

As the temperature rose and the snow melted, it gave Joseph, Ian and me the opportunity to take our first walk together on the moors. Feeling a lot better, I was determined to enjoy myself for the first time since my lengthy self-imposed isolation from the community.

'Good morning Leslie, are you ready for today's walk?' asked Joseph, who was dressed in his warm hiking clothes. 'I've made the sandwiches and a large flask of soup for the three of us, which we'll need out there on the cold moors.' It was the first time I had seen him without his habit on.

Around 9 am, walking with a seasonal spring in our steps, we went through the large imposing Heythrop Monastery gates, our rucksacks full of hats, gloves and food, determined to enjoy ourselves. We continued walking through the quiet village, where local people went about their everyday business just as their forebears had done, and we took a well-trodden track that led us onto the moor. The land was rock hard, and most of the ground cover plants were lifeless, yet somehow the wild animals found food to survive the harsh conditions that natural selection had chosen for them. Even the ling, shivering in the morning glow, looked like it was made of many strands of wire.

With cold air streaming out of our nostrils like the steam of a miniature railway locomotive, we took a track through Higg Wood, a small conifer plantation. Although it was less than ten years since they were planted, the Scots Pine had grown considerably. Many birds, including the crossbill, hen harrier, goshawk and long-eared owl had begun to colonize them. Many of those birds were attracted to this type of wood for the abundance of food that was available such as smaller birds and rodents, who themselves found shelter amongst the dense trees.

Near Keld Stack Farm, we took a detour, as Joseph wanted to show us an old disused cemetery, which was now overgrown by various wild plants. People had been there recently, as discarded beer bottles littered the ground. Joseph explained that the cemetery contained the souls of men, women and children who had died of disease during the construction of the railway. He added solemnly, 'Families took in lodgers to earn more money, but a lot of the time those navvies carried disease which they in turn gave to others. It is consecrated land'.

We continued walking the 1,500 feet, huffing and blowing, until we eventually reached our destination of Newton-on-Rawcliffe, about five miles north of Pickering. 'Rawcliffe was once a small productive farming village,' said Ian, whose piercing blue eyes shone like diamonds in the cold. 'There were several smallholders here that produced pork and mutton, but the land, as you can see, was unsuitable for farming. For some unknown reason, the place became uninhabited many years ago, although the remains of one of the old cottages and the sties have now become habitats for various animals.'

There was something odd and mysterious about Ian. He appeared, most of the time, to be from another world or dimension. The development, probably, of practising an intense spiritual life.

We found a dry place in one of the old small sties to have our food and heart-warming soup. The three of us sat in silence while we watched a short-eared owl perched on a nearby fence, holding a small mammal in its beak. For about three minutes the brownish-buff bird just looked curiously at us with his large penetrating eyes.

'How are things with you now, Leslie?' asked Ian, who was lanky, slim, educated and about 40 years of age.

'I feel a lot better thanks. At one time in me dormitory I felt really rough and frightened, but thanks fer all the support you lot gave me,' I said sincerely. 'Ow long you bin at Heythrop, Ian?'

This was a question I had been longing to ask ever since I first saw him, some time ago.

'I've been living at Heythrop Monastery for over ten years and I've enjoyed every minute,' was his enthusiastic response.

With the temperature now beginning to drop, the two Brothers decided it was time we started to descend, but using a different route so that they could show me different areas of the moors. We walked more to the west, taking in Sprigotts pig farm, Queens Plantation, which had eight-year-old conifers that were at least forty feet tall, and New Hambleton, once the home of the moorland poet James Gregory. He, incidentally, wrote prose about the various wild moorland animals and used to camp there for several days at a time observing their behaviour. For the final mile, as the light of the day began to fade, we joined an old well-worn droving road that took us into Pickering.

After another prolonged and enjoyable stay at the monastery, it was once again time to return to London. Even though I had lost my relationship, and employment, I was so pleased to have spent time with human beings who actually, I assumed, liked me, even loved me, for who I was. My understanding, practice and faith in Christianity had deepened on this occasion. Why? I was unaware of the power that faith had over me. It was as though something was growing inside me, and every time I stayed at Heythrop it was nurtured by the spiritual atmosphere. I didn't know what was happening to me, but it was good for my well-being.

The challenges, however, would come when I found myself living back in London, where everyday life is usually difficult, dangerous and alienating for most people. Whether my so-called growing faith was strong and resilient enough to withstand the pressures of London life when I took into consideration my bouts of depression, or whatever it was, I would soon find out. But the one strong conviction I had, as I stood outside the main gates of Heythrop, prepared for my homeward journey with my trusty old rucksack on my back, was that I would return some time to live with my friends again.

It was Brother Joseph who once again drove me to Thirsk Station. But on this occasion, unlike the last, we were both quiet and contemplative. One of the most frustrating things in life is that you never know what another person is actually thinking. In that respect, I always felt separate from my fellow beings.

I hugged Joseph goodbye outside the grimy looking station. 'Thanks for everything Joseph. Thanks for your 'elp. I 'ope we meet again,' I said, as tears fell down my cheeks.

'You take care Leslie. You are always welcome at Heythrop. I shall be praying for you,' replied Brother Joseph, who had a serene smile on his tender looking face.

Chapter Twelve

Lost soul

Thirty minutes later I was on the London-bound train as it sped through the lush green countryside, where numerous farm animals were preoccupied with their heads down, munching the grass that would eventually fatten them up for market. I often wondered if those animals think or feel similar to human beings? Do they have consciousness? What short and painful lives they have; after a few months, they end up being carted off to some abominable abattoir. And I, and many like me, add to their suffering, I thought, by eating them.

Halfway through my journey, I became aware of the council housing estates that had been built, or were in the process of being built, for those working-class families who had a moral right to them. Hitherto, industrialisation had failed to house local peoples, whose lot had been sub-standard accommodation not fit for habitation. Local authorities up and down Britain were now empowered to build those much-needed houses for families to bring up their children in homes with inside toilets and bathrooms, decent-sized bedrooms and gardens to play in or the opportunity to grow your own vegetables. It reassured me to know that my parents had a secure tenancy on their Peabody Trust flat for the rest of their lives.

As the train with its eight teak-brown carriages slowed down, it was clear that we were seeing the dirt and grime that clung to most London buildings. Fossil fuels and smog, fog made heavier and darker by smoke and chemical fumes, were the main culprits for the pollution in London and other cities that caused many thousands of premature deaths, especially among older people. But major transformation was all around me, as I sat on the no. 35 bus taking me to Rowton House in Whitechapel. Many old and dilapidated tenement buildings, similar to David Road, and roads of slum terraced houses, had been knocked down and replaced with new homes for families. Although I wasn't impressed by the new high-rise blocks of flats, they did provide new homes for many people who had previously lived in squalor. My main concern was that some of those young men who had fought in the war, those heroes, now had a new home in which they could settle down with their young families and look forward to a better life. New churches, schools and shops had also been provided to improve living conditions for those who had experienced war, high unemployment and economic depression. Inter-war slum clearance had clearly made considerable progress, but very many new buildings were still needed.

After the optimism of living in Heythrop Monastery for several months, gloom once again descended upon me as I walked through the impressive timber and glass doors of Rowton House.

'Allo Les my son. What you doing back 'ere? I thought you moved out of 'ere to live with your partner somewhere,' quipped Sandy Jardine, a short, fat, nasty Scotsman aged about 50, who had worked at this Rowton House for years. Given the opportunity, he was one of the few employees who gave you a hard time. Many residents told him to fuck off, but not being a confident person, I was most reluctant to argue with him. Besides, Whitechapel Rowton House was my home, and with that always in mind, I had to make the best of it. Mind you, I would have loved to have smashed Jardine's head in with a sledgehammer, or even worse, stick gelignite down his throat. I always tried my utmost to avoid conversation with him, as I usually thought of him as an ideal sergeant major due to his aggressive attitude, which undermined others. In his company, I was constantly reminded of those words by Thomas Hobbes, that life is 'nasty, brutish and short'.

Aware that Rowton House was far superior to the gruesome squalid lodging houses, I was more than pleased to hear there were vacancies. 'Sign 'ere Les boy,' said Jardine. 'One shilling and sixpence a night. You know the score by now laddie. You get a cubicle to yerself and use of our excellent bathrooms, but no wanking yerself off. There's still strict discipline 'ere don't forget. That means no cooking bangers and fuckin mash. We 'ave a good dining room. No playing cards or bringing back 'ere any women of the night. Get me son?' He smiled scornfully at me.

With bedclothes, towel and rucksack in hand, I climbed two flights of disinfected tiled stairs, following the steps of many dispossessed men before me, to find my cubicle twenty feet down the light brown corridor.

'Awight son?' asked one old bloke, who was lying on his bed reading a copy of the *Daily Worker*. I put my few chattels on the floor and threw myself onto the single well-sprung bed. As I lay there thinking about my predicament, I wondered about all my predecessors who had slept on this bed since 1902, when it had first opened, and what had become of them. They surely, I thought, must have had dreams and aspirations for themselves, but in time they were overridden by the weight of life. Uppermost in their minds must have been the need to earn a few shillings to feed and house themselves. If they were lucky, then perhaps they had a beer or two, or rarely a visit to the cinema, theatre or music hall. I wondered how many of them had committed suicide, unable any more to live a meaningless life devoid of any joy or pleasure. I wondered how many had been incarcerated in various institutions through no fault on their own? How many, indeed, had fought in the Boer War and World War 1, and returned home to absolutely nothing whatever? And most importantly of all, I painfully wondered how many of those men who had lain on this bed, just as I was doing, had ever seen their mothers, fathers, siblings or children again!

After a long night's sleep, I awoke the next day feeling depressed, but realised that I must get out of bed to find myself a job, as the three pounds I had saved would not last very long. After washing and changing some of my filthy clothes and managing to avoid conversation with other residents, I found myself standing on the noisy Commercial Road. With no friends, job or family of my own, I stood there wondering if life was worth the effort. It would be easy and quick, I thought, to jump in front of an oncoming lorry or bus and get it over without any fuss. No one would miss my presence and life would go on just like before. I had had enough of trying to exist in a world that had no time for me. I was no one, had nothing and was never likely to have anything to call my own, I thought to myself.

As a big blue lorry approached me I tensed myself and closed my eyes, ready to jump in front of it. My mind went blank; I froze as I stood in the gutter waiting for the end. 'Get out of the road yer silly bastard! You'll get yerself killed standing there!' shouted the irate driver.

Confused, I walked on until I found a café full of working men having their breakfasts. The café had dirty brown walls and worn-out lino and was full of cigarette smoke.

'Cuppa tea please,' I asked the fat old woman serving.

'You alwight son? You don't look very well,' she said.

I sat down at a table with three other blokes all talking, smoking and drinking large mugs of tea. I didn't want any company, but no other seats were available.

'Ow yer going Les?' asked a young man sitting on the next table in front of me. I sat still and kept looking down at the table in front of me, making out I hadn't heard him. I felt I wanted to be anonymous. I felt I didn't want to go on living.

'Les 'ow yer going? I 'aven't seen yer for ages,' asked the same bloke.

With great reluctance I lifted my head. 'Allo Ted,' I replied.

'You still a costermonger for Billy Wendle? The bastard sacked me for fiddling.'

'I left ages ago,' I replied as I walked past him on my way out of the café.

Things looked bleak for me, but I had to keep going and somehow find a job to earn at least enough money to pay for my bed in Rowton House. Without a roof over my head at night I would have to go back to those squalid, flea-infested lodging houses full of lost souls.

The thought shuddered me into action. After walking up and down the busy Commercial Road several times to clear my head, I walked into the local labour exchange to find a job, knowing that with over three million people unemployed my chances were slim. The place was full of working-class blokes like me. Most were dressed in overcoats, boots and caps, and were reading the various job vacancies attached to the dirty cream-coloured walls. Several well-dressed men and women were behind desks interviewing people.

'Get in that queue if yer wanna be interviewed fer a job, or if yer wanna receive unemployment money,' a scruffy young bloke ordered me.

After twenty minutes of waiting, I was eventually asked by a plump young woman with ginger hair and thick red lipstick to sit down in front of her desk. She politely asked my name, address, age and previous employment. She didn't sound that impressed or optimistic that my employment record would find me anything grander than toilet attendant or bottle washer.

'Although you are now over 25 years of age Mr Tatter, you have not done a great deal with your working life, which means your opportunities are very limited indeed,' she said, sighing. She gave me the addresses and phone numbers of three companies who were looking for unskilled factory workers.

'What about unemployment money, Miss Clarke. Can I register for that?' I asked. So she filled out the various forms, and I signed and dated them.

'Come back in a week and you should receive some money to live on, but not a great deal. Meanwhile I shall send confirmation of your unemployment details to Rowton House,' she said.

Back out on the road, with information about three vacancies in my pocket and anticipating at least fifteen shillings next week, I felt more confident things would change for me as I made my way towards the Salvation Army café in Cable Street, Stepney. The Salvation Army had been there for many years, and provided accommodation and food for men who were mostly in dire straits, just like me. Most of the Army sites were managed by decent volunteers, guided by their own religious convictions, who wanted to help those worse off than themselves

When I entered the ground floor café , I was confronted by a menagerie of human beings the likes of which I had not seen in one place at the same time before. It was even worse than the café I first used in Thirsk! There were winos, tramps, prostitutes, unemployed, drug addicts, patients from the local mental hospital, passing travellers, costermongers, blokes selling stolen, cheap second-hand clothes, a few former soldiers from World War One and others I found impossible to classify.

The place reeked, understandably, of filthy unwashed clothes and the bodies of men who had slept under the stars. You couldn't see from wall to wall due to the heavy smoking. You would have thought the café was full of the infamous London smog. As I had given up smoking, I had a quick cup of tea and left before I got into conversation with others. The City of London, through to the Mile End and beyond, was notorious for rough sleepers. Most of them weren't even welcome in some of the most squalid lodging houses, where conditions were still Dickensian. A lot of the rough sleepers were transient, moving around from place to place, but unlike walking tramps such as Sammy, Percy and me, they kept to towns and cities. Like me, none of them qualified for any of the new dwellings that were being built all over London. Wherever they walked, county councils, established in 1888, would keep moving them on to somewhere else. The London County Council, set up in 1889, had a similar attitude. In general, the London County Council did very little at the time even to house families.

For the next few months, I walked, most of the time, aimlessly round London seeking my fortune, which, of course, didn't exist. Twice weekly I attended the labour exchange, vainly seeking a job; at this demoralised stage, even a toilet attendant job looked appealing. Not even the well-intentioned Miss Clarke and her colleagues could find me a suitable job. I was fast becoming unemployable. At least the unemployment payments covered my posh cubicle fee, and with the small amount of money that remained I could buy cheap food from various places around London. Soup kitchens were always there for tea and bread. Not once was I successful at getting daily cash-in-hand work down the docks unloading lorries, or clearing up the day's rubbish at one of the many markets. Some days, demoralised, I used to walk many miles out to Epping Forest, and return the same day, although on two occasions I did sleep there in one of the council sheds accompanied by rodents.

On one occasion, I took the train to Tattenham Corner station. During the journey I noticed that countless new private houses were being built. From the station, I walked round Epsom racetrack and over the wide blustery downs before walking down a long narrow lane, with racehorses in fields either side, into Epsom Town. There was a grand Victorian clock tower in the middle of the high street. The town had a strong aura of affluence about it. The local police kept eyeing me to see if I were there to cause trouble. I soon scarpered back to the 'smoke'.

On several occasions, I walked 20 miles to Box Hill in Surrey and made a small camp on the top near the remains of a castle. There I was at peace with myself surrounded by trees, where no one could see or interfere with me. I made myself a small but comfortable canvas tent from material I had brought with me. I boiled water for tea and ate my food, and enjoyed the many days I lived there wandering in the beech woods collecting kindling for my fire. Most mornings grey squirrels would sit outside my tent anticipating, correctly, that I would feed them bread. They were followed in turn by rooks, crows, blackbirds and sparrows.

The only downside to travelling around for more than one day at a time was that I sometimes forgot to inform Rowton House and the labour exchange staff of my absence. The former were sympathetic to my wanderings so they kept my bed available for me, except when the modern *Mephistopheles*, Sandy Jardine, found out. He deliberately gave me a hard time. On two occasions I had to phone the labour exchange to explain that I would be unable to register to collect my unemployment payment due to my mother being unwell in hospital. On both occasions they were unsympathetic, until they sent me, with an official letter in my hand, to the posh Clarendon Hotel, Mayfair for an interview as a kitchen porter.

With my insecurity deepening and my confidence at rock bottom, I walked up to the marble-clad reception area and asked a dazzling-looking blonde woman, resembling a Hollywood Queen, where I could find one James Bellini, the head porter. Minutes later a short, well-built, stern-looking regimental chap, wearing a light brown suit with gold braid, presented himself.

'Welcome to the Victorian-built Clarendon Hotel, Mr Tatter. I'm informed you are here to be interviewed for the kitchen porter vacancy. Is that correct?' asked the formidable-looking head porter, who was about 50 years of age, and who, from his name and appearance, I assumed to be of Italian extraction.

'That's right governor, sorry, sir. The labour exchange sent me 'ere,' I explained rather nervously.

I followed him down a long, brown carpeted corridor until we reached an office with his nameplate on the polished brown wooden door. He offered me a seat in the small, pink-wallpapered office with bookcases and an expensive-looking leather chair, which he sat on.

'What do you know about kitchen work, Mr Tatter?' the Head Porter asked. In reality, I thought, nothing.

'Not a great deal. I've done washing up in several small companies where I've worked in the past, but I 'aven't worked officially like for years due to travelling,' I muttered.

'Well the work here is hard. You will be on the go all day or night, depending on which shift you are working. Ten hours per day or sixty hours per week. Meals and uniform provided. The pay is £2-15 shillings per week. You can start tomorrow at 8 am, but please remember this proverb when working with your more experienced colleagues - *'A wise man learns by the mistakes of others, a fool by his own!'*

With such words of wisdom began my career, if that's what you could call it, in February 1931 at the expensive London Hotel. It was impressed upon me from the outset by the senior kitchen supervisor that riff-raff employees like me must not at any time be seen by the wealthy clients coming and going from the hotel. In essence that meant using a narrow side alley which was obscured from paying guests, which meant most of the rich Americans would not see the paupers like me who attended to their every needs.

From the outset I homed in on the banter used by my East End colleagues. Not surprisingly, most of them had been in one institution or another. Of the six blokes I worked with on regular shifts, most had been in children's homes, prison or mental hospital. Same old familiar tragic story, but they were all diamond blokes. Once they realised who you were and where you came from, all things were possible away from the prying eyes of management. For example, Robbie, a young tearaway from Poplar, used to regularly fleece the Americans of part of their steak meals. Once the meal had been cooked, he used to cut several pieces of the meat from each plate and share it with his colleagues. The waiters never had any complaints from the rich North Americans, who, incidentally, always complimented the chef on his fine culinary skills. We nearly always went home after finishing our shifts with our bellies full of good, wholesome food which in everyday life was out of our reach to buy.

Working ten hours a day down in the bowels of the earth, underneath a great hotel edifice, wasn't easy, believe me. The way I used to cope with such deprivation was constantly thinking of a picture of Jesus Christ guiding me from above. And most of the time it worked for me, especially when we had hundreds of pieces of cutlery and crockery to wash after an extravagant meal above in the large restaurant. Yet I kept the Jesus thing close to my chest, just in case one of my colleagues found out. If it leaked out to my fellow workers that Jesus was my guiding light, they would have thought I was ready for the laughing house. Especially Robbie, and another two colleagues, Martin and Joe from Bow; they would have given me a merciless ribbing for hours on end. All three rogues had been incarcerated in various institutions where religion was incessantly stuffed down their throats.

Any mention of religion in the large, well-equipped kitchen would probably have caused mayhem for our supervisor/chef, Chris Page. Mind you Chris had worked at the hotel for years, which gave him justified rank above all others in the kitchen. And to his credit, he turned a blind eye on most of our immature behaviour. It transpired that he had fought in the Great War and had got injured by flying shrapnel, which had left him with a severe limp.

When I was working night shifts at the hotel and couldn't sleep during the day at a Rowton House, I occasionally used to visit my parents in Shadwell on one of the newly-introduced trolleybuses. They were cheaper and quicker than most local transport.

'Good ter see yer Mum. How yer keepin luv? Still cleaning the flats 'ere?' I asked Mother, who appeared to like her job as it gave her the opportunity to meet other tenants, have a cup of tea, and along with several other women, listen to the radio. In those days not many homes could afford a radio, so neighbours used to congregate round the homes that did. Now 46, she got lonely on her own all day as Father, 47, worked ten hours a day in Aldgate market. That pleased me as the coal delivery job was causing him back pains, but according to Mother, he now felt a lot better selling fruit and vegetables. Susan, 22, still worked full-time for Davies Shipping, but had been promoted to senior clerical assistant.

'I'm well, Les. The money I get from Peabody for cleaning the stairs and steps is very 'andy in buying most of the groceries. They're good ter me, yer know. Cos when I was orf tom and dick [sick] they still paid me. Fuckin' good that Les. And 'ow about you son? Where yer bin? Are yer workin yet?' Mother asked in her usual quiet manner. Her head tic was now more pronounced, but I didn't mention it.

'Got meself a kitchen porter job at the posh Clarendon Hotel in Mayfair,' I told her enthusiastically. 'Not bad money, and we get free meals on duty. The place is full of Yanks, but they got plenty of green music [money]. And I'm living at the Rowton House in Whitechapel. For one and six a night you get yer own bed with a cubicle. That gives me privacy. You can 'ave a good old soak in the bath when you like. There's several 'undred residents and we 'ave a smoking room, reading room, large clean dining room and our own shop. Good bloke that Rowton geezer, weren't he?'

My mother had lines all over her face and was looking prematurely old. 'Yer grandmother's now working as a cleaner in Guys Hospital,' she said. 'She loves it there, and the patients love 'er. The best treatment they'll get there, I bet.' she grinned and winked at me. Over gallons of strong tea and tasty mutton stew, Mother and I continued chatting for several hours.

When I was not working or visiting my parents,

which wasn't often, I used to take the train to various places in Surrey, Kent and Sussex, and just go walking, even though I didn't know the country areas at all well. Many times I got lost wandering over fields and woods, where the ubiquitous sign 'TRESPASSERS WILL BE PROSECUTED' made you feel you were in another country, instead of being only 15 or 20 miles from London. Those signs didn't act as a deterrent to me. Besides, how can they prosecute you when all you are doing is walking over land that many millions died for?

I visited a few country places several times, and I must say, I enjoyed it each and every time. The numerous pubs I visited were all friendly and welcoming, except on one occasion when a smart arse of a customer, posh and well spoken, thought the East End of London to be full of thieves. Well, he was right! 'Hallo young man, what are you doing in this neck of the woods? Not getting up to any mischief are we?' he arrogantly asked me.

Walking down the English country lanes and passing old cottages and quaint pubs was for me a most wonderful activity to spend my time when I was away from work and Rowton House. Of all the times I got lost walking in the countryside, I only had to sleep out twice through missing the last train. It didn't bother me one bit that I couldn't get back in time to sleep at Rowton House, because now I was working, I could afford to pay them weekly in advance. Besides, when it came to walking, sleeping rough and coping, I was now pretty good at it. At the right time of year there were ripe fruit and vegetables that I used to help myself to, no doubt to the anger of the owners. One old farmer shouted at me, 'why don't you fucking gypsies buy yer own fruit?' But for the past few months my depression had not reared its ugly head.

Most of all it was the countryside churches that really inspired me to keep returning to walk round and learn all about their history. I visited a mix of Catholic and Anglican churches, and they all had many riches inside their austere walls, which were covered with plaques showing the names of vicars, Fathers, churchwardens, military people and family members long gone. Some of the churches were built in Norman times. One of the great marvels of these churches was the large, ornate multi-coloured stained glass windows, some of them standing about twenty feet in height, depicting various biblical characters and stories. I had briefly been inside a few churches, to nick anything, when I was younger in the East End, and of course, had prayed and recited the bible at Heythrop, but never before had I had this golden opportunity to wander, unimpeded and on my own, for hours around old country churches.

As I sat for some time on an old wooden pew during a visit to a small Anglican church in Hollingbury, it dawned on me what great skills the people who made the altarpieces, organs and wall murals had. Nearly all the churches I visited had well-maintained graveyards. Many graves belonged to local people who had grown up, worked and died without ever leaving the parish. Several graves belonged to young men, of different ranks, killed in the Boer Wars and World War One. One of the most inspiring rural sights was the ploughman and his large tough harnessed horse pulling the plough all day, turning over soil thousands of years old. And all around was silence - silence!

Most parishes had churches, which were connected by small tracks that were big enough for farmers to drive their cattle to pastures after being milked. Visiting rural churches, waving at a ploughman working in a field, having the occasional pint of local ale or walking the old roads, tracks and byways made me feel that life was a good place.

That good feeling about life was often, unfortunately, squashed when I returned to my grim everyday life in London. Yet most days in the London hotel kitchen were a good laugh. You had to have a sense of humour, or otherwise the drudgery of the work would have sent you over the top of Westminster Bridge. At the beginning of every shift the Head Porter, Mr Bellini, would appear without fail to make sure everyone was present, well-dressed in hotel uniform and working hard. With so many people unemployed you had to make sure you were busy, or you made out you were working hard, and say 'Good morning Governor' when Field-Marshal Bellini first appeared. You had to give them the flannel (flattering talk), and let them think they were superior to us, which of course they were in most respects.

But when he disappeared, he left us alone to our own devious devices. Within seconds Joe and Colin were in the toilet having a smoke. Given the opportunity, Robbie unfailingly threw a bucket of water over the top of the toilet door, soaking them. Philip would make gallons of tea and Chunky, as he was known to everyone, cut up large slices of ham, beef or chicken to fill our doorstep-sized sandwiches. Chunky Cripps, aged about 30, tall, the size of three men and just as strong, came from Hoxton. He had served six years for armed robbery and spent two years in a mental hospital for threatening someone with a chopper. Not the sort of bloke you took home to meet the family, but I always found him friendly and honest. Except that is, when he used to hide butter, meat and chocolates inside his extra-large overcoat without telling anyone before taking it home. Mind you he used to have everyone in stitches of laughter from the time he started work until we left after ten hours of mind-numbing graft.

The chef didn't mind what we got up to so long as we did our work competently. Amongst others things that meant keeping the waiters constantly supplied with customers' meals. It pleased me no end that my colleagues, who were all characters, took the limelight, because around this time the barking black dogs were returning, after several months of relative calm, to haunt me. I kept a brave face in front of them during working hours, but back at Rowton House, I retreated to my enclosed space for comfort and security.

Just two weeks later my family and I celebrated my 26th birthday, although it wasn't a rip-roaring success. When I arrived at my parents' home late in the afternoon of 6 June 1931, all four of them were waiting for me. 'Appy birthday Les!' they all sang in unison as we toasted my anniversary.

'What yer bin up to Les?' asked my dear old grandmother, Bessie, who was still energetic and full of life.

'I'm working at the Clarendon Hotel as a kitchen porter. Not a bad number, and wiv three million unemployed, you can't be choosy, can yer? And I'm living at Rowton House in Whitechapel. Right decent place Bessie. Got me own cubicle which allows me privacy. I like it there. We got our own shop, reading room, dining room and smoking room. 'Ome from 'ome Mum,' I explained half-heartedly. 'By the way Bessie,' I remembered to tell her for the first time in ages, 'I've still got the medal you gave me all those years ago. Wherever I go, that medal goes wiv me'.

I turned to Dad. 'You got a new job Dad, down the local market I 'ear. Any good?' I asked.

'Yus boy, long hours but I gets plenty of fruit and veg to bring 'ome,' answered Father in his typical upbeat manner.

'And Susan, I 'ear you're still workin at Davies Shipping and got promotion. Well done gel. When yer getting married? You can't live 'ere for the rest of yer life,' I said jokingly to my sister, who had grown both physically and intellectually during the past few years and was now a fine young lady.

'Susan can fucking live 'ere for as long as she wants to Les,' Mother retorted, which was most unusual for her .'I don't want 'er to live in some old run-down bedsit with winos and dossers.' She was probably thinking about the predicament I was in, and knew she didn't want her daughter to follow in my footsteps.

'Cheers once again on your birthday Les,' said Father as he poured out another large glass of red wine.

We all tucked into Bessie's delicious home-made

steak and kidney pie. What a treat, I thought. I remembered I enjoyed eating her great pies when I was about five years of age, and have done so many times since. 'That'll put some lead in your underused pencil', said Bessie, pointing the finger at me. How right she was.

Three hours later, feeling rather relaxed and confident, thanks to several glasses of wine, I thought it was time to broach the subject of my depression with my family. Although I had explained some of my problems to them, no one knew the depth and extent of my depression and my involvement with Heythrop Monastery.

'I've got somethin' important that I'd like to explain to all of yer,' I started. 'Well 'ere goes. I will try my best to make sense. For many years now, since I was a teenager, perhaps before, I've suffered wiv depression, at least that's what I think it is. I 'aven't bin to see a doctor about it because I was frightened they would shove me in the laughing 'ouse. When it's bad I feel like shit. I just wanna hide away, which is what I do if I can. That's what I like about Rowton 'ouse, you can hide away in your cubicle and people leave yer alone. I get the horrors in me 'ead and sometimes I feel like killing meself. The depression comes and goes, but I never know when it's coming. The monks at Heythrop 'ave bin very supportive to me, and one day I might go and live there for the rest of me life. The Christian faith appeals to me. I don't seem to fit in anywhere else'.

With that out of my system, I began to cry. My father put his arms round me for the first time in years.

Two months later, on one of our rare days off, I encouraged my colleague Martin Hill to join me for a walk on the North Downs, east of Box Hill. We caught the packed bus to bustling Waterloo Station, where we managed to buy an awful cup of tea, which smelt like cats' urine, before boarding our train. There were other young men and women dressed in their walking gear, similar to Martin and me, all laughing and joking, anticipating, I assumed, an enjoyable day's walking ahead of them.

Before Clapham Junction, the train passed the busy Southern Railway locomotive sheds of Nine Elms, Stewarts Lane, Bricklayers Arms and Longhedge. Just before our train arrived at Epsom station, I realised we had passed many new housing estates that were being built. There must have been thousands of new homes, but whether they were council homes or not I didn't know. It was, nonetheless, reassuring to see the Government's 1919 Housing Policy in action. Most Londoners in those days viewed Surrey and all the other counties around London as the 'sticks' (rural).

We got off the train at the Victorian-built Boxhill and Westhumble station. The small station was deserted. Not even a porter was visible. There was just an elderly woman sitting on a stall smoking and selling flowers. The electric train with its four green carriages slowly pulled its way out of the station bound for Dorking, where the other walkers must have been heading. We stood on the platform to look at my newish map to make sure we knew where we were going. Martin looked smart and convincing wearing his new boots and rucksack, no doubt prepared, as I was, for a good day's walking in the densely-wooded hills full of wildlife.

Half a mile down the narrow road from the station, we crossed a busy main road and the fast-flowing river Mole, where mallard ducks lazed the day away nesting nearby. We passed an early Victorian hotel, with large expensive cars parked at the front, climbed several hundred feet up a steep hill over low-lying box and yew until we found ourselves on top of Box Hill. We turned round to gape at the exhilarating view of the Weald below us.

For the next three miles or so we walked through brambles, nettles and box, but we both enjoyed the challenge of eventually finding our first destination, Waybury Chalk Pits. There we saw many feral kittens being fed by mature cats. Neither of us had seen so many of them in one place before. Most of the old warehouses in East London had kept feral cats to stop rats and mice from eating the owners' fabrics.

'Shall we stop 'ere for a sarnie Martin?' I asked my affable colleague. In the warm sun, we sat down on the short, chalk downland turf, ideal for the local rabbits, and started eating the food we had pinched from the Clarendon Hotel. All around was quiet and peaceful. I imagined that I was sitting alone in the garden at Heythrop Monastery watching the birds pecking at the apples in the orchard. Time seemed to have stopped.

'What a contrast to living up the Smoke,' said Martin, who was short and good looking, aged about 30, and had long blond hair. At work he pretended to be one of the lads, but I realised in time that he was a quiet, studious sort of bloke who enjoyed reading science fiction. Born in

Bow, East London, he had lived alone with his mother for the first sixteen years of his life, until her boyfriend moved in.

'Yeah, his name was Paddy O'Sullivan,' he said. 'He worked on building sites and was nearly always pissed. He used to 'it me mum most of the time. He was a right bastard. He started sexually abusing me most nights. Me mum didn't believe me at first, but eventually she cottoned on to what he was doing to me and told 'im to fuck orf. A few years later, when I was about 19, I saw 'im in a pub, somewhere near Lime'ouse, drinking with other navvies. I followed 'im home down an alley, where I knocked the fuck out of him. Beat 'im up right good and pissed all over 'im and took his money. I never saw the cunt again.' Martin was seething with contempt, understandably, towards the person who had abused him.

Sadly this was another familiar story, like so many I have heard over the years, including my own experience, of children and young people being sexually and physically abused by adults who cared for them. In Martin's case, I could understand how it had affected his confidence and prevented him from maturing.

We continued walking east for the next six miles through a large wood of oak, beech, birch and yew which was on one side of the track, with sheep grazing on open pasture land on the other. The gregarious rooks and crows were making a huge din high up in the canopies of the tall old oak trees. Rooks form large flocks, whereas crows tend to be more aggressive, but are usually found in pairs. Both these large birds, with a 17-19 inch wingspan, used the parks around Stepney, where they were guaranteed scraps of food from the local tramps. Later on we saw two more common woodland birds, those further down the food chain; the blackbird and the tree sparrow. The former had an enchanting song and made me feel good when I was depressed.

The warm summer sun filtered its way through thick foliage down onto the dry, well-trodden earth paths. Thick green ivy straddled and wove its way through an old piece of former farming fence as we dreamt our way through the last mile of our interesting walk. Just before Merstham, we came across a patch of red poppies standing tall and proud just inches off the track. According to a magazine article I read in the dentist's surgery in Pickering, artists once used the black poppy seeds to mix oil paints before they were replaced with linseed oil

An hour later we were back on the train heading for Victoria. 'Did you enjoy the day's walking Martin?' I asked my colleague, who appeared to be full of energy.

'Yeah I did Les. Hopefully we can do another walk someday,' he replied.

'I hope so too.'

The following day I saw Martin and my other colleagues grafting back at the London Hotel, and after saluting General Bellini good morning, the day continued much like any other. We did our work, had a good laugh and ate what we could steal, either from the customers or the kitchen pantry. However, when I woke the next morning in my bed, I felt paralysed. I was unable to move and started shouting for God to help me. The old chap in the cubicle next to me came in to see what was happening.

'You all right son?' asked Barney, a former building worker.

'Please send for God to save me please. I'm unable to move. God will help me!' I shouted incoherently.

A few minutes later I was being physically shaken by Mr Davey, an employee at Rowton House. 'What's the problem with yer? Are yer not well Les? Are yers in pain?' he frantically asked me.

'I don't feel well. God will protect me from all suffering!' I yelled at whoever was round my bed.

Apparently, sometime later Mr Davey returned with his manager, Mr Fulton, to try and sort things out. 'Are you not well, Lesley? Would you like me to call a doctor for you?' asked the concerned manager.

'No no, no doctors for a spiritual person like me. Only God will do!' I rambled on.

The manager helped me to sit up in bed, gave me tea and toast and told me to stay in bed for the day, and not to worry as he would inform my employer that I was unwell. Other than managing to walk, rather unsteadily, to the toilet several times, I slept in bed the rest of the day. The next two days things were the same. I shouted incoherently throughout the day about needing the love of God in my life. The manager brought me food and drink, which I didn't touch, as I thought it had been deliberately contaminated to kill me.

In the early morning of the fourth day, I was woken by a middle-aged, well-spoken man asking me to get out of bed. He told me the two blue-uniformed men standing next to him wanted to take me to hospital.

Chapter Thirteen

In and out of the Laughing House

With a 14-month career as a mental patient ahead of me, I was reminded later what Dante had said: *'All hope abandon, ye who enter here'.* Not surprisingly, I could remember very little of the journey from Rowton House, by ambulance, to Colney Hatch Hospital. All I can recall was that there was a flashing light on top of the white vehicle, an attendant was sitting next to me asking questions, and the driver was using a two-way radio (Motor ambulances, incidentally, replaced the cumbersome horse-drawn ambulances during World War One.).

Upon my admission to Colney Hatch Hospital on 20th August 1931, I was taken to a recently-built villa for male patients, Nightingale House, to be assessed for my mental competence. According to the young doctor who interviewed me, I had suffered a nervous breakdown brought about by a long illness of undiagnosed depression. Or something similar to that! I was still unclear, even some considerable time later, what I did originally suffer from. But of course, taking into account my lack of education, it could well have been something to do with delusions. Anyway, whatever the illness was, a young male nurse gave me an awful-smelling liquid medicine to drink (later I found out it was called a sedative) and took me to a small dining room, where other patients were eating their lunch. I remember most of the male patients were quite elderly; some were shouting, at whom I didn't know, and the rest appeared to be staring down, with fixed eyes, at their dinner plates. Another young male nurse brought me something inedible to eat.

Minutes later, I became very relaxed and light-headed and things gradually began to feel unreal. The room and ceiling started to spin round. I became disorientated. I must have passed out, because when I woke up I found myself in bed wearing oversized dirty pyjamas.

That's all I can recall of the first month or so in Nightingale House. I was greatly relieved when Dr Dalgleish, an ageing Scottish psychiatrist, informed me that as I was responding well to treatment, he would reduce the medicine. Within a few days, I gradually became aware, to a certain degree, of what I was thinking and feeling, and could appreciate my immediate surroundings. Somehow I just felt more human, and my depression had lifted.

Nightingale House was built about 100 yards from the main hospital; it had four wards numbered from 1-4, full of rows of metal beds that were all neatly in line, resembling a military barrack. At the end of each ward was a small office for staff. Two dining rooms, with toilets and bathrooms at one end, separated the wards. There was also a patients' smoking room and library. The whole inside of the building was brightly painted and pleasant, unlike the Victorian asylum nearby, which was rather austere and forbidding in appearance. Within the original hospital there were six miles of corridors, and many patients could be seen shuffling endlessly and aimlessly up and down them all day shouting at their inner voices; it resembled a road outside the cheap lodging houses in the East End. Many times I witnessed some poor soul, dressed in despicable-looking clothes, who seemed lost in an institution that had, essentially, been forgotten by the outside world. The Great War had bankrupted Britain. People in Colney Hatch, and all other similar places, were at the bottom of the heap when it came to expense. It was possible that a significant number of patients in the hospital were former soldiers, but I didn't actually know.

Nightingale House was kept unlocked; in other words, none of the patients were deemed mad enough to be certified insane. It was reassuring to know that I hadn't gone completely off my head. Patients were free, therefore, to come and go, when they weren't working, for a walk, smoke or to sit on their own in the garden to ponder on their existence in Colney Hatch Hospital. From Ward 3, my humble abode for the duration, I used to enjoy walking out on to the colourful patio to sit at the black metal tables provided for inmates and write to various people after my illness started to improve. At least that is what the medical staff told me. When no one was around, I used to read the bible and other religious literature that I found in the ward library. I didn't want to be labelled a religious fanatic, as patients would then assume my admission to hospital was due to some false belief that had overtaken me. Mind you, that could well have been the reason for being in hospital. I kept God to myself, which I thought made me safe from those who might ridicule or harm me. There was a chapel that was available at weekends for patients to use, but I never ventured in, because at times I thought my depression could have been exacerbated by my experiences at Heythrop Monastery. I gave the place a wide birth.

Most of the elderly patients, unless cajoled to do otherwise, would sit all day in the smoking room listening to the radio or sleeping. Beyond the patio was a small garden, full of various flowers that patients had been encouraged to plant and maintain at their own initiative. Many of the younger patients, including myself, worked on the 75-acre farm providing the meat, vegetables and fruit that made the hospital self-sufficient in food. In total, including the gardens and surrounding farmland, there was about 120 acres of land in the hospital. Patients also worked in the large laundry or the main hospital kitchens, cleaned the never ending corridors, maintained the many gardens, repaired hospital clothes and equipment and so on. All the work was supervised by various hospital staff. The hospital was a well-oiled industry staffed by patients, which kept costs down to a minimum.

After a few weeks, I had been passed fit to work and was able to participate in everyday hospital life. I was back in the land of the living, and the regime of strong medicine and wearing filthy ripped pyjamas all day had ended. A typical working shift, unlike weekends, which were more laid back and quiet, changed very little from day to day. In Ward 3 the day started around 5.30 am, when two male nurses - nearly all the nurses were men - rang a bell for patients to get out of bed, use the toilets, wash, get their medication and go to the dining room for breakfast. This usually consisted of tea, toast and porridge. Due to the powerful effects of the medicine, most patients said very little, unless spoken to by staff. Occasionally you got something resembling a sausage or an egg.

A lot of the older men coughed incessantly day and night, and belched and shouted at anyone who was around, which sometimes put me off eating my breakfast. Some nights on the ward it was impossible to sleep due to the cacophony of noise made by the older patients. When it got unbearable for the night staff, not the patients, they used to give those patients medicine to make them sleep. Most of them had been transferred from the old asylum and were in various stages of becoming institutionalised. The younger patients, understandably, became belligerent towards some of the staff, who used to shout and swear at them.

Many times I overheard nurses call a patient a shit-house, nutter, wanker, moron and so on. On separate occasions three different nurses called me names that really hurt me, but there was nothing I could have done about it. I soon realised that nurses were all-powerful in the ward, where they made up the rules for their own convenience. If you were stupid enough to make a complaint against any member of staff, the consequences were dire.

After breakfast most of the younger patients from all four wards would be marched two hundred yards by two of the hospital staff down to the farm. After the rancid smells of the ward - sometimes it was overpowering - I particularly looked forward to those early morning walks in the enjoyable fresh bracing Middlesex air accompanied by the singing of various birds.

After we had finished each day's work, we used to have our midday food in the farm shed, we would all be marched back, like a platoon of soldiers, to Nightingale House for our evening meal, which was usually well cooked and the best meal of the day. As usual in institutions, regimentation dictated that we wash our hands, change from our dirty farm clothes into something a little cleaner, though sometimes ill-fitting, and line up to take our food to the dining table. By this time the old patients had either eaten their meals or had not even bothered to turn up. If we said too much at the dinner table, or laughed too loudly, some nurses, depending who was on shift, would show ill will to those who had the audacity, in their eyes, to be different.

After dinner most patients went to bed early due to a combination of tiredness and the side effects of their medicine. Others would take tea onto the patio, listen to the radio or read books, magazines or newspapers. All these activities were encouraged by the nursing staff. But other than formal interviews in their offices, medical staff never spoke to patients. I felt they consciously kept their emotional distance from inmates like me.

My regular job on the farm, depending on the time of year, was usually digging, planting and weeding along with about eight other patients. All of them were from the East End of London. We were a motley crew if I ever saw one. Some of them wore hospital clothes that were too short, too long or far too big. It was a lottery as to what working clothes you were handed by ward nurses. We wouldn't have looked out of place in a Yiddish music hall or children's pantomime. There were days when some of the patients even forgot to put their teeth in.

Nonetheless, we had a laugh most of the time taking the piss out of each other. One of the worst inmates for throwing cow-shit at people was Sandy, who used to sell jellied eels for a living. "Ow long you bin 'ere then Sandy?" I asked him during one of our tea breaks.

'Fuck knows boy, I've forgotten. Could be six or seven years. Most of the time I've lived in the big 'ospital. They sent me 'ere when the Villa was built. I 'ated it in Primrose Ward. They gave me strong fucking drugs to stop me 'earing voices. One treatment they me made me 'ave, I shook like a jelly for ages afterwards. I fucking 'ated that,' explained Sandy, who was short, slim, stammered badly and aged about 60. Prior to be being hospitalised, he had lived with his elderly parents somewhere in Poplar. Most of his family, he said, had been in and out of stir (prison). No one ever visited him, as with most of the other patients, especially the older patients, who were probably confined to the hospital until they died.

When Sandy said he shook like a jelly, he was referring to insulin shock or coma 'treatment'. Patients were repeatedly injected with large doses of insulin to induce comas over a period of several weeks. It was first introduced by the Austrian-American psychiatrist Manfred Sakel, and used mainly for treating schizophrenia, so I was informed years later by a nurse.

Another character was Peter Brabrook, who was a dwarf, being no taller than four feet six inches in height. Not surprisingly, he was called 'titch' by everyone. Peter was well known for being a professional cat burglar. He was adept at shinning up any building to break in and steal what was available inside. He was well known in the Mayfair and Chelsea areas not just by the police, but also by local residents. They reckoned Peter climbed as though he had glue stuck to his hands and feet. His hands were the size of dustbin lids and were even bigger than my tramping friend Percy's hands.

'After several stretches in stir, the last time I was in court the Judge thought, at the age of 48, I might benefit from 'ead treatment in a mental hospital,' he explained.

It's a right doddle 'ere Les boy and far easier than doing stir in Wandsworth or Pentonville prison. 'On the ward...'

He was interrupted by our prison farm supervisor. 'When are you bunch of cunts going to do some work?' snapped Mr Mortimer, a tall, well-built chap of about 50 who originally came from Manchester, and now lived in hospital property along with his wife and teenage children. On his good days he left us alone to our own devices, but other times he shouted, swore and bellowed at us. After working at Colney Hospital for about 25 years, he was as mad as some of the inmates.

I had written several letters to my family; six months later, I felt well and confident enough for them to visit me at Nightingale House. As all five of us sat quietly on the patio, drinking tea on a coldish February afternoon, Mother broke the ice.

'Ow are you, love?' she asked.

'I'm a lot better now. When I first came 'ere, I was quite ill, so the shrink told me. As you know when the 'ospital wrote to you, I was taken from Rowton 'ouse by ambulance to this 'ospital in a mad state I suppose. They gave me this medicine, which I found overpowering, but they reduced it after a few weeks. That made me feel better. Ever since things 'ave improved. I've bin workin' on the farm for some time now. I like it there. I work wiv a lot characters from the East End. Right bunch of nutcases they are.' I was hoping my family would understand.

'I'm so pleased to 'ear that love,' remarked my smiling mother.

In silence we finished eating the large currant cake

and meat sandwiches that mother had brought to the visit. Everyone looked tense and anxious, which was not surprising, as they were in a mental hospital for the first time. These institutions were austere places.

An hour later, I escorted my family to the front of the Villa, where my father's car was parked. With tears in her eyes, mother said to me, 'Take care love. I'll write to you soon'. I was pleased to see my parents, Bessie and Susan all looking so well. But there was still a part of me that felt resentment towards my parents, and my mother in particular. The reason for that I still don't really understand, years later.

Even though a mild form of depression had returned to haunt me, I never told anyone about it, especially not any of the staff, whatever rank they were. To have done that would have meant certain confinement to the ward, where stronger drugs would have been put into my body in the name of mental treatment. Working on the farm with the gang of crazy patients was enjoyable, kept me fit and, hopefully, it impressed the doctors so that some day, sooner rather than later, they would sanction my goodbye from this stinking hell-hole. Mind you, I was not a certified patient so I could have left earlier than I did, but no one informed me of that small point.

One of our farm supervisors, John Silsbury, thought we should have been given a voice to speak on things that undermined us in the hospital. John was young, gregarious and funny. At the time he lived in Leytonstone with his wife and two children. His mother had been confined for years in a large asylum, so he realised that the people he was supervising had had working lives and families before being patients at Colney Hatch. He used to give us cigarettes, fresh fruit to eat and various books to read during our dinner breaks. We were all at first reluctant, even afraid, to converse with him and laugh at his jokes, but after a while you were confident that he was genuine.

'What you in here for Les?' John asked one day during a tea break.

'I've suffered from depression for years. I came in 'ere about nine months ago for treatment. I'd lost my girlfriend and my job and was sleeping in Rowton 'ouse, although I liked that place,' I explained.

John was short and heavy and tattoos covered both his arms. Often he would spontaneously burst into song like a thrush or blackbird. He should have been on the stage treating people to his wonderful renditions, not wasting his time in a huge asylum, earning peanuts to keep his soul together. Mind you, patients received even less for working hard all week on the farm; a few shillings bought us tobacco or confectionery.

'Don't worry about girlfriends and sex too much. It's all overrated, if you ask me. I read something the other day that made me laugh: Lord Chesterfield, whoever he is, said about sex, 'The position is ridiculous, the pleasure momentary, and the cost enormous'.

I learnt a lot from John Silsbury. Above all else, he encouraged me to question, to challenge things that especially involved me, and seek answers that could help resolve my own difficult situation. It was so reassuring for a working-class lad like me, from poverty-stricken Stepney, to know that I had the power, potentially, to question authority. Although materially life had improved considerably since those bleak 19th century days down the East End of London, people still didn't feel empowered to really challenge the status quo.

A few weeks later, with the optimistic song of the blackbird echoing around the gloom of the place, I received with joy a letter that I had been anticipating for some time from the Abbot of Heythrop Monastery. I had written to him for the first time in many months explaining my admission to Colney Hatch Hospital for depression. Over several warm evenings on the patio outside my ward, I carefully crafted a letter to Father John-Paul detailing my life, as skilfully as my intelligence allowed, and asking him to consider my request to live at Heythrop as a probationer monk. I had been agonising for some considerable time whether I should take the spiritual plunge by writing to the one person who could help change my life for the better. My prospects of a good material life were very remote.

This was something I had discussed at length with John Silsbury, explaining to him that I anticipated and hoped that I would be discharged from the hospital quite soon after making a formal request to my psychiatrist. But I omitted any mention of religion to him. Not surprisingly, Dr Woosnam suggested I stay for a few more months to make sure I was as fully prepared as possible to re-enter society. The important point was I did not want to re-enter society; I wanted to live the religious life where, I thought, my salvation lay.

After a long hard day's work digging and sowing on the farm, my hands shook slightly with excitement as I opened the Abbot's letter. 'My dear Leslie,' it began, 'how wonderful to hear from you after all this time'. It continued further on, 'I'm so pleased to hear that you are recovering from your depression. Let me know when you have been discharged and we can make arrangements for you to visit us here at the monastery'.

To say I was elated at reading those few powerful words would have been an understatement. Here I was, a young man, a patient in a large mental institution along with two thousand or so other unfortunate individuals, working on a farm for a few shillings a week. I realised I had to change. Otherwise, I could envisage ending up here for years as an institutionalised old man, a wizened frail ghost of a person with only death as my liberation. That wasn't going to happen to me, no matter what it took to fool, cajole, lie, feign, or come what may, to the powers that be so that they would let me leave this place of human suffering as soon as possible. After nearly 14 months of treatment and refuge, my mind was made up that my time had arrived to depart. For that I was grateful. I felt less fearful, more confident and stronger, even though I was at times still preoccupied with the freedom that butterflies engendered in me. By this time, I had realised that my preoccupation with butterflies could have represented the spiritual potential latent within me.

Having made arrangements with the Abbot at Heythrop to contact him after my discharge, I entered Dr Woosnam's bright, wallpapered office with some anxiety, knowing he would do his utmost to keep me in the hospital for a longer period.

'Well, Leslie, I hear you want to be discharged,' he said condescendingly. 'Do you think you are well enough to live on your own once again, taking into consideration the problems you had at your last place of residence?'

'Yes I feel well and confident,' I replied 'I'm going to live wiv me parents for the time being and me dad's found me a job as a navvy in Stepney.' Not one word of it was the truth. You had to beat these people, I thought, at their own game.

'Very well, I shall sign your discharge from this hospital for seven days' time, which will be the 12th October 1932. I will arrange medicine for you to take if your depression gets worse. I wish you well. Goodbye,' he said with a wry smile.

On the day of my discharge, my father was waiting for me outside the large steel gates that hung from the huge stone pillars that gave Colney Hatch Hospital its imposing stature. As I opened the passenger door of my father's old Ford car, I looked back, for the last time, at the grand hospital brick building with its lofty central round tower flanked by two much smaller square towers just 200 feet from the road. Before I could get my breath back after the realisation that my nightmare was over, father had already driven several miles along the quiet, clean suburban Middlesex roads leading us back into the East End of London. Every mile he drove he drove me nearer to my family, the only people I was concerned with seeing right now. As Father drove through north-east

London heading towards Shadwell, I was amazed by the way some areas had been transformed by new council housing and high-rise blocks of flats. In places it looked as if a new world had opened up at last up for young working families; such a contrast to older generations who had experienced so much poverty in the old slums. What a change they were from those private homes built for profit and to guarantee the owners an ever-increasing income, to the detriment of working-class people. Nonetheless, it must be remembered that as unemployment was at a record high, families were still finding it hard in the 1930s to feed and clothe their children as a result of Britain's involvement in the Great War.

Father and I walked to where mother, Bessie and Susan were all waiting for us with beaming faces and outstretched arms to welcome me home after many months of hospital life. I immediately kissed and hugged all my family as we stood on the lawn of the communal garden. Susan in particular looked mature and attractive.

'You look healthy son,' said mother, as she wiped tears from her eyes. Looking at her sad, ageing face, I could tell that my confinement in a mental hospital for over 14 months had been an ordeal, not just for my mother, but for the rest of the family.

'It's so good to see yer son. 'Ow do yer feel yourself?' asked Mother.

'Well Mum, being in the laughing 'ouse wasn't all bad. I met some decent blokes from the East End who 'ad various mental problems. A few of the staff were decent to us. One of 'em was a diamond geezer, named John, who was fucking good to us. When I was discharged the shrink gave me a few bottles of medicine to drink if fings got worse for me. I think it's called a sedative.' I went on to explain that mental hospitals could play an important part in your recovery, but they also diminished your independence if you weren't careful.

'What do yer think of our new radio Les?' asked Mother. 'Yer dad bought it less than six months ago from Newlove's shop not 200 yards from 'ere. It's 'bout bloody time we bought one. Some days there must 'ave bin at least twenty women in old Flo's flat listening to her radio. But she didn't mind. She is a good old sort is Flo. Besides, she got her bent [stolen] radio cheap from one of the local costermongers'.

'Anyway son, I've bought a large bottle of bubbly to celebrate your 'omecoming,' said Bessie, as she filled five glasses for us to drink to my freedom. 'And don't forgit Les, you're sleeping 'ere with mum and dad tonight. But as there's not enough room for yer 'ere, from tomorrow you can stay with me at my newish council flat until we can sort something long term out for yer. Is that alwight son?' My dear old grandmother had sorted things out already, whether I agreed or not. You didn't argue with Bessie.

The following morning, I awoke early after several hours of fitful sleep on Mother's second-hand settee. During the past year or so I had been used to a regimentation that allowed for very little personal initiative. You were told when to get out of your hospital bed, get washed, have breakfast and take your medication, and then marched to work. But, of course, neither the hospital staff nor anyone else could take away your mind, your thoughts, feelings, dreams, desires and so on, unless powerful medication had in time taken over your inner life.

My inner resources were inspired most of the time in hospital by two small objects that I cherished daily. First my forebear's medal reminded me of the suffering he must have endured on the battlefield. He was my hero. Second was the gold crucifix that John-Paul had given me, which reminded me of Jesus suffering on the cross. I too could live a religious life, free of suffering and supported by friendships, to seek salvation. I realised that such a life demands generosity and renunciation of oneself. I was willing, I pleaded to John-Paul, to try and cope with a life of austerity dedicated to prayer.

These heartfelt words, among many others, I wrote in my letter to the Abbot at Heythrop Monastery, asking once again to join his holy orders, first as a postulant for six months, and if that went well for me, for two years as a novice, after which I could take my vows. That meant the first vow was for a minimum of three years. I realised that after those three years I could leave or choose to take my solemn vows for life.

It was during the third week, while I was living with my grandmother in her council flat near the Mile End Road, that I received the most important letter of my life. It was from Father John-Paul. The letter started, 'How wonderful to receive your inspiring letter, Leslie'. It concluded, 'Yes I agree that you can join us here at

Heythrop as postulant for six months. I shall write to you soon with further details that will explain what is required of you and your position here in the community'.

'Bessie, Bessie!' I shouted to her in jubilation, 'the Abbot has accepted me as a six-month postulant'. 'Well done son. At last fings are beginning to move for you. What's a postulant, sweetheart?' asked Bessie.

'Well it's a kind of asking for admission into a religious order. Something like that,' I tentatively explained.

'You've come a long way son. I'm proud of yer,' said Bessie. She nearly squeezed the life out of me as she hugged me with her strong old arms.

'Thanks a lot Bessie, for all your support over the years, especially, when I was young and unable to fight for myself. You were there to sort people out,' I said. Floods of repressed tears fell as we held each other.

After saying goodbye to my parents, Bessie and Susan with a heavy heart, I didn't want any painful display of emotions at the station because I wasn't sure I could trust myself not to break down in floods of tears. I made my way on the 32 bus to Kings Cross station. Realising that this momentous day, 17th November 1932, was the start of a potentially life-changing journey, I walked up to the ticket office and asked for a *single* ticket to Thirsk.

There was no going back now. I had committed myself to living the religious life as best I could, aware that along the way I would question my decision to live at Heythrop Monastery. But fellow monks and friends would be around to support me when I started to experience insecurity. Strong concerns about how I would cope with depression, if it reared its ugly head, did bother me constantly. Would those barking black dogs in my head, which caused such resentment, anger, and so on, return to haunt me? And would I resort to the butterfly symbol to help me escape from the powerful grip of depression? When things got really hard for me, would I run away or retreat into my own inner cocoon? Only time would tell.

After five years of religious study, I am nearing the end of my first vow. I was encouraged to read around other subjects, which has informed the writing of my memoirs. The Abbot and the other monks have been marvellously supportive, suggesting ways to improve my writing, pointing the way to analyse various subject matter and helping me transform it all into a book. The end result has surpassed my wildest expectations for such a deeply insecure man. If my former teacher ever found out, I would be truly happy if she gave my book her sincere approval.

My religious training has been challenging, frustrating and emotionally painful, amongst other experiences, but I have been encouraged by the unstinting love of my fellow monks to stay with it, to persevere. It was reassuring to be told, by the Abbot, that I had matured since I joined the order. That development has come about, I hope, through the power of daily reciting the book of prayers, which is central to my contented life here.

Is the religious life all an illusion, I constantly ask myself? When such experiences arise, I remind myself of what Joseph Conrad had to say: 'It's only those who do nothing that make no mistakes'.